Berkley Sensation Titles by Catherine Mann

DEFENDER
HOTSHOT
RENEGADE
PROTECTOR

PROTECTOR

CATHERINE MANN

BERKLEY SENSATION, NEW YORK

THE BERKLEY PUBLISHING GROUP
Published by the Penguin Group
Penguin Group (USA) Inc.
375 Hudson Street, New York, New York 10014, USA

Penguin Group (Canada), 90 Eglinton Avenue East, Suite 700, Toronto, Ontario M4P 2Y3, Canada
(a division of Pearson Penguin Canada Inc.) • Penguin Books Ltd., 80 Strand, London WC2R 0RL,
England • Penguin Group Ireland, 25 St. Stephen's Green, Dublin 2, Ireland (a division of Penguin
Books Ltd.) • Penguin Group (Australia), 250 Camberwell Road, Camberwell, Victoria 3124, Australia
(a division of Pearson Australia Group Pty. Ltd.) • Penguin Books India Pvt. Ltd., 11 Community
Centre, Panchsheel Park, New Delhi—110 017, India • Penguin Group (NZ), 67 Apollo Drive,
Rosedale, Auckland 0632, New Zealand (a division of Pearson New Zealand Ltd.) • Penguin Books
(South Africa) (Pty.) Ltd., 24 Sturdee Avenue, Rosebank, Johannesburg 2196, South Africa

Penguin Books Ltd., Registered Offices: 80 Strand, London WC2R 0RL, England

This is a work of fiction. Names, characters, places, and incidents either are the product of the author's
imagination or are used fictitiously, and any resemblance to actual persons, living or dead, business
establishments, events, or locales is entirely coincidental. The publisher does not have any control over
and does not assume any responsibility for author or third-party websites or their content.

PROTECTOR

A Berkley Sensation Book / published by arrangement with the author

PUBLISHING HISTORY
Berkley Sensation mass-market / March 2012

Copyright © 2012 by Catherine Mann.
Excerpt from *Guardian* by Catherine Mann copyright © 2012 by Catherine Mann.
Cover design by Annette Fiore DeFex. Cover art by Daniel O'Leary.
Interior text design by Laura K. Corless.

ISBN: 978-0-425-24699-3

BERKLEY SENSATION®
Berkley Sensation Books are published by The Berkley Publishing Group,
a division of Penguin Group (USA) Inc.,
375 Hudson Street, New York, New York 10014.
BERKLEY SENSATION® is a registered trademark of Penguin Group (USA) Inc.
The "B" design is a trademark of Penguin Group (USA) Inc.

PRINTED IN THE UNITED STATES OF AMERICA

10 9 8 7 6 5 4 3 2 1

ALWAYS LEARNING   **PEARSON**

"I count myself in nothing else so happy,
As in a soul rememb'ring my good friends."

—WILLIAM SHAKESPEARE

To K. Sue Morgan, Joanne Rock, Deborah Hale, and Winnie Griggs. Thank you for being my friends at the start of this writing journey, and for being the dearest of friends still today!

ACKNOWLEDGMENTS

Sometimes when an author is writing a novel, a secondary character whispers from the page, "Give me my own book." Captain Chuck Tanaka did just that when I wrote *Defender*. By the time Chuck showed up again as a secondary character in *Renegade*, he more than whispered, he demanded, "I deserve my own happily ever after!" And I'm thrilled to answer, "Here it is . . . Chuck Tanaka's book."

Many thanks to my editor, Wendy McCurdy, and my agent, Barbara Collins Rosenberg, for also wanting to hear Chuck's story. Much appreciation to my dear friend and critique partner, Joanne Rock, for reading this story again and again until I got it just right. Hugs, love, and thanks to my four children—Brice, Haley, Robbie, and Maggie—for understanding that deadline mom is a zombie mom. Ands always, I'm so grateful to my air force hero hubby for his help with the military details. Love you, Rob!

ONE

"I've lost my edge, Colonel."

The admission burned its way up Captain Chuck Tanaka's throat, each word like acid on open wounds inside him. But he was an ace at embracing pain, and he'd be damned before he would endanger anyone else by taking the colonel up on his offer to put Chuck back in the action.

F-16s roared overhead, rattling the rafters in the gaping hangar. Colonel Rex Scanlon stood beside him as airmen prepped for deployment to the Middle East with immunizations, gas masks, duffel bags full of gear. Close to two hundred warm bodies going to war.

Including his crew. His old crew from the top secret test squadron.

Pilots Jimmy Gage and Vince Deluca lined up with loadmaster Mason Randolph standing in a long, long line for a gamma globulin immunization along with an assload full of other shots to prepare them for the diseases overseas. He remembered well how the huge needle left a lump that made for uncomfortable flying. Back when he'd been their navigator. Before his injuries grounded him for life.

These days he was the squadron mobility officer. He ensured all deploying personnel were up to date with training, shots, equipment.

In a nutshell? He rode a desk and pushed paper.

Musty gear and a low hum of chitchat filled the hangar. All familiar. Jimmy, Vince, and Mason shuffled forward, flight suits down around their ankles in boxer shorts while the doc shouted, "Next."

"Tanaka?" Scanlon leaned forward, staring him down from behind black-rimmed glasses. "I need you on this mission. You're the man. You have the skills."

Not the skills he wanted, not the job he wanted. Better just to exist.

Chuck took a folder from an overeager airman and signed off on the bottom of a form. One more ready to deploy. Around them, uniformed men and women carried large green deployment bags stuffed full of equipment picked up at numerous stations. Security cops were posted throughout, watching and talking into radios. Off to his left, a dozen more who'd completed drawing equipment sat on the floor fitting the ballistic plates into their body armor. Another group checked over their weapons, disassembling and putting them back together.

His fingers twitched with muscle memory from performing the same tasks countless times. In the past. Speed mattered, and he couldn't trust his hands or his feet any longer.

Chuck slapped the folder closed. "I figure I've given my fair share to Uncle Sam. He won't mind if I sit out the rest of my commitment to the air force at my desk, rubber stamping paperwork."

Scanlon scrubbed his face, sighed hard, his eyes too full of the hell that went down when they'd both been in Turkey two years ago. "Without question, you've sacrificed more than your fair share for your country. But this op, this enemy, these people . . ." His jaw clenched, and the pity shifted to something harder. "This is our chance to even the score for what they did to you and those other servicemen they kidnapped."

Hunger. Mind games. Torture. Chuck's grip tightened on his clipboard.

Thankfully, his thoughts were broken by another airman thrusting a folder at him. He opened it and took a few minutes to calm himself by reading the checklist before signing at the bottom. He embraced routine and monotony through the days and sweated through the nights.

Chuck passed the folder back to the airman and waited until he stepped away before meeting the colonel's gaze dead on. "A very wise nun in the Hawaiian orphanage where I grew up always told me holding grudges is bad for the soul."

"In case you didn't notice, I'm not laughing."

Neither was Chuck these days. But he was getting by. Surviving one step at a time, as he recovered from the ass kicking he'd taken overseas at the hands of a sadistic bitch bent on prying secrets from servicemen, then selling the info to the highest terrorist bidder.

She hadn't gotten jack shit from him about the covert test missions he used to fly or the cutting-edge equipment he developed in the dark ops squadron. But he'd paid a heavy price for keeping those secrets.

"Pardon my bluntness, Colonel, but have you taken a look at me lately?" His eleven broken bones had healed as well as they ever would, and he was lucky to be on his feet again. Reconstructive surgery had taken care of most of the scars. External ones, anyway.

His ex-girlfriend claimed he was still an "emotional cripple." Whatever the hell that meant. "Sir, I know exactly what I'm worth these days, or rather how little. You're not fooling anyone here. Offering me a mission is the equivalent of a pity fuck. Sir."

Scanlon's thick eyebrow hitched upward through two shouts of "Next" before he pulled the clipboard from his hand and gave it to Chuck's assistant, a surprised master sergeant.

The colonel guided Chuck away from the bustle and behind some pallets loaded for the deployment. "Chuck, this mission could be the backbreaker for what some of the intel spooks think is a major attack here in the States. Our equipment, equipment you helped test, is the only way to exploit the one hole we have been able to find in their organization—"

"Not interested," he interrupted, desperate as hell to stop the colonel from taunting him with what he could not have anymore.

Scanlon continued as if he'd never been interrupted, "You'll go in undercover as a blackjack dealer on an Italian cruise ship next week. You won't be going in alone. I'll have your back, and David Berg will be running the surveillance equipment on board the *Fortuna*. Think about it. At worst you'll get some sun and great food. And at best, you'll bring down a terrorist cell."

Hunger for the chance to fight back gnawed at his gut. "You don't need me as the front man." Maybe . . . "Why not let me operate the gadgets? Nobody runs the packet analyzer and translator algorithms as well as I do. It's more art than science."

Shit, he was already envisioning himself there. "Forget I said that. I'm exactly where I should be—"

Pop! A gunshot blasted from the other side of the pallets. A chunk of wood splintered into the air.

Chuck jerked hard and fast, looking over his shoulder even as he knew it had to be some dumb ass who'd slipped a round in his weapon then seriously screwed up with an unintentional discharge. He looked across the hangar—

And stared straight into the cold, emotionless eyes of a gunman who looked too damn much like one of their own firing wildly into the clusters of airmen.

So fast. Shouts and more pops. Bullets. From the gunman and the security cops, but no one could get a decent aim as the guy ran and bobbed. The gunman turned toward Chuck's old crew. Fired. Jimmy spun back as a round caught him in the shoulder. The gun tracked Jimmy for another—

Chuck drew his sidearm before he could think and centered on the uniformed gunman's chest. *Pop. Pop. Pop.* He squeezed off three shots, center of mass.

Everyone and everything in the hangar went unearthly still. The only sound was a haunting echo of Chuck's shots.

The gunman crumpled to the ground a second before the acrid scent of gunfire bit the air.

Chuck's fist clenched around the familiar weight of his 9 mm. The hangar seemed to freeze frame, imprinting itself in his brain. Cops with weapons drawn. Others with their fists wrapped around the butt of a gun. The unarmed huddled, hugging their heads protectively.

Slowly, sounds of sirens outside pierced his consciousness and snapped the frame back into motion. Security cops swarmed the downed gunman. His old crewmate, Jimmy, sat up, clutching his shoulder with blood pouring between his fingers while the rest of the crew checked him over. No one else had opened fire, but the edgy need to stay on guard seared the air as three other injured held on to a bleeding leg or arm. No one dead, though. Thank God.

Chuck scoured the hangar. Adrenaline coursed through

him, his pulse pounding in his ears. The gun felt right in his hands. Taking out an enemy felt even better.

The colonel secured his unfired weapon back in the holster and stared at Chuck's smoking gun, now pointing upward. "Still think you've lost your edge, Tanaka? Because from where I'm standing, it appears you just stopped a massacre."

Chuck lowered his weapon slowly, the inevitable flooding his veins with each slug of his heart. "That same old nun also told me gloating is as dangerous as grudges."

"Fair enough, Captain. I take it then you'll be joining Berg and me at the morning briefing?"

He nodded once without taking his eyes off the unconscious gunman.

"Good, good." Scanlon righted his black-framed glasses. "Meanwhile, you may want to brush up on your blackjack skills."

Chuck thumbed the barrel of his weapon, an undeniable thirst filling him. The need to get back in the fight. The need to defend his comrades.

The need to avenge.

There were still a lot of blanks to be filled in, but then that's what briefs were for. He didn't need to hear any more well-executed persuasive arguments. He already knew.

He was going all in.

★ GENOA: CRUISE TERMINAL OF
  PONTE DEI MILLE

"Who wants eight the hard way?"

"I'll take that. Gimme twenty on eight."

"Come on, little Joe from Ko-ko-mo!"

Jolynn Taylor parted the pervasive smoke with her body, winding around slot machines and frenzied gamblers. Her eyes stung, and she tried to blame the moisture on the thick cigarette haze. She wanted to be as far away from this sleazy, sometimes dangerous world as she could get.

Why hadn't she just ignored the message and stayed in Dallas rather than racing all the way to Genoa, Italy? Security for intercontinental flights was hellish right now after that attack at the Nevada military base last week.

Sure, her father was recovering from a heart attack. But he employed plenty of people to care for him while he recuperated at a local rehab center and then in total luxury on one of his cruise ships. *He* was the one who chose to live overseas floating from port to port, Italy, Greece, Croatia . . .

She slipped between an aging Italian contessa playing the slots and a newlywed couple plastered together by the one-armed bandit chanting out their desire in French. The casino's nerve-tingling clamor contrasted in her mind with the quiet sterility of a sickroom . . . her father's sickroom, which she couldn't avoid much longer. Nothing short of hearing he was at death's door could have drawn her back into his seedy realm.

Bells chimed and lights flashed as she elbowed through the crowd in search of her cousin, Lucy, the director of operations. Once she dropped off her luggage and got the latest lowdown on her dad, she would drive over to his rehab center.

"Hello, love." A Brit with slicked-back brown hair held a pair of dice in one hand and palmed her leg with the other. "Be a dear and blow on my dice. A pretty bird like you could change my luck."

Jolynn offered him her best insipid drawl reserved for

soused morons who put on fakey accents. "Wish I could help you out, sugar." She moved his hand firmly. "But I can't be giving anyone a house advantage."

She tapped her laminated security pass, resisting the urge to tell him to "sod off." Forging ahead, she passed a young couple walking from machine to machine, silver mining for loose coins.

The ship's lounge singer took the stage and started off her next set with a morose Italian ballad to some moony-eyed guy, which only darkened Jolynn's already bottomed-out mood. She wanted no part of her father's world. Yet she missed him with an ache as annoying as the blister developing on her heel.

Jolynn shouldered through the press of overheated bodies until she escaped the circle of gaming tables into the hollow center designated for dealers and the pit boss. The open area provided a clearer, and calmer, vantage point from which to scour the area.

She pivoted, only to pitch forward. Her feet tangled with someone crouched near the blackjack table. Her arms pinwheeled before smacking the floor, halting her gangly tumble. Jolynn's body bridged the huddled individual's back. A man's back. Pressed against him, she could feel every whipcord muscle of his slim physique. His musky male scent pleasantly distracted her from the casino's smoky odor.

"Excuse me." She walked her fingers along the carpeted floor, inching up and using the man's broad back as her final boost. "I didn't see you down—"

"*Ooof.* Careful. That's my kidney."

His protest tickled her ears, his American accent bathing her in familiar sounds of home. Jolynn skimmed her hand over his spine to his shoulder, enjoying the sinuous trek a little too much. "So sorry. I was preoccupied and didn't look where I was going."

She grabbed the blackjack table for leverage as she stood. She shook her skirt in place with a little shimmy, not wanting to know how much she'd exposed during their impromptu game of Twister. "Did I inflict permanent damage?"

"Everything seems intact."

"Good." Jolynn looked down at the kneeling man staring back up with mesmerizing mocha dark eyes.

She'd never been much of a romantic, but his eyes seemed to glint with hidden depths . . . Okay, okay, light from the crystal chandelier may have added something to the dreamy effect. Even so, she couldn't look away.

He shook his sleek black hair into place again. His forearm rested on his bent knee, his other hand pressed to the floor. He had a broad forehead, a firm chin, and fine creases around exotic eyes, perhaps with a hint of Polynesian ancestry. He was a total package kind of guy, with a strong, handsome face. She judged him to be in his late twenties or early thirties.

He rose, finally stopping just at her level, around six feet in her heels. Perfect. In her father's world of burly men and overblown personalities, she found calming reassurance in the man's understated power.

Safe. Sexy, yet safe. "Are you sure you're all right? Your kidney, I mean."

"I've taken worse hits and survived," he said softly. "How about you?"

Better than three minutes ago. She welcomed the opportunity to think of something, anything other than where she was. "Just fine."

"Glad to hear it." He nodded slowly, his thick hair sliding over his brow.

Smiling, she backed away—and bumped into a waitress who shouldn't have even been in the pit area. A tray of drinks flew from the woman's hand and crashed to the floor. Jolynn winced.

Not even back in her family circle for a full day and already she'd reverted to her gangly teen moves. Years of cultivating a poise that rivaled her father's multitude of Greek and Roman goddess statues evaporated with a simple glance from this guy.

He grinned, creasing dimples in his cheeks. "Sorry to trip you up like that—again." He extended his hand, offering her the silver token gleaming in his palm. "I didn't mean to start such a ruckus just to retrieve this."

"No harm done." Jolynn accepted the token with an ironic smile.

"I'll be happy to pay for your dry cleaning."

"You don't have to do that." She would settle for another one of those distracting smiles instead.

"At least let me help you dry off." He grabbed a stack of cocktail napkins and reached out to blot her travel-weary suit jacket. His fist clenched just beside the damp fabric covering her breasts.

He passed the wadded clump to her. "You may, uh, want to take care of this yourself."

"Uh, thanks."

Fantasy gave way to reality as she refocused on the man in front of her. He wore the standard casino uniform of creased black pants, a loose white shirt, a red bow tie . . . and a name tag. *Charles Tomas: Blackjack Dealer.*

Her safe, beautiful man was a two-bit blackjack dealer. Of course he was. How could she have forgotten where she was?

Jolynn resurrected the vapid facade she used as a defense against the smarmy losers she attracted like flies to sticky paper. "See you around, sugar."

She watched his smile fade.

"Jolynn Taylor!"

The high-pitched squeal of her only cousin carried over the mayhem, breaking into any further temptation to daydream.

Long ago, when she'd learned the truth about her father's international mob connections, Jolynn had quit believing in fantasy princes. Trusting in fairy tales got people killed. She'd toughened up fast and didn't plan to change.

As soon as she helped her father settle in on his floating barge of iniquity, she'd be back on a plane to a normal life. By then, the nagging ache to reconnect with the old man would be soothed and all thoughts of dark-eyed princes would be left behind with the Mediterranean Sea.

* * *

Chuck Tanaka watched Jolynn hug the casino's director of operations, before the cousins commandeered stools at the bar.

When the leggy redhead had charged through the casino, he hadn't even needed to glance at her security pass to clue him in. He'd recognized Jolynn Taylor, knew her bio in the report he'd received on Josiah Taylor's operation. The past week had been spent packing his head full of information, preparing as the CIA brought in the NSA as well as the air force OSI and their special ops test unit.

Some of the briefing had been done in person, some by telecom, some anonymously. For their own protection, supposedly, but it sucked not knowing who all the players were.

For his own protection, they'd assured him. But then he already knew he couldn't only rely on his test squadron brothers.

Implementing their setup and cover stories had been

easier than expected with the rest of the world preoccupied with the soldier who'd open fired on the deploying troops.

Thank God no one had been killed.

He brought his attention back to the moment. He was in the game again. A last-ditch effort to resurrect himself. Do or die.

Already he'd almost fumbled when the colonel had slipped the warning about Jolynn's unplanned arrival. Chuck had nearly botched calling the game when from across the room Colonel Scanlon had pointed her out by that British dude.

Chuck had known it must be important for Scanlon to break their established routine of exchanging info at designated times. The colonel had whispered the alert under the guise of asking for directions to the lounge to hear his Italian girlfriend sing. The warning that Josiah Taylor's daughter was due in for an obligatory sickbed visit had come just in time for him to toss himself in her path, literally. Not one of his smoother moves, but his klutz act had gotten the job done. Contact had been made.

Except she'd rocked his balance right back.

He monitored Jolynn and her cousin as they ordered drinks. He'd made the requisite attempts to cultivate a low-key relationship with the director of operations. But she was too wrapped up in her security guard fiancé to talk about anything other than wedding plans.

Chuck mentally reviewed the facts on file about Jolynn Taylor. Boarding school education. Six-figure accounting job in Dallas and dating life that made the social pages. The rumor mill churned with stories of Josiah's estranged daughter.

His systematic analysis faded as he remembered the press of her breasts against his chest. He'd almost forgotten to breathe. She'd come too damned close to finding his Beretta strapped in the ankle holster.

Across the room, her auburn hair gleamed like a warning light. Damn, he'd been too long without. His breakup was already six months old and that relationship had been, well, a mixed-up mess.

He was better served staying clear of female entanglements. Making contact was one thing. Letting attraction get the better of him was another. A mistake he'd made two years ago and it had cost him. Big-time.

Chuck turned his back on Jolynn Taylor and dealt the next hand. He wasn't done with her yet. Thanks to the surveillance device in the token he'd given her—which she'd so accommodatingly placed in her purse—he would be reviewing tapes of her conversation well into the night.

TWO

Colonel Rex Scanlon had unfinished business.

And if there was one thing he'd learned since coming to grips with his wife's sudden death, he knew life could screw you over in a heartbeat. So a guy had better fix what he could, while he could.

He closed the door, sealing him inside the standard cruise cabin, deep in the belly of the boat with no windows or portals to compromise security. Rex double bolted the additional locks and swept aside a striped privacy curtain. The space wasn't much larger than a walk-in closet, but perfect for Major David Berg to set up his surveillance equipment along the wall with narrow bunk beds over it for sleeping. They'd declined maid service. The spot was perfect.

The engine room on the other side of the wall even offered the perfect disguising noise. Not to mention very few would ever bother taking a leisurely stroll down here.

David "Ice" Berg waved without looking away from his computer screens, one earbud plugged into the system. The token Chuck has slipped to Jolynn was one of their solid standby toys with a boosted range and an imperceptible signal. No one would ever know they'd been bugged. But of course, they developed listening devices that worked from fifty thousand feet. This part was a cakewalk.

Rex swept the curtain back over the door. Although chances were next to nil that anyone other than he, Berg, or Tanaka would get past the high-level security locks.

Berg was a driven perfectionist and workaholic, still reeling from a messy divorce. His ex had walked out on him and both kids. The older child, a boy, had been from her first marriage so he went to his biological father while Berg had custody of the daughter.

Life was definitely too complicated to miss out on settling unresolved business whenever possible.

Hopefully, this mission would tie up a number of loose ends at once, tightening until they formed a net around a particular Al-Qaida cell that had wreaked havoc on his squadron. He needed this. Chuck had to have this win in order to move on.

Not that Rex would have brought him along unless he was the best. Tanaka's lightning-quick reactions during the hangar attack proved he was the man for the job. The hell he'd endured merely honed him.

Rex dropped into a silver plastic chair beside Berg. "We really gotta get you better seats in here."

"My ass would thank you for that, sir." Berg unplugged the headset and switched to speaker. A conversation softly filled the air. Jolynn Taylor talked with her cousin Lucy.

And an Italian love song echoed in the background sung by Livia Cicero. *His* unfinished business.

Her husky voice crooned over the airwaves and straight into his senses like a shot of undiluted liquor. Top quality. High potency.

"Heard anything interesting yet?"

"Give it time, sir. I've barely unpacked my flip-flops yet," Berg said dryly, clicking through images on the split screens, one of which focused on Chuck Tanaka flipping cards between fingers that doctors had once considered amputating.

Tanaka had taken a beating at the hands of a bitch intent on prying secrets from his brain and selling them to terrorists. Yeah, this mission was more than a little personal. The woman was in jail. But they were still chasing down higher-ups in the network.

The boat would leave port tomorrow at noon. Word had it Josiah himself would slip on board in the morning—against his doctor's advice. Further affirmation something big was shaking down.

Thank God for the tip he'd gotten from Livia Cicero, an almost lover who'd never been an item in his life but someone he'd never been able to forget. In semiretirement from singing, she ran with a high-power political crowd throughout Europe and Asia. People assumed she was dense.

Stupid people who were dense in their own right. Livia had brains and spunk to spare.

Five minutes into hearing what she'd observed on the cruise ship, Rex had called Eagle Eye, a counterterrorism clearinghouse. Because of her tip, they'd pieced together bits from intercepted cell phone chatter to know that someone major in the terrorist network would be getting on board at one of the stops, while making his or her way across Europe and into the United States. The ultimate goal? Set off a dirty nuke in a major subway.

Now they had to figure out who, when, where that person would climb on the ship, and hopefully, details of the attack.

Failure wasn't an option. "Are the parabolic devices generating anything of interest?"

Attached to windows, the device could pick up the vibrations on the pane, reading conversations. "No major red flags, but I'm piping data back to our lab techies for detailed review."

"What about Jolynn Taylor's suite?"

"I'm on it. I'll have something for Chuck to work with by morning."

"Good, good." He stared at the technology in front of him and wondered if it would be enough. "Anything I can get you before I go back up?"

"A sunlamp?" The former South Carolinian semipro golfer scrubbed a hand over his shaggy hair. When on base he kept his mustache and hair trimmed to regulations. But he was known for letting both grow out during undercover missions. "I'm gonna be so pale after this maybe we can change my call sign to Dracula."

"Your country appreciates your sacrifice."

"Yeah, yeah, yada, yada, whatever. Don't forget to toss some bread and water in every now and again, sir."

Normally Berg oversaw entire test programs these days, but this mission made Rex itchy, nervous. He'd pulled David Berg to join in even though he was technically overqualified. Because if—God forbind—Chuck couldn't deliver, they needed all the muscle possible to haul his ass out of the fire.

Berg tweaked a knob, filtering through noises as he zoomed in the camera on Jolynn Taylor chatting with her cousin. Rex looked quickly from screen to screen and realized he wasn't the only one watching her—Tanaka and the British gambler were both trying to be covert, but from this angle there was no missing it.

Rex scraped back his chair. "Okay then, Berg. Time to take in some culture."

The Italian singer's voice summoned from the screen. He could only trust himself and two of the best from his squadron to keep her safe.

★ ★ ★

Jolynn used the tiny straw to stir her seltzer water with lime, the love ballads beginning to grow old fast. Didn't the Italian songstress know anything else? Maybe the woman was depressed over losing her pop star career and having nothing left but to hit the cruise ship circuit.

"Hello?" Lucy tapped a manicured nail against her glass, ting, ting, tinging for attention. "How did it go when you saw him?"

Jolynn blinked fast and worked to keep her eyes off the blackjack dealer. How had Lucy noticed—

Wait. Her cousin meant how had it gone when she saw her father. Which she hadn't. And God, but she needed a distraction.

"My flight was delayed because of tightened security. That attack on the base in Nevada has all the airplanes on higher alert." She shivered at the raised terror level. "I've been wanded, frisked, not to mention dog sniffed by very thorough canines. By the time I arrived here, it was too late to go by the rehab center."

Lucy reached into her pocket and pulled out a tiny travel bottle of hand sanitizer—orange nectar scent.

Smiling, Jolynn extended her hands. The day Lucy joined her at boarding school had started the happiest time in Jolynn's life. Lucy, a pixie of a woman with bobbed blond hair, possessed an effortless charm that had won over the private academy cliques in a way Jolynn never would have managed on her own.

Sometimes she could almost forget that her father paid his niece's tuition out of guilt. "How's he doing? Really?"

"The old man's hanging in there. He says he prefers to recover on one of his ships, with his own doctors around him. That an eight-day cruise is the tonic he needs . . . blah, blah, blah. I'm not so sure it's the wisest decision, but no one can make him do anything he doesn't want."

Lucy squeezed her hand. "Let's talk about happy things . . . like how you sure can make an entrance."

She tossed her straw aside on the clear acrylic table. "My feet tangled with your clumsy blackjack dealer."

"He's new. I hired him about a month ago. His name's Thompson, uh, Turner, or uhm—"

"Tomas. Charles Tomas." His name tasted new and memorable on her tongue.

"So you noticed, did ya? Join the crowd. Mr. Tomas has everyone in skirts working their chops off to gain his attention. The waitress probably flattened him out of desperation." Lucy gave her friend an assessing once-over. "We've all been wondering what it would take to sneak past his defenses. You may be just the ticket."

"Me?" Jolynn forced her eyes to stay off him. "Forget it."

"Coy doesn't suit you," her kittenish cousin said, tucking her hair behind her ears. Lucy's hair was razor cut, shorter in the back, trailing in the front. "We've got a running bet on which lucky lady he'll ask out. I'd go after him myself if I weren't already engaged. As of this minute, I'm putting my money on you, Red."

More than ready to talk about something else, she said, "So when do I get to meet your fiancé?"

"You're gonna love Adolpho . . ." Lucy paused. "Hey, nice try, but don't change the subject." She waggled a finger, bracelets chiming like the chink of coins from a jackpot. "Help me out. I need the cash I could rake in from winning this one to pay for some of that beading on my wedding dress."

Jolynn stared at Charles Tomas and cursed her bad instincts with men. Chanting encouragement to the crowd, he sailed cards toward Mr. Blow on My Dice, who'd abandoned craps in favor of blackjack.

"No offense, Lucy, but this visit is as close as I want to be to Dad's business." Remembering the day she'd witnessed her father's business practices in action, recalling the acrid smell of blood, she shuddered. She'd learned at twelve years old not to trust anyone, even her own dad. She hadn't met a male since who'd changed her mind.

"Hmmm." Lucy twisted her bracelets around her wrist.

"What?"

"Did I forget to mention his application says he's saving up to return to the London School of Economics? A late-in-life career change, or so he said in the interview. Apparently he's taking online classes at some American college now . . . But I'm rambling. Suffice it to say, he's hot, smart, and available."

Something warm unfurled inside Jolynn, something that felt remarkably like hope. She reassessed Charles, envisioning him as a professor, or maybe a banker. Sexy, smart, and *safe*.

Definitely a deadly combination.

As if he sensed her gaze, he peered over his shoulder at her. His face dimpled into a sheepish grin.

Dimples. *Angel kisses*. She savored a rare memory of her mother explaining the tiny indentations as special kisses from heaven.

The straw bent in her hand. Dallas definitely would have been safer.

* * *

Chuck closed his locker with a restrained click. Slamming wouldn't come close to releasing the pent-up frustration inside him. He slung his backpack over his shoulder and cut a path through the other workers in the employees' lounge. He hoped for a bit of luck so he could slip out for a drive before the ship left in the morning.

Focus. He couldn't afford to let his mind wander, especially while on the *Fortuna*.

He strode through the gaming area into the enclosed gangplank. His footsteps echoed with hollow thuds until the confines exploded into an array of color splashing through the spiky crystals hanging overhead like something out of Superman's home planet of Krypton. Glass double doors waited like a piece of salvation beyond a goddess fountain statue. He flashed his employee ID to the guard keeping track of those going on and off the ship on his way out.

Safely on solid land—or concrete—Chuck tipped his head back and inhaled the fresh night air, grateful to leave behind the chaotic world belowdecks. He hoofed it away from the cruise terminal of Ponte dei Mille. He would meet up with the colonel and Berg later, after his concentration steadied.

Instinctively, he surveyed the area around him. At his four o'clock, a couple of teens with assorted pierced body parts were cruising the nightclubs. At ten o'clock, a vendor hauled covers over wooden stalls and a drunken businessman type stumbled toward a trash can.

He forced back memories of late night in another foreign city. In Istanbul. Of a woman who'd lured him. Drugged him, then . . .

Breathe. Overcome it. Don't let the past steal any more of his life.

As if in defiance of Chuck's need for order, Jolynn Taylor appeared at his twelve o'clock. Even with the tight suit gone, she didn't offer much relief with its replacement. Crisp white jeans and a shiny yellow shirt hugged her slim body. Her hair, gathered with a band, trailed a fiery path between her shoulder blades.

The aching tendon in his neck kinked tighter. He ignored the pain. What was she hiding?

Her brush-off at the casino had stung, then stirred the coals of his banked anger. Apparently Ms. Taylor didn't hang with the help.

Chuck leaned against a lamppost under the pretense of searching through his backpack. Tomorrow would be soon enough for a second "meeting" with her, once the colonel could update him, and once he'd gotten his damned hormones under control.

She slid long legs into a Maserati Cambio Corsa with the cruise ship name on the license plate—*Fortuna*—the Roman goddess for luck. Jolynn slammed the door then riffled through her huge designer purse for what seemed like an eternity.

Why wasn't she leaving? Something was off. He couldn't just leave her here vulnerable.

But he wouldn't be caught off guard again, either.

Crouching, he pulled his Beretta from under his pant leg and tucked it in his waistband. He readjusted the loose folds of his shirt, concealing the gun.

As he checked the tattooed teens again, a movement slid through his peripheral vision. The drunk businessman straightened.

Too alert, the man veered away from the trash can, his

focus on the Maserati. He stalked toward Jolynn with lethal grace. She struggled with the ignition, hunching over the steering wheel. The vulnerable curve of her neck glowed under the hazy streetlamps.

Adrenaline pumped through Chuck, tightening his scalp. The familiar metallic taste stung his mouth. He padded across the cement, his muscles bunched, ready to unleash into action. The businessman cocked his head to the side and turned—the slick British guy from the casino who'd hit on Jolynn. His narrowed gaze connected with Chuck's, the feral gleam unmistakable even in the dim garage.

Chuck knew his time to plan was over. His feet picked up speed as he closed in on the Maserati convertible.

THREE

"Damn it." Jolynn pounded the heel of her hand against the dashboard. She tried the ignition again and—nothing. Her head slid forward to rest on her arms hooked over the steering wheel.

She let two tears slide free, tears for her father. After years of shuffling her aside, he had asked for her.

It had taken a massive heart attack, but he finally needed her, and like a sap, she'd come running across continents to his side. Only to freak out before she could knock on his door.

She'd told everyone—herself even—she couldn't visit him because of flight delays, but she was a liar. Only back in her dad's world for a few hours and already she was falling into old bad habits.

Like drooling over her father's employees.

If she could just have a ride to clear her head, she would be fine, in control again. Flopping back on her seat, she tried to envision what could be wrong with her Maserati. She was too tired to peek under the hood, and a darkened street didn't seem like the wisest place to do it while alone. She should take this as a sign that she couldn't keep running forever. Time to call Lucy and ask about another ride.

Jolynn rummaged through her cavernous bag and pulled out the cell phone, dialing the number from memory. Phone calls and visits with Lucy had been the only link Jolynn had allowed herself to her father over the years.

While waiting, she tried the ignition again, on the outside chance it might work. The dull "click" popped in the pitch black, along with dance club music in the distance. Too distant. Her skin prickled. Footsteps echoed in the darkened alley, coming closer. Fear ballooned up to her throat.

"Everything okay?"

Charles Tomas. At the sound of his voice, Jolynn melted into the supple leather of her seat. She peered through the window as he rested an elbow on the roof.

Her momentary relief shifted. What did she really know about him? What if Charles turned out to be some baby-faced killer? Would anyone immersed in the nightlife even hear her?

"Hello. Hello?" The muffled sound of Lucy's voice drifted from the cell phone.

Jolynn sagged with relief. As long as she let Lucy know where she was, and whom she was with, she should be fine. She lifted the phone with one hand, rolling down the window with the other. She wanted Charles to hear her conversation and realize she'd identified him to the outside world, just in case.

"Hi, Lucy, it's me." Jolynn could feel his heat reach to her through the open window.

"Do you know what time it is? Oh, no, is it your dad? Tell me where you are. I'm on my way."

"Wait. I was going to see him—" Lying again already? "Except the company car is giving me trouble. Your new blackjack dealer has come to the rescue."

The predictable laugh drifted from the receiver, before Lucy launched into a litany of "I told you so." Only half listening to her friend's ramblings, Jolynn allowed herself an unrestrained look at Charles.

He stepped back from the car, arms crossed over his chest. With the casino uniform tie discarded, his white shirt fell open at the collar. A silver chain nestled in the part.

Why couldn't she have the traditional, delicate whisper of butterflies tingling her senses? No, something more like a hummingbird knocked around inside her.

Charles looked so normal, probably an everyday guy from a regular family. She wanted to trust her instincts for once but she knew better.

"You're with him right now, aren't you?" Lucy's voice vibrated through the phone.

"We're not in high school anymore," Jolynn said.

Charles leaned against the cement wall, glancing around the side alley. She followed his gaze to a businessman jogging away, toward his car. Apparently in a rush, the guy peeled out and away from the cruise terminal of Ponte dei Mille.

Leaving her alone with Charles.

"Jolynn . . ." Lucy's voice turned bossy. "Now's the perfect time for you to play the helpless female."

"Stop it." Jolynn wasn't sure she had the emotional energy at the moment for any man, no matter how sexy. "Can you—"

"Oh, come on. You don't have to worry about him being some weirdo. He's a pussycat."

Jolynn hoped Charles would give her at least another

minute to gather her composure before he did something drastic, like smile. "I'll call back if we can't get the car running."

"You'll call with details first thing in the morning."

He smiled.

"Good night, Lucy." Jolynn looked away. The frantic little bird in her gut wanted out.

Charles cleared his throat. "Looks like you're having trouble with the car. Are you leaving already?"

She deactivated the phone, tucking it back inside her bag. "It won't even turn over. And no, I'm not leaving."

Jolynn released the latch and circled to the front of the car just as he lifted the hood. She passed him a flashlight.

"Hmmm." He rolled his sleeves to his elbows, before extending a hand. "Charles Tomas. We were never formally introduced inside."

"Hello, Charles. I'm Jolynn Taylor." She waited for his expression to change to apprehension or greed as he realized she was the boss's daughter. And she waited . . . But nothing.

"Nice to meet you, Jolynn Taylor." He shook her hand in one smooth motion. "Let's see what's going on with your car."

She didn't bother letting him know if the vehicle could be fixed without a computer in a shop, she could do it herself. Let him assume what he wanted. To argue that while she loved high heels, she hated cooking and adored crawling beneath an engine, well, that would mean she cared what he thought, which was far more hazardous than depending on his help for a few minutes.

Charles crouched beside the Maserati, peering underneath. Standing, he rested the heels of his palms on the front of her car. He reached inside, tweaking caps and hoses, while he "hmmm'd" in that time-honored manner she'd always found an amusing part of the male strutting ritual.

Bent over the engine, he displayed his incredibly cute, narrow-hipped tush. Her gaze moved up past the taut sinews of his back she'd explored a few hours earlier. "Find anything?"

"Not yet." He leaned farther under the hood. "If you don't mind my asking, where are you headed this late?"

"Going to visit my father." And as she said it, she realized she had to make the trip tonight, no matter how late. Delaying gave her father too much power over her emotions. "Uh, you may have heard that Dad had a heart attack."

She pushed down the cuticle of her thumbnail and wondered what she would say to the man she hadn't seen in ten years.

Charles shifted to the side, dipping his head to look at her. "Not much of a family reunion."

"Nope." His flash of compassion reached to her, touching a corner of her lonely heart.

"Why don't you try to crank it again?"

Jolynn slid into the driver's seat and pressed the ignition button and . . . Still nothing. She ducked her head through the window and looked around the mirror. "Well?"

"Beats me." Charles shrugged, his greasy fingers dangling in front of him. "Sorry."

She thought about those nimble fingers scooping up cards . . . stroking her flesh. She fished around in the glove compartment for something to clean away the grease and came back with a box of Kleenex.

Jolynn joined him in front of the car. "Here."

"Thanks." He took the tissues and swiped his long fingers. "Wish I could have done more to help so you could enjoy that ride. Guess I'm just not all that great with electronics. Can I walk you back to the stateroom? Wouldn't want you to run into trouble out here alone at night."

"You tried." Jolynn watched each swipe until she forced herself to focus on something mundane, like a radiator.

"At least let me escort you onto the ship."

Dilemma. Big-time dilemma. She stared under the hood, directly at the wire hanging loose beside the distributor. Every feminine inch of her screamed, *Leave the car alone. Come back out and fix it after he leaves. You don't have to prove a thing.*

She clenched her fists by her sides and willed herself not to show this man any part of herself beyond what she chose to let him see.

Her hands reconnected the wire to the distributor.

She whipped the tissue box from him. Maybe he'd known that all along and had just been conning her as a way to spend time with her and get close to the boss's daughter. Reluctantly, she looked into his eyes. Rather than surprise, she found—admiration.

"Well, Jolynn, I bet it starts now."

Sure enough, the Maserati purred to life. "Thanks anyway."

"No problem."

Envisioning their next encounter, she imagined her blackjack dealer toppling his table as a shield against the Amazon threatening him with a socket wrench. But damn it, she'd had to learn to take care of herself. She'd had no choice in a world where even her own uncle wasn't safe. She needed to leave now.

Charles glanced at his watch and frowned.

"Is something wrong?" Why couldn't she just go?

Charles rubbed his hand along his jaw. "Hey, why don't I go with you to the hospital? It's late, and while you're an undeniably capable lady around an engine, a dark hospital parking lot isn't the safest place to be alone." His face dimpled into a smile. "Please, don't deny me my life's dream of riding in a Maserati convertible with a redheaded lady mechanic."

Panic pattered in her gut. She should tell him no. But then just as she'd avoided her father, turning down this man's polite and logical request to accompany her late at night in a foreign town . . . it just wouldn't make sense.

She eyed him, eyed the car. Why not? Lucy had already given him her stamp of approval. Compared to the risk in coming home, how dangerous could a short ride be through the heart of Genoa with Charles? "Get in."

* * *

Relief slammed through Chuck harder than the closing door.

Thank God he wouldn't have to scrounge for more excuses to accompany her, or worse yet, follow her and risk being made. But he needed to be sure nothing more came of that brush with the Brit.

And no way in hell could he pass up a chance for a face-to-face with her father. A meet with the mob boss could be good for their operation.

He rubbed a hand along the kink in his neck, still strung tight from his near-confrontation with the guy who'd very likely tampered with her car, a guy who'd been close to her more than once on the cruise ship. "Is it okay if I store my backpack in the trunk?"

"Go ahead." She passed him the clunky key chain.

"I'll be right back." He stowed his bag.

He'd thought he could keep her at the ship by not fixing

her car—ironic as hell since he specialized in testing military jets and weaponry for a living. Or rather he had . . . Before . . .

Who would have thought Jolynn could tell a distributor wire from a battery cable? Chuck couldn't suppress a smile remembering her chagrined expression after reconnecting the distributor.

His smile faded. A wilting flower wouldn't be as tempting.

He had more important concerns. His cursory inspection of the undercarriage and engine hadn't uncovered any sign of explosives. The last thing he needed was to explain away a brick of C-4. Nothing more could be done except to stick with her and make sure she got to and from the hospital in one piece.

"All set." Chuck eased into his seat, "accidentally" knocking her purse to spill on the floor. "Sorry about that."

Leaning forward, he checked under the dash for as long as he dared. The bumbling facade made a decent cover at times, but he hated acting the fool in front of such a competent woman.

Be honest with yourself, Tanaka. That she was an *attractive*, competent woman made the pinch to his ego all the more uncomfortable.

Not that he planned to pursue her.

"Here you go." Chuck stuffed the contents back in her bag.

"Thanks."

Jolynn's fingers brushed against his oversensitive palm. Her obvious awareness of the moment bothered him. The jolt of her touch bothered him even more. Damn.

His body didn't seem to care she wasn't his type. But then his body had betrayed him before.

* * *

Jolynn wrestled with guilt during the drive to the rehab center in the forested outskirts of Genoa. After passing two churches and a basilica, her conscience was kicking into overtime. She should be focused on her father's condition— checking on him—finding out why the hell someone hadn't bothered to let her know sooner. How could she be so into talking with someone she barely knew?

Maybe because he was actually a good listener. They discussed his return to college, her job. Lightweight stuff, and just what she needed to take her mind off what awaited her inside the rehab center.

By the time they reached the hospital parking lot, she decided not to overanalyze her reaction to the blackjack dealer–math whiz. Her jumbled nerves calmed with Charles Tomas in the seat next to her. She couldn't remember when she'd simply talked with a man, her defenses always too high for anything more than banter.

She shut off the car outside the five-hundred-year-old Renaissance Italian villa that had been converted into a posh rehab center. Tuscan columns and Roman arches shone in the floodlights strategically placed along the garden grounds. And the statues . . . fewer and more subdued than the ones her father favored, but without question, he felt at home here.

Turning, she faced Charles, the small space in the luxury car suddenly smaller, more intimate. "Thanks for coming along so late. I hope you won't fall asleep at work tomorrow."

"No problem. I'm used to working crazy hours across time zones." He tipped his head to the side, rubbing a hand along the back of his neck. "Are you ready to go up now?"

"You don't have to come with me." She avoided his gaze under the auspices of gathering her purse. "If you want to get something to eat, I can find you when I'm through."

"I'll pick up coffee for both of us and meet you afterward." He pulled out a sleek new iPhone, a model so slim it looked like a serious upgrade from even hers. "I can keep myself occupied."

As he bent to help her, Jolynn raised her head, and they bumped painfully. Chuckling, he pulled away. "Do you think we should alert the paramedics anytime we're in the same place?"

His light teasing eased the tension coiled in the pit of her stomach. "Thanks, Charles. I needed a laugh today."

"Glad I could help." He held her eyes with his intense dark stare. "Take as long as you need."

Without knocking over a gurney or flattening any nurses bearing trays full of blood samples, they safely entered a private wing of the rehab center, where her father had been recuperating from his heart attack. The smooth sounds of Italian spoken quickly flowed over her ears. Her mother had loved coming here, the reason her father had set up his first international office in this region. Memories of her mom were few, but the sound of her sitting in a beach chair practicing the language with a tutorial tape . . . She swallowed hard.

Her gaze swept the empty leather sofas—antique reproductions with carved cherry accents rather than the standard Naugahyde and steel that filled normal hospital settings. Finally her eyes landed on the welcome sight of her father's friend and longtime head of security sprawled in a carved throne chair watching a television tucked in an antique armoire.

"Hello, Hebert." Jolynn savored the soft Cajun pronunciation of the old man's name, *Ay-bear*.

Hebert Benoit's familiar, square face creased into an asymmetrical smile with a chipped front tooth. He ambled to his feet and crunched her into a hug. "Welcome, welcome. 'Bout time you came."

"Then perhaps you should have let me know about his heart attack when it happened."

"And maybe it shouldna taken that to bring you into the family fold again."

Except things weren't that simple with her family. Even her feelings for this longtime protector of hers were tainted with the possibility of darker duties he must have carried out for her father over the years.

"Is he awake?"

"He never sleeps, same as always." Hebert mopped a handkerchief over the sweat beading along his bald head. Spidery veins and bluster stained his smiling face.

"What's he thinking, recovering on a ship, away from a fully outfitted hospital?"

Hebert brushed back a lock of her hair with a beefy hand. "He's old, just like me, and when you're running out of time, you just aren't willing to waste any of it being somewhere you don't wanna be."

So where did that leave her now with the decision to come to Genoa?

Hebert gestured to Charles. "What's he doin' here?"

The blackjack dealer lounged against the door frame with his backpack dangling from one hand. "Good evening, Mr. Benoit."

The older man grunted.

Jolynn placed a hand on Hebert's arm and squeezed.

"Charles helped get my car started. He rode along in case it gave me trouble again."

"Thanks, Tomas." Hebert's brows lowered in a deep scowl. Bushy spikes of hair touted defiance to the bare scalp. "I appreciate your watchin' over our little girl."

"Bear, nobody's called me *little* since my tenth birthday." Sighing, she realized she'd exhausted her stall tactics. "Charles, I really could use that coffee. Extra milk, two packets of Splenda."

"It'll be waiting." The brief flash of Charles's dimples bolstered her for the ordeal ahead.

By the time she'd reached the end of the hall, her feet seemed to drag her body into her father's private suite, which had to be costing a mint. Nothing simple for Josiah Taylor. The pricier, the better to prove to everyone how far he'd come from his poor roots.

He'd started his operation with a simple sawdust joint—a nonluxury gambling club on the Texas-Louisiana border. As legal constraints on gambling put a choke hold on expansion, he'd redirected his business into a riverboat casino with seed money from a less-than-reputable source and his business expanded overseas.

Or so the story went. Not that anyone had ever been able to prove anything. And not that her whispered childhood confession of what she'd seen was ever believed. Her nanny had gone to her father . . .

He'd told her she was mistaken. It hadn't been one of his employees who'd shot Uncle Simon, but one of their enemies and he would pay. She must have been traumatized by what she'd really seen.

Her father's face then merged with now as he lay in a hospital bed surrounded by antiques that still didn't re-create any sense of home. Whatever medicines they'd put him on left his features bloated, his complexion pasty. Time had dulled his full head of red hair to a rusty copper with glints of silver.

"Daddy," she whispered with all the feeling of a child waking from a nightmare in search of comfort.

God, how she wanted to keep driving with Charles, far away from Genoa. To London maybe . . . which made her think about the guy with the fakey Brit accent back on the ship.

No escaping.

Her father's eyes moved beneath his lids. Jolynn backed away. His lids fluttered open, and he scanned the room for a moment in a vague, unfocused manner before halting on her. Father and daughter looked at each other for the first time since she'd graduated from college.

Jolynn plastered what she hoped was a hundred-watt smile on her face. "Hey there, old man."

"Hello, Punkin'."

The childhood endearment stung. Eyeing the doorway, she wondered what Charles would think if she burst back into the waiting room and begged him to run away with her to a London garret on the Thames. He could study quadratic equations while she admired him in nothing but a pair of jeans.

"You . . ." Her father cleared his throat with a grimace. "You all settled in on the ship?"

"There's not much to unpack. I'll be leaving in the morning before the ship pulls out." Before she could stop herself, she said, "I could stay for an extra day or two if you need me."

He shook his head gruffly. "No need. I've got plenty of suck-ups on the payroll for that."

She tamped down the sting. She should have kept her mouth shut. "I'll just go then. You should try to rest."

She moved toward the doorway, the need to hug him a force almost stronger than her pride. Why couldn't she fly into his arms the way she had with Bear? Bear had to be every bit as guilty as her father. Any employee that high up in her father's chain couldn't have clean hands.

"Hold on," he said.

She hung her head, waiting without turning. That London garret was looking better by the minute.

"Jolynn Taylor."

Lifting her chin, she faced him. "What, old man?"

He struggled to speak, but a fit of coughing stopped him. She flinched at the labored breathing. Concern smoked through her brain. Had she been told everything about his condition?

"Want you to do something." Her father coughed again and clutched the small hospital pillow against his rib cage.

Why couldn't they just hug each other instead? "What, Dad?"

"When you go back to Dallas, stay there this time." He gripped the pillow and coughed again, the fluid rumble resonating.

Watching him struggle to breathe past the pain, Jolynn wondered how he still held the power to confuse her, to sting her feelings. She hadn't expected a brass band reception, but had hoped for something more than this. She hated him for hurting her and loved him simply for existing.

But while she'd chosen a different—more honest—path than his, she was still his daughter, with a nose for a scam. Something more was going on here. The new suspicion made her dig in her heels. She would never have that traditional safe place with her father that other daughters seemed to have so effortlessly. But she could stick around and fight for him to stay clean long enough to get well. She wasn't going anywhere just yet.

"When are you going to realize I'm your daughter? I'll leave when I'm damn well ready." Feeling as weary as her father looked, Jolynn shoved through the door and came face-to-face with Charles Tomas.

FOUR

★ ───────────────────────────────────────

Chuck drummed his fingers against the coffee mug cradled in his hands and wondered how long Hebert would maintain the staring contest across the waiting room. Not that this looked like any waiting room he'd ever seen.

God, he hated hospitals. Even the scent of Italian java steaming upward couldn't disguise the antiseptic scent.

He'd spent over six months having his body pinned back together again. There hadn't been enough morphine to kill the pain. And the stark military facilities had been far from "homey" with steel-framed industrial furniture and medical personnel in uniform. They'd patched him up. He'd even had his head shrunk by a Freud wannabe in camo.

After all he'd been through, there wasn't much Hebert Benoit—parked in some kind of antique throne—could do to intimidate him. The old dude was worse than some father on a front porch with a shotgun. Of course, knowing that Benoit served as Taylor's unofficial bodyguard added an

extra level of danger beyond the mundane threat of a Rem-
ington double barrel.

Benoit cracked the knuckles of one fist against his other
palm. Chuck kept his hands loose on the arms of his chair
and counted the many ways he could disable the man, using
only his pinky. Benoit reached into a leather bag on the floor
by the carved mahogany chair legs.

Chuck tensed.

Okay, he might be willing to use both hands, if need be.
Or even his Beretta tucked coolly against his back.

Benoit pulled out a brown paper sack. Chuck scooted to
the edge of his seat. Was Jolynn worth the added risk?

An image of her chagrined look after she'd fixed the
Maserati flashed through his head.

He caught himself up short. She wasn't his reason for
being here. The investigation, putting his past to rest, and
most important of all, stopping a possible terrorist attack—
that's why he was hanging out in a five-star luxury rehab
with an overprotective henchman.

Chuck zeroed in on the brown paper bag as Hebert slid
his hand inside and withdrew, slowly, deliberately, a container of vanilla bean yogurt and a Chinotto—a local fruity
cola.

Touché. Chuck yielded the point to Mr. Benoit, toasting
him with a lift of his coffee mug.

Benoit twisted his bottle open, the hissing of the vacuum
seal resounding in the late-night silence. "I'd be mighty
upset if anyone hurt that little girl."

"I don't doubt it for a minute." Chuck took a much-needed
sip of his coffee, brought to him minutes ago by one of the
countless people on staff here who moved about with a
silence the CIA would do well to study.

Setting the mug beside the one he'd gotten for Jolynn, he leaned back, crossing his feet at the ankles, watching, assessing, cataloging details to use later if the opportunity came for a peek inside the old mobster's mind.

The door from Taylor's suite swung wide, banging hard against the wall. Chuck shot to his feet a second ahead of Benoit. Reflexively, Chuck grabbed for the Beretta tucked in his waistband under his shirt, ditching his mug on the end table with a slosh. The old guy's yogurt and drink clattered to the floor.

Jolynn blasted into the waiting area. Benoit's shoulders slumped and he knelt to clean up his snack splattered on the floor. He reached for his napkins, only to stiffen again the minute Jolynn smacked him on the back of the head.

"You lied to me." Jolynn circled, whacking her hands against Benoit's barrel chest. "I can't believe I was such an idiot. I thought you were the one person I could trust, and you lied."

Standing, Benoit scowled. "Now, watch your mouth, little girl."

Only moments prior, the muscular mobster had a seasoned dark ops aviator on the edge of his seat. Now Hebert held his hands in front of him, fielding blows like a boxer until he managed to grasp Jolynn's wrists.

No doubt, she had spunk.

And he wasn't an aviator anymore.

Without warning, the energy radiating from her evaporated. Jolynn sagged like a limp rag doll hanging from the clutches of a dejected child. "Bear, why did you tell me he asked for me?"

Her voice sounded small in contrast to the dynamic woman who'd blasted through that door. Viewing the unguarded moment between the two, he felt more voyeuristic than during any surveillance operation in his aircraft.

The older man avoided her eyes. "Because he did ask."

"Try again." Her accusing gaze narrowed.

Benoit slid an arm around her shoulders. "I know he wants you here. He just doesn't know how to say it."

So Taylor hadn't asked for his daughter. What had her father said in there to elicit such a strong reaction? Worth checking out once he paid Berg a visit in the computer hub and reviewed the tapes picked up with the chip in Jolynn's bag.

She slid her wrists free and hitched her purse higher onto her shoulder. "Come on, Tomas. Let's blow this pop stand."

With a toss of her auburn hair, she strode down the corridor.

Chuck scooped up his backpack, feeling it rest just over his gun. He nodded once to Benoit and turned away.

"Tomas."

Chuck glanced back at Taylor's bodyguard.

"You watch out for her, boy."

Not what he'd expected from the old guy, but he nodded again, then wondered when the two of them had gone from being adversaries to allies.

Chuck jogged down the corridor, too late to catch the elevator. He took the stairs double time. In the lobby, he spotted her bright yellow shirt outside the glass doors and pinned his eyes on her. He needed to hang tough. Gather information. See her safely to the ship, then get back to work.

Her long legs raced across the parking lot until she stopped by the Maserati. She crossed her arms on top of the *Fortuna*'s car, resting her forehead in the crook of her elbow. A sigh shuddered through her.

That simple sigh kicked him in the gut harder than any implied threat from Hebert Benoit.

Steam radiated off the asphalt with stored heat from the afternoon sun, relieved only by the kick of the ever-present sea breeze. Chuck looked at Jolynn and felt an answering heat inside himself. What the hell was it about this woman?

He swiped a forearm over his brow and waited for her to speak, using the moment to scan the area. Work used to offer him distance, control. Not tonight.

Jolynn lifted her head and extended her arm. The key fob dangled from her fingers. He stared into her glistening green eyes, then flipped his palm up, snagging the controls just as she dropped it. "Where do you want to go, Red?"

"Drive, Tomas. Top down and as fast as she'll go."

Without another word between them, he opened the door and secured the convertible top for an open-air ride. Thank God she was pretty much out of it, giving him a chance to check the car for further tampering.

He slid into the driver's side, and the seat embraced him with a seductive blend of expensive leather and Jolynn. Somebody could market that scent for a mint. Chuck barely suppressed his groan at being behind the wheel of a car any man would give his right arm to drive.

Beside him sat a woman most men would give both arms to spend one night with. But he wasn't here for sex and neither was she.

He snapped his seat belt. The defiant lift of Jolynn's chin, he expected. The quiver, however, sucker punched him. Chuck reached across to secure her seat belt with a soft click. A quick flash of gratitude tipped at the corners of her mouth, making him feel like a fraud.

Hell, he was a fraud. Was his first instinct right? That he'd lost his edge, that he'd left it somewhere in a dank

torture cell back in Turkey? If so, Berg, the colonel . . .
Jolynn would be the ones to pay the price.

If she was as innocent as he thought, but that brought
him right back to thinking his instincts were in serious doubt
these days.

Regardless, his best course of action was to spend more
time with her, and a drive to blow off steam sounded like a
damn good idea.

Checking for tails, Chuck guided the convertible through
Genoa on a deliberately convoluted route. Once confident
they weren't being followed, he turned onto a two-lane highway snaking along the Mediterranean shore and edged the
superbly engineered car toward the speed limit.

God, but he appreciated a well-tuned engine, whether it
powered a car, or military machinery. He'd been a part of
testing upgrades of everything from unmanned aerial vehi-
cles to a hypersonic jet.

The power surged through his hands on the wheel, his
foot on the gas. He'd been so long out of an airplane, his
body soaked up the rush. The car wasn't quite the same as
being airborne, but the rush of power and speed was amazing all the same as he damn near flew past the trees, a
crumbled castle ruins, a restored villa. The past and present
merged the farther he drove.

Jolynn's yelp of exultation carried on the wind. She
ripped the tie from her ponytail and tossed it into the blur-
ring shoreline. Her hair trailed like a fiery banner in the
wind.

For the first time in the two years since he'd been taken
captive, he was flying. The howl in his gut echoed with the
roaring wind.

He floored it and left Genoa behind.

* * *

Cupping a forties-era microphone, Livia Cicero submerged herself into the schmaltziness of "Bewitched, Bothered, Bewildered." The stars outside the glass ceiling gave the whole night a vintage paper moon feeling she soaked up in her soul so parched for artistic outlet.

Her voice wasn't what it once was, not since smoke inhalation had wreaked havoc on her vocal cords and ended her rising career. But she was alive and otherwise healthy. These days she sang for herself, something she could live with most of the time.

Although it felt damn good right now to use her voice again for a higher purpose, something beyond just herself.

Over the past months singing on the *Fortuna*, she'd noticed a number of repeat travelers. Again. And again. Suspiciously so until it made her think of how the terrorists that pulled off the 9/11 attacks had reportedly made multiple practice runs.

Her government had logged her report, but something in their distracted, overworked eyes didn't reassure her. Without thinking, she'd run straight to the only man who'd ever broken her heart. Damned ironic she still trusted him more than any human being on earth.

Colonel Rex Scanlon.

He lounged in a velvet chair with silver piping that matched the threads at his temples. He wore a gray suit tonight rather than his uniform, but his military bearing was unmistakable. His long lean body, his intense stare still turned her inside out and he'd never done more than kissed her. He still loved his dead wife. Livia understood that all too well, yet she still wanted him.

But not enough to play second fiddle.

There hadn't been any real choice for her but to reach out for his help. Much about his career was secret to her, but she'd believed he had connections. Important ones. Apparently she'd been right because the next thing she knew he'd followed up her lead and here they were—the colonel and the team members she knew from the op in Turkey where they'd met, only to spend more time together once she relocated to the States for a while.

She'd agreed to assist the military, her country and the United States working together on something she could not know in detail. She would work with him and two others she'd met during a USO tour. She felt certain other servicemen and women were undercover on this ship, but some things in life were better unknown.

Her heart would certainly hurt less if she'd never known Rex.

The last note melted on her tongue, mellow and with a slight rasp that hadn't been there before. Applause rippled through the crowd already half-drunk on the excitement of their cruise departure in the morning. After an afternoon of foxtrot lessons on deck five and limbo around the main pool, the partying passengers would have cheered for a karaoke singer.

Standing, Rex clapped steadily, his eyes still on her intently as he walked toward the stage with long lean strides. As she approached the top step off the stage, he was already there to meet her like an attentive boyfriend, extending his hand to help her descend.

Her galloping heart had to remember it was all an act.

"Bravo," he said simply. "An escort to your room?"

"*Grazie*." She fit her hand into his and he clasped her with strength, stability, all the things she'd never had in her life.

Inching up the hem of her red satin gown, she took the steps slowly, careful not to let her bad leg buckle beneath her. The limp was another souvenir from the explosion that damaged her voice. She'd minimized the limp with rehab, and could make it all but indistinct if she didn't rush. But still it served as a daily reminder of the attack during her USO tour, when she'd met Rex.

As if she could forget him. And now they had to pretend to be lovers for the next eight days.

Nearby, the couples who'd been slow dancing to her song were only just beginning to break apart, their martini-fueled reaction times slowed by the Mediterranean heat. An Eastern European man in an expensive suit lifted his glass in a private toast to her behind Rex's back. She'd known better than to date fans, even on the few occasions she'd been interested. With Rex beside her, she scarcely saw anyone else.

Tucking her hand around his elbow, she walked slowly alongside him away from the stage. Since calling him in a panic about her suspicions, she hadn't been alone with him. Until now.

She stared up at his warm chocolate eyes melting over her until her skin overheated even in a strapless gown, air conditioner blasting. "What happened to your glasses?"

He thumbed the bridge of his nose where the black horn-rimmed glasses usually rested. "I took your advice and got contacts."

Idle conversation felt strange, drawing too much attention to how they'd left things between them. Rex was willing to pursue an affair. She wasn't willing to shadow dance with the memory of his dead wife.

Voices swelled in the hall, an aging contessa coming into view holding the arm of her arm candy, a much younger man who looked like he'd just stepped out of a Versace photo shoot. Rex's forehead furrowed as he studied the mismatched couple.

Livia tugged his arm and his attention, leaving the poolside DJ to entertain the late-night crowd that veered between overtly sleazy and pleasantly intoxicated. The scent of seawater and grilled tapas hung in the air as the next shift of wait staff took over food services. "Why not have the surgery, the uh, Lasik?"

"It's only recently been approved and I haven't gotten on the list. Before that PRK was okayed about ten years ago, some studies say it's more resistant to ejection trauma . . . But I would have to take time off work."

Giving up those glasses was obviously difficult for him, like letting go of the past. "You're making those changes with infant steps."

"Baby steps." He gave her a half smile. "Right."

He looked younger without his glasses, but over fifteen years separated them and she knew it bothered him. Still, after being around Rex, she found men her own age—immature.

Rex stopped outside her suite. She slid her room card from a pocket in the folds of her gown.

"*Grazie,*" she repeated, unable to meet his eyes. "I will see you tomorrow."

His hand flattened against her door. "I should look over your room and check for any overzealous fans."

She wished he wanted to come in because he ached for her desperately—needed to have her in his life no matter the case. But his implication in the invitation was clear. Things weren't as they seemed here. She had to be careful.

She swept past him into the corner suite. The curved

window overlooked the dock and come tomorrow would offer a to-die-for ocean view, a perk of being A-list entertainment by cruise ship standards. Closing the door behind her, she watched Rex move around the heavily gilded furnishings with stealthy grace. Her body couldn't have him but she couldn't resist indulging her eyes. He oozed confidence and knowledge and power, his moves sure as he checked out every corner of her cream-and-espresso-colored sitting area—of her bedroom. He paused beside a photo of a Roman statue of Hercules, and she couldn't help comparing her ideal to the epitome of Roman manhood. Colonel Scanlon won that battle as far as she was concerned, his muscles heated from within, unlike the smooth marble.

Finally, he stopped in front of her, resting his cheek just beside hers, speaking softly in her ear. "Your room is clear and my people haven't detected any listening devices or cameras."

The crisp scent of his aftershave, the heat of his breath against her ear sent her sagging against the door. Attraction wasn't smart or reasonable. Or timely.

They weren't here for each other. She focused on his words about her surveillance-free room his "people" had checked over.

People. Plural. She knew about Chuck Tanaka, a military man she called a friend after having visited him as a morale booster for a wounded soldier. As a part of the operation, she'd vouched for him—as Charles Tomas—when he applied for the job as a blackjack dealer. Why hadn't she gone to Chuck instead of Rex with her worries?

A moot point now. "Rex?"

"Yes?" His hand flattened on the door. The lean length of him was so close.

The urge to slide her hands up his chest was almost irresistible. Her breasts ached with the need to press against him, to deepen their dating cover with some reality.

Just a kiss. A simple turn of her face toward his and their mouths would meet. She could claim it was accidental and maybe even convince herself, too.

Out of the corner of her eye, she saw his hand move toward hers. Her heartbeat hammered harder in her ears as she held still. His knuckles skimmed her wrist, upward along her bare arm until goose bumps prickled her skin, her nerves alive. Higher, higher still he stroked silently until his fingers curved around her bare shoulder.

Her eyes slid closed. *Mio Dio* . . .

"Livia." His American accent, his Texas roots gave her name such a foreign and distinctive sound. "I've missed you."

Missed her? He had a damn strange way of showing it, considering he hadn't so much as called in two years. Yes, she had walked away from him, but if he wanted her, really wanted her . . .

She opened her eyes and gripped his chin. "No."

He stared back, his gaze so intense without glasses diluting the power. How was it that the stroke of his eyes over her face stirred her more than anyone else's tangible touch?

This was so, so dangerous.

"No," she repeated, stronger this time and adding a shove to his chest before she weakened. "I understand my role in helping you with"—she lowered her voice again—"whatever covert operations you have in the works. I realize it will help both of our countries, and in spite of rumors about my vanity, I do love my country more than myself."

"I never doubted that for a moment." He crossed his arms over his chest, his half smile grating on her already ragged nerves. Damn his condescending ass.

"Good." She whipped past him and into her suite. "You need to go now. Bad things happen to me when I am around you. In Turkey, I was almost blown up. In your country, a serial killer kidnapped me. And I survived it all just to have you fracture my heart. I believe you will understand if I do not want to spend any more time around you than necessary."

His smile widened.

"What?" she demanded, her hands flaying the air. "Did I get another of your American idioms incorrect?"

"It's nothing." His smile eased. "You are just so damn magnificent when you're fired up. Good night, Livia, and do not forget to lock the door."

He turned to leave, and it was all she could do to keep from tossing an ice bucket at his head. And yes, her Latin heritage was showing, but she couldn't help herself around this man.

Rex Scanlon loved his dead wife, and Livia did not intend to compete with a ghost or settle for second place in any man's heart. She'd patched her life, her body and heart back together, a long and painful process.

She had eight days to restrain herself from the colonel's undeniable appeal. Eight days holding strong as they traveled from Italy to France, down the Italian shore to Greece, then back to Italy. Eight days, she could handle.

The seven nights, however, worried her all the way to her toes.

FIVE

★ _____

Staring up at the night sky, Jolynn felt the need to explode swell with each mile of foaming waves and Italian country-side that sped past. Emotional and physical exhaustion inched toward frenzy.

Charles downshifted the Mazarati, slowing, veering toward a waterside rest area near three crumbling stone columns beside an arch. Ruins were a dime a dozen around here, yet her American mind-set still gasped at the ancient ruins around every corner.

She felt small and insignificant in comparison.

The pillars cast long, fat shadows across the small paved lot lit only by the moon and a lone lamppost humming in the night. A few straggler tourists strolled in the distance, snapping photos with weak camera flashes that would never capture the majesty of this land.

The Maserati's motor idled, a soft purr. Charles shook his black hair into place.

He turned to face her. Something wild and mysterious

lurked in his dark eyes. "You've had a long day with the transcontinental flight . . . then seeing your dad. We should head back."

Maybe the day didn't have to be a complete disaster.

Sure, she didn't know Charles very well, but he seemed to have insinuated himself into her life in a hurry. He'd been so thoughtful to stay with her at the hospital, so kind to drive when she'd been too emotional to steady her thoughts. Was it all just because he worked on the ship? Did he remain with her to stay in the family's good graces? It surprised her to realize how much she resisted that idea, but she would be foolish not to take that into account. Still, something drew her to the blackjack dealer who seemed so competent. So . . . hot.

And bottom line, she'd had the day from hell.

"Not yet. I'm not ready." She unsnapped her seat belt and flung herself from the car, twirling in the abandoned lot, waves foaming lap after lap against the rocky beach. "Let's walk, Mr. Charles Tomas."

She spun away without waiting for his answer and scrambled down the stony embankment to the narrow shoreline, grabbing hold of an olive tree on her way, branches rustling, seeming to whisper caution. Would he leave her to walk alone? Unable to bear the thought of another rejection so hot on the heels of her father's, she sprinted into the gritty wind, embracing the friction of sand against her skin.

The Maserati silenced, and she heard Chuck's steady progress until he eased beside her with quiet grace. Hands stuffed in the pockets of his black work pants, he kept pace, his shoulder close, but not brushing hers. But he might as well have. She could feel him near her all the same.

Comfort—distraction—waited a few inches away. Did she dare take it? She certainly couldn't imagine hurting worse than she already did.

"My father wants me to go back to Dallas first thing in the morning." She punted a small rock, weaving her way along smooth, worn stones, broken in places by the determination of many generations of weeds coming up through them, a testament to the stubborn.

Ache and anger twined as she wove around a small boulder, past a tide pool. After her father had sent her away that last time, after college, she'd vowed never to set herself up for the rejection again. She was a grown woman, damn it.

"Maybe you *should* leave." Charles nudged the small rock farther along with a brush of his foot.

So much for him offering her consolation. Jolynn snatched the rock and flung it into the sea, before spinning to face Charles. "I was considering going home, but now? Who knows? I go where I choose, when I choose. Maybe you don't know it, but I'm an overindulged only child. Like my father, I don't do well with the word *no*."

She studied his brown eyes, searching for some indication that he might be different, a man to trust. His hands clenched visibly in his pockets. Silently, he tipped his head from side to side, working away a kink in a gesture she was beginning to recognize as habit.

"Why doesn't he want me in his life?" Her voice sounded pathetic, even to her own ears, and she hated herself for the weakness.

Chuck blinked, unveiling eyes more guarded than when they were closed. "Anyone who would send you away is a fool and doesn't deserve you. Go back where you belong, Jolynn."

Could she have heard him right? Was he somehow as tempted as she was? Staring back, she savored the edge of danger. Maybe she was her father's daughter after all. "What if I already am where I belong? Could be it's time to quit running."

"And if running keeps you safe?" His hand lifted, jerky, as if weights tried to tug him back until it steadied just beside her face. He brushed her cheek lightly.

His hands were scarred and calloused. Hands that had grabbed hold of life up close.

His touch soothed, healed—excited. He cupped her cheek and she swayed toward him. She didn't even bother trying to resist. She wanted this. Wanted to find out if he could deliver on the promise in his molten dark eyes, in his surprisingly gentle touch. Her whole body ached to feel him closer.

The scent of his soap and a hint of perspiration from the warm night mingled on the salty breeze with each breath that seemed to come faster and faster until her eyes fell to his mouth. Her lips parted in anticipation. She arched up onto her toes, her arms rising—

He clamped his hands around her wrists and backed away. He shook his head once, sharply. Either to say no or to clear his head, but either way he dropped her hands and turned away.

With long, no-nonsense strides, he walked back along the shore, up the rocky incline toward the crumbling pillars.

No. "Wait just a minute, Charles Tomas." She left men. They did *not* leave her. "You can't look at me that way, touch me that way, and just walk off. You insisted on coming with me tonight. A man doesn't throw around signals all evening the way you have without feeling something. You're damn right I deserve better, from my father and from you."

He braced his shoulders and continued walking. His

leaving, after a day too full of disappointments, pierced her bubble of frenzy.

"Do not turn your back on me," she shouted after Charles and, yeah, maybe at her father, too. "I won't follow you. I mean it. I am not moving from this spot."

He kept walking, not missing a step, as if he hadn't even heard her.

Her chest tightened, and she gulped in heaving breaths of the humid night air. "Do you know what they'll do to you if you show up at the *Fortuna* with that car without me in it? You won't be in any shape to deal cards for quite a while."

That stopped him. The roll and retreat of pounding waves filled the silence. Her threat may have been mean and small, but she didn't care. Any reaction was better than being ignored.

Her heart had been pretty much yanked out of her chest while still beating this evening, so if she was operating now without it, she had a damn good excuse.

He pivoted back toward her, slowly, looming above her in the stone archway. Moonlight slashed across his scowl. "Finished with your temper tantrum?"

Temper tantrum? She'd flown halfway around the world for a man who didn't care to see her. A man who dared to call her daughter. A man who would be happy to go the rest of his lifetime without another visit from his *beloved* daughter. "I'm just getting fired up." Jolynn flung the words at him like rocks from the crumbling ruins, knowing full well she was being unfair and yet completely powerless to rein it in. Yes, she was shouting but who the hell cared.

Not that there was anyone to hear her now, the tourists disappearing, finding their way into distant bars and restaurants.

Leaving the rocky beach to the two of them.

She drew in a shaky breath. "This has been one of the worst days of my life."

Okay, the day Uncle Simon died and she'd realized the depth of her family's dirty business had been far, far worse, but times like this brought that one right back to the fore until it felt like she was in the middle of that horrific moment all over again. "Say something, damn it."

"Poor little rich girl didn't get all the attention she wanted from Daddy. What a tough life you and your cousin Lucy must have lived, tearing up the town with your old man's money." He shook his head. "You're breaking my heart to bits."

His disdain grated over her as he stood silhouetted by moonlight. Like an avenging angel, he dispensed judgment on her superficial existence. As if she hadn't worked her ass off to create a life in Dallas that didn't involve her father. As if she still collected some kind of trust fund allowance for being part of a richly corrupt clan. Pale beams shone through the loose folds of his shirt, outlining his trim waist, his broad chest.

Surprise, surprise. He thought she was another airhead heiress just like half the women traveling on the *Fortuna* this week. She felt herself deflate, knowing this argument wasn't worth the time. That he had every reason to think that of her when he didn't know her at all.

Slowly, she climbed up the incline until she faced him, toe to toe, heated breath to breath. "I can't believe I thought there was something halfway interesting about you." She pushed him, preferring even anger to his continued calm. "You're just like every other man I've met from Tuscany to Texas, too scared of my father to take me on."

If the storm clouds in his murky eyes could produce, she would be drenched to the skin. Jolynn sidled a step closer, so full of pain she felt the need to unleash some of it on her nearest target. "You're afraid of him, but you want me anyway. I can feel it. You're not as cool as you want me to believe."

His throat convulsed in a long swallow at odds with his impassive expression.

Encouraged, she tucked her hand inside his collar and lifted the chain free. She caressed a finger along the links, stopping at the dangling medal. His body heat lingered on the silver.

She tugged harder until the chain went taut, but still he didn't come closer.

Grabbing her wrist, he pulled back. "You're just using me to lash out at your father."

His hoarse tone dashed away doubts she might have harbored about her effect on him. "So what if I am?"

Jolynn angled forward until her mouth sketched over his. She nipped his bottom lip and tugged it between her teeth. The simple touch flooded along her skin like an icy waterfall, invigorating, almost painful.

He lifted his hands, the magnificent hands she'd watched at the casino, and cradled her face in his palms. His fingers slid into her hair with the same ease he'd employed to sail a card across the table. He drew small circles against her scalp, his touch shimmering through her.

His brown eyes closed. Charles flinched as if in pain, a feeling Jolynn understood too well.

His lowering face eclipsed the moon as he claimed her mouth. His lips skimmed over hers with gentle strokes that quickly turned hungry and bold. The pounding waves echoed the pulsing of blood through her veins.

Her arms looped around his neck. She reveled in the luxurious glide of his hair between her fingers. His tongue met hers, stroking, possessing.

She pressed closer, sealing herself to him. A distant part of her brain understood that she was seeking some assurance of her worth, even on the most basic of levels. That didn't stop her bruised heart from accepting the comfort, the blessed forgetfulness brought by his hard and honed body against hers.

Charles's mouth slid away from hers, and she moaned her regret until he slid his parted lips across the tender flesh of her neck, kissing, tasting. His hands drifted low on her hips, lifting her against him, offering an unmistakable message of desire broadcast even through his pants, her jeans.

Her hands roamed along his back, scratching a path over the cotton of his shirt, the cut of his muscles bulging with tension. Her fingers raked lower down his back until her wrist nudged against something solid tucked in the back of his waistband, like a cell phone maybe? A shiver washed over her as she thought of all the men in her father's world who carried guns as casually as others carried pagers and phones. She'd barely had time to register the thought when he pulled away.

The breeze sweeping across the river encircled Jolynn, jolting her as goose bumps popped along her skin. Charles stood a foot apart from her, with his hands braced just above his knees. He hung his head, drawing in labored breaths.

"Damnation." He hissed the curse through gritted teeth. "Jolynn, go back to Dallas."

His words, mirroring those of her father, slapped her. How she'd been sent away after her uncle's murder. How often she'd been shuttled from boarding school to boarding school over the years. She was an adult now. She didn't have to put up with this crap from anyone anymore.

Living in Dallas, tearing through the business world with the same wildness she went through men, wasn't getting her anywhere. God knows, hitting on Charles Tomas hadn't accomplished anything other than dishing up a whopping helping of humiliation.

She didn't even want to think about the weakness she'd shown him out here—an unwilling witness to a meltdown that had probably been ten years in the making. Since when did she let her guard down like that?

If she'd learned anything climbing her way up the corporate ladder, she learned that when something didn't work, don't be an idiot repeating the same mistakes again and again. Try something new.

It was time to stop letting her unresolved issues with her father mess with her decisions. What just happened here solidified what she'd just begun to grasp in her father's hospital room. She wasn't going anywhere until she had answers from her father about her past and his present.

No more secrets. She would be persistent, digging as deep as she needed to resolve things with her father once and for all.

"Return to Dallas? I must have forgotten to tell you. I'm spending some quality time with the old man after his whole health scare. What better way to do that than go on an eight-day cruise with him?"

His jaw went slack, his eyes guarded.

Reveling in her hollow victory, she marched past him toward the Maserati, the *Fortuna* license plate mocking her every step.

* * *

Jolynn drove like a maniac.

Undeterred, Chuck hooked his elbow on the passenger door of the Maserati and just watched the coast speed by. Wind whipped through the car, the coastal highway perched close to the rocky ledge with the sea crashing hard on the shore below.

Although she expected to freak him out by driving like an Indy 500 pro, then she had another think coming. This was small potatoes in comparison to the missions he'd flown as an air force test aviator.

This woman, however, was giving him emotional whiplash. The first brush of her lips against his had almost sent him to his knees like an untried teen. What was he thinking allowing himself to lose control?

Allow? Just looking at Jolynn Taylor made him question his sanity more than his military shrink ever had. The woman was dangerous to his concentration, not to mention his mission. He turned away to look at the rolling waves again, sea mist hanging in the air and stinging his face.

Thank God she'd left her purse—and the silver token surveillance device—in the car so no one else heard him kiss her like an idiot with no will. Like the fool he'd been two years ago. He should have listened to his instincts back in Nevada. His edge was gone.

He refused to consider what could have happened if Jolynn hadn't nudged his gun as she stroked his back with insistent, arousing hands. Luckily, he'd still possessed a fragment of reason and recognized the insanity of what he was doing. She was the daughter of a major suspect.

She could be involved.

Believing her "poor little rich girl" act was dangerous. If she was acting, people would die.

And if she wasn't acting? Then the best thing he could do was keep his distance because she would be hurt a helluva lot more when his role in bringing down her father came out.

Another scenario—even worse—exploded in his head.

What would her father's underworld buddies think if they discovered she was hanging out with an undercover military operative, someone with dark ops connections?

Once they got back to the *Fortuna*, he needed to focus his fact gathering on someone else, like the director of operations. The colonel could chat up Jolynn.

And the knowledge that Scanlon wouldn't hit on her since he was far gone on Livia Cicero?

Mighty convenient.

Hell. He was so screwed.

Another gust of wind tossed an auburn lock across his cheek, plastering it against his skin for four heartbeats before it slithered away.

His body throbbed rock hard just that fast.

There was no denying it. He wanted her. And that in and of itself knocked him on his ass all over again.

After his capture, after the torture and beating in Turkey, he hadn't had sex with a woman for nearly a year. He hadn't even woken up with morning wood. Eventually, he'd had a girlfriend and a couple of flings. But things still weren't right in his brain.

What a helluva time to learn his libido at least was one hundred percent in working order.

* * *

Parked back beside Berg at the mobile command center, Rex couldn't deny that his old habits were alive and well.

Rex could almost hear his dead wife tsk-tsking at him for using work to avoid things he didn't want to deal with. Countless times, Heather had walked up behind him at the computer and slipped his glasses off his face before sliding into his lap. Then she would work on providing ample distraction—

His brain screeched to a halt on the thought. Yeah, he

was also trying to push away the feelings stirred by Livia by ramping up memories of Heather. Of how damn unfair it was that his wife had died of a heart attack at only forty-one years, for God's sake. Normally, that offered the splash of ice water guilt he needed. For some reason, it wasn't working so great tonight. The exotic scent of Mediterranean herbs and flowers—Livia's perfume—lingered so tangibly he could almost swear it clung to his clothes the way she clung to his memory.

And now he saw that she hadn't stayed in her stateroom, damn it all. She'd returned to the casino for God only knew what reason. Livia always had done whatever the hell she wanted.

He spotted a pair of their CIA compadres in the gambling crowd cruising the slot machines. Reassuring to know they had Livia's back even when he couldn't. There were far too many other eyes tracking her moves.

She was beautiful, fascinating—and yeah, sexy as hell. He would have given his left nut to kiss her back in her suite. But she'd made it clear that she refused to compete with the memory of his dead wife and that time had passed for them. Which made him feel like a damn stalker watching footage of her when he really should turn in for the night.

Past your bedtime, Grandpa?

Not for the first time, the age difference pinched him. Hard. Those CIA agents in their prime were more her age. His knuckles cracked.

He stared at his hands, surprised. When had he made a fist?

"Something wrong, Colonel?" Berg asked, glancing over.

"Nah, I'm good." He forced his attention back to the present. "Is the listening chip Tanaka passed over to Jolynn Taylor working again?"

"Seems to be, not that Chuck's doing jack shit to pry any information out of her while driving back here." Thumb scratching his mustache, Berg leaned back in the chair—and almost hit his head on the wall behind him in the narrow space. "It's the damnedest thing. Signal shows it's working fine, but there are strange stretches of silence. Actually more than silence. It's as if the sound was flatlined by one of our own noise cancellation devices."

Confusion chewed his gut. He was sure, as absolutely certain as he could be, that Chuck was trustworthy. Hell, the man had passed the worst test imaginable at the hands of his captor, never breaking.

What was he up to here?

Rex scanned the split screen video on the multiple views inside the cruise ship, two dedicated to the outside, where the city was beginning to shut down for the night. The skyline glowed at half power.

Although the parking lot stayed well lit. Feed showed Chuck walking past security with Jolynn Taylor. Nothing appeared wrong with Chuck . . .

But Ms. Taylor? Something was definitely off as she charged two steps ahead.

What had gone on during those noncomm minutes? Chuck himself had said he feared his edge was gone. For the first time, Rex questioned himself. Straight up, he felt guilty as hell for what had happened to Chuck. While he couldn't have done anything to prevent it, the kidnapping had happened on his watch as commander. Had he chosen Chuck for this mission just to prove to himself the past was behind them?

If so, he would have failed Chuck again.

Rex shot to his feet. His chair skidded back against the wall.

Without acknowledging the fact that Berg was studying him curiously, Rex made tracks out the door, down the corridor, taking the stairs two at a time. He didn't question why he was searching for Chuck. He just knew he had to look the young captain in the eyes, a damaged man he'd sent undercover.

Rex hit the deck by the pool just as Chuck rounded the corner. Alone. Jolynn must have gone to her exclusive suite, obviously nowhere near the more bare-bones accommodations where the staff lived.

The deck was sparsely populated, most everyone else having turned in for the night. Waves lapped a rhythmic tune. A couple made out by the rail. An older guy lounged in a deck chair sneaking a smoke, his cigar glowing in the night. A cleaning crew mopped the deck in sections while a bartender shut down his station for the night, lining up bottles and emptying ice buckets. The pool glowed with a submerged purple light, giving it an eerie cast.

It should be safe enough to pretend to ask Chuck for directions since his shirt bore the *Fortuna* staff logo.

"Excuse me?" he called out to Chuck, stopping beside a stone fountain with a goddess pouring water into the pool. "Could you help me out with some directions?"

Chuck's head snapped up, his eyes sharpening fast. Reassuring to see. He glanced over his shoulder and walked to Rex by the fountain. "Sure, where do you need to go?"

By now, they stood near enough to each other and the fountain, far away from the stray night owls. "What happened tonight? The sound went out."

A generic enough statement if anyone happened to overhear, but Chuck would understand full well what he meant.

"Sorry, but I don't have an answer for you. I was out walking with a friend."

Walking with Jolynn Taylor. "Nice night for that."

"A very wise nun once told me that spending time with a woman is always a good idea."

Rex studied him through narrowed eyes, ready to press him for more when a sound from across the deck shut him down. He glanced over his shoulder quickly to find a drunken woman—the contessa—stumbling toward an upper deck with her boy toy. Rex waited for them to pass before lowering his voice.

"Well, we need to win this one," he said softly while gesturing to a freestanding map of the ship so it would look as if he were discussing the directions. "And make sure you keep us in the loop next time. I don't like losing contact."

Chuck nodded once, then turned away. His steps were slow and even. Rex watched for any signs of physical stress or strain. Chuck's body had taken such a beating, his recovery was nothing short of a miracle. But the fact remained, he couldn't fly any longer due to a burst eardrum. Further, injury to his spine put him at risk for paralysis in ejection seats or parachuting. He had so many pins in his body he would set off metal detectors in airports.

What the hell had he been thinking insisting he put himself back into the line of fire this way?

Watching the door close behind Chuck, Rex stuffed his fists into his pockets. Damn. His hands were shaking so hard he couldn't dodge the truth.

He hadn't rushed to see Chuck to make sure the man was alive, to be sure the captain still had his edge.

Rex was making sure he hadn't lost his own.

★ ★ ★

Hugging her knees, she sat in the damp grass at the edge of her father's garden, peering around a bush sculpted to

*look like a battle horse. She'd been waiting for her dad,
hoping to have some time with him on her own. Since her
mother died, all he ever did was work.*

*She squeezed her eyes shut for a minute against the sting.
She was twelve years old, for Pete's sake. Too big to whine
like a baby because her dad was too busy for her. Pissed
off at him and herself, she pitched a big fat rock at the Venus
de Milo fountain a dozen feet away. Her father collected all
those stone statues of big-breasted women like his own personal harem. She started to throw another stone at the leg-
endary beauty when—*

*A noise startled her. She dropped the stone beside her,
and looked again. Anticipation eased the ache in her
chest . . . But it was just Uncle Simon. Rats.*

*Uncle Simon was with two men in dark suits, and boy,
were they all mad at each other. They were pushing and
shoving each other past a circle of iron benches and chairs
until they stopped beside the fountain. She pressed her back
to the leafy horse's leg and searched for a way to sneak
away without them noticing.*

A shot popped through the air.

*She jerked, her eyes snapping back to the sound. Back
to the three men. Back to her uncle. She bit her hand to hold
back a scream. Horror, however, bubbled inside her until
she could swear it was in her sweat.*

*Blood oozed from a single bullet wound behind his ear.
One man caught him on the way down, staggering against
the fountain. The other man, the one with the gun, tucked
it under his jacket as he turned. Toward her.*

*Panic bit harder than the prickly branch slicing into her
hand as she scrambled backward. The gun guy in a black
suit stared. Straight. At. Her. And she knew him.*

She knew Charles Tomas . . .

Jolting awake, Jolynn rolled off the edge of her bed and hit the floor. Hard.

"Damn it!" She grabbed her elbow, the charley horse stabbing pain through her.

Charley horse? Even her aches linked up to Charles after only a couple of days on the ship together. She blinked to adjust her eyes to the shadowy suite, the first rays of morning sun casting a minute orange glow through her balcony window.

She'd spent the past two days on the cruise ship visiting with her father and ignoring Charles. And it hadn't done her one damn bit of good. The man invaded even her dreams. Intellectually, she knew he wasn't there the afternoon Uncle Simon had been shot behind the ear, execution style, but the eerie horror of her dream wasn't so easy to shake.

Swinging her legs to the floor, she padded barefoot past her circular bed perched into her sitting area. A deep rose, red, and bronze color scheme bathed the stateroom with a fire-and-brimstone decadence.

God, her dream was making her melodramatic. Used to working sixty-hour weeks, she really had too much time on her hands. Marseilles had come and gone, and they were set to drop anchor in Sardinia today, but she'd visited the ports countless times in the past on one of her father's earlier ships, and sightseeing alone held little allure.

She needed something to fill her mind with anything other than worries for her dad. And thoughts of Charles. She needed to be more insistent with Lucy about helping out with office affairs while her dad was under the weather. She had an accounting degree after all. Surely it wouldn't sound out of the realm of possibility that she would offer— and it would give her a great chance to snoop.

And digging around in her father's files would prove

much more productive than just standing around on a balcony, the water below reminding her of her midnight walk with Charles.

Jolynn pulled a bottled fruit juice from the small refrigerator tucked under the counter next to the minibar and twisted the top off. Her great plan for peace wasn't working out. Staring out the balcony window at the endless ocean, she rolled the cool bottle between her hands. There wasn't much she could do about her relationship with her father during this cruise other than hang out for a bedside vigil and fluff his pillow.

But when it came to Charles Tomas, ignoring wasn't working out for her. Her hands slowed . . . She frowned, looking harder at the balcony.

And the masked man staring back through the window at her.

SIX

Jolynn screamed.

She wasn't hiding in topiaries these days. She shouted at the top of her lungs while running for a phone. A knife from the kitchenette would be a welcome bonus. And never once did she take her eyes off the black-clad figure on her balcony. A man. At least she thought it was a man, lean, tall, agile. And masked.

Whoever it was reached for the sliding door.

Her hands shaking, she jabbed the number for the operator.

Ring.

Ring.

Pick up, damn it.

The ringing stopped. "*Fortuna* hospitality, how—"

"Jolynn Taylor. Someone's breaking into my stateroom," she gasped.

The door slid open. She grappled behind her, her hand closing on the coffeepot. He stepped inside. Screaming, she ripped it from the wall and threw it across the room. She dropped the phone. Grabbed for whatever her hands landed on. A lamp. A book. Her purse. And she screamed. God, how she screamed.

Her door rattled from the outside and the man stopped in his tracks.

She raced to unlock the door. "I'm in here. Help!"

As she fumbled with the lock, she kept expecting a hand to land on her shoulder. A force to grab her from behind.

The door swung open. Lucy stood on the other side with a key card and a hulking big guy. He charged past her and Jolynn spun to see the dark-clad man swing over the balcony—and disappear.

Arms slid around her and she jerked instinctively before she realized. It was just Lucy comforting her.

"It's okay," her cousin chanted, hugging her hard. "Adolpho will take care of everything."

Jolynn glanced back fast at the hulking man with a thick mop of dark hair. Adolpho—her cousin's fiancé—leaned over the balcony, looking down where the intruder had disappeared. She sagged back against Lucy, her cousin's French perfume radiating off her.

God, she'd come on this cruise to regain control of her world, only to have it unravel all the faster.

* * *

Chuck lounged on the low brick wall that encircled a lobby fountain. His laptop computer was open beside him, a legal pad on his knee, pencil in hand as if he needed to make some notes.

Between sips of coffee, he typed, the screen filled with what appeared to be college course work—macro-econ. The student cover story provided a great excuse to justify his computer time. In actuality, he was sorting through some repeating number sequences that Berg had come across from select slot machines. He hadn't known what to make of them and passed them on to Chuck for another set of eyes. Working in plain sight could sometimes make the best cover while passengers headed out for a day in Sardinia.

If he parked himself out here long enough, he figured his path would cross with Jolynn's—as per the colonel's command.

He'd been surprised to see her at the casino the day after their kiss by the river. But true to her word, she was sticking around. Although she'd done her best to stay out of his way and it chapped his hide to think he'd blown a possible lead.

Every time a piece of her clunky jewelry sparkled in the casino lights, he'd reminded himself he was better off— she was better off—staying away. Except he didn't have the luxury of ignoring her back.

He stared into the depths of the casino lobby fountain being replenished by Venus de Milo. He could still call to mind the pert tilt of Jolynn's nose, the unexpected wide innocence of her green eyes. Her image seemed to ripple in the watery fountain.

His body tensed until the lead point snapped against the paper. He pitched the pencil into the shimmering pool. The mental picture of Jolynn shattered into a band of expanding circlets.

"That wasn't very nice."

Her mirrored face converged in the water.

Damn.

He glanced at his laptop to gather his thoughts, but he wasn't any more successful than he'd been figuring out what a bunch of numbers from slot machines meant.

That's what he got for not being straight up about what

happened back in Genoa. Just past his laptop, he saw crimson toenails peeking from sandals. Elegant arches seemed to beg his fingers to wrap around them.

He would have to focus on his job soon enough, so Chuck allowed himself the momentary pleasure of gazing all the way up her incredible length of leg. Her sleek body was equally appealing, and then, to his surprise, he found a smile on her face.

Chuck closed his laptop. "So you're done with the silent treatment."

"Seems rather juvenile." Her nose tipped a touch higher with a defensive air, file folder with *Fortuna* logo clutched to her chest. Her face was pale, but gorgeous as ever.

"That it does." He drummed his thumbs on his laptop.

Confusion flickered through her eyes before she looked down at his mouth. Awareness of that out-of-control kiss snapped between them, memories of how close he'd come to saying to hell with it all and sinking to the ground, ocean pounding against the shore while he gave in to the need pounding through his veins.

Jolynn cleared her throat, her smile steadying again. "Should I relieve you of any further weaponry?"

Chuck stilled. He carefully set aside his laptop, buying himself time to think. "Pardon?"

"Are you planning to toss any more lethal pencils my way?"

Relief coursed through him. "Nope. The rest of the lead arsenal is stored safely in my backpack."

Given the assorted security equipment in his computer, strapped to his leg, and sometimes tucked in his ear, Chuck took heart in knowing he wasn't really lying. His career field necessitated a hefty dose of subterfuge over the years. He tried to stick to the truth whenever possible.

She grinned again, more relaxed and genuine this time, her lips plump and shiny with gloss. "I wish you weren't so funny."

"I wish you weren't so sexy." *Shut up, Tanaka.* That's not what the colonel meant by spending more time with her.

She assessed him through narrowed eyes. "Thanks for that much at least. My ego could use the boost after our midnight stroll a couple of days ago."

Since the colonel had ordered him . . . "Do you want to sit?"

Chuck settled into the idea of a conversation, reassuring himself he only intended to gather information about her father.

So far no luck in figuring out who had tampered with the car. And they couldn't be sure if that person was after her in particular, or just taking a shot at Taylor's empire in a vaguer fashion. Without question, the old crook had his fair share of enemies.

I'm only doing this for her safety and the integrity of my case. Chuck could have sworn he heard the statue's laugh mingle with the rippling water.

So he wanted her. He wouldn't do anything about it. His head was on straight now that there had been time to regroup. "Do you want to sit or not?"

A quintet played chamber music standards nearby, the ship half-deserted while they were docked in Sardinia. A ponytailed cruise director gave a lecture on Italian artistic treasures to prep the guests on board for some of the sights to see on a tour of Sicily tomorrow.

"Are you going to throw me in the fountain? Because your scowl sure says as much."

"Didn't even cross my mind."

"Can I trust you?"

"Of course."

"Yeah . . . You seem to be a pretty straightforward, honest guy." She lowered herself onto the brick wall with a grace that made Chuck long to plunge himself into the icy fountain waters before he did something stupid.

Jolynn tapped the top of his laptop. "Schoolwork?"

And a reminder everything they said could be overheard. "Macro-economics."

"Pretty heavy stuff for a dim brain like mine."

So she was still determined to play the pampered wild child. Problem was, he was beginning to get a different picture of her. Chuck hated moments like these. He was going to have to lie, and lies made old scars ache.

Having reviewed her personal file, he knew she was an accountant with grades that made his look like chicken feed. He couldn't even console himself with the fact that he'd worked his way through college, and Miss Overprivileged Taylor had received a free ride.

He didn't believe in making excuses. The nuns at the orphanage in Hawaii where he'd grown up weren't big into self-pity. They were all about a person making the most of God-given talents and taking charge of the future.

Besides, he admired Jolynn's intelligence. Although why did she go to such lengths to hide her brains? Easier to manipulate the unaware? Or were those hints of vulnerability for real? He wasn't particularly comfortable with the deepening image as compelling as the way her supple body had moved against him when they kissed.

"Charles?" She waved her hand in front of his face, her knee brushing his as she shifted. "If I'm boring you, I can leave."

The simple brush of her knee against his lingered. He focused on her face, on the moment. If you gotta lie, keep the story simple. Spy School 101. He tapped the laptop again. "I'm distracted. Online test Monday."

"Good luck."

"Well," Chuck prompted, reminding himself to do his job, gather information. "How's your father?"

"Enjoying the sun on his balcony." She clutched the file tighter.

"What's that you've got there?"

She glanced down at the file as if she'd almost forgotten she held it. "I was at the office this morning after, uhm . . . My cousin and I were talking to some security folks," she said evasively, "and I decided I needed something to keep me occupied, so I'm helping out with the *Fortuna*'s scholarship fund."

"Security issue?"

She clicked her fingernail against the edge of the scholarship file. "No big deal."

Alarms sounded in his brain. There was something there. "For someone who was willing to sit with me, you're not all that chatty."

"Maybe I'm waiting for the apology you owe me."

Apology? She had kissed him . . . And he had made the most of the kiss for a damn long time. He was undercover and investigating her father. He'd had no business taking advantage of her that way.

"Jolynn, I am sorry, sorrier than I can say—"

Lucy Taylor rounded the corner, and Chuck wasn't sure whether to be relieved or disappointed. Either way, he knew he was in hot water. There was no deluding himself that the kiss had been a freak, onetime attraction.

Just sitting next to Jolynn Taylor for a few minutes, catching a whiff of her cologne in the air, aching because of a simple brush of her knee against his, and already his body was burning for her.

* * *

Hugging the file folder to her chest like a shield, Jolynn watched her cousin weave through tourists with cameras around their necks, toting overlarge bags. Lucy was headed straight toward the fountain—straight toward her and Charles. Jolynn tamped down disappointment at having her time with him interrupted. It was probably for the best to have a buffer between her and the confusing guy next to her. But he'd made such a welcome distraction after the nerve-wracking start to her morning three hours ago.

"Hey, cuz." Lucy sat beside Jolynn and peered around at Charles. "Well, hello, Mr. Tomas."

"Miss Taylor." Chuck nodded simply.

"Did Jolynn tell you about the peeping Tom that jumped onto her balcony?"

His eyes narrowed, his muscles flexing under his shirt almost imperceptibly. Almost.

"Lucy—" Jolynn elbowed her. "It's no big deal."

Charles didn't let up, those tight, roped muscles still twitching. "That's why you met with security."

Lucy hooked an arm around Jolynn's shoulders. "I would have been a basket case if that happened to me, but no"—she tugged at the file—"my über-efficient cousin just asks for something to keep her occupied so she won't worry."

Jolynn kept her hold firm on the file. "I would think you'd be glad for my help with this project."

The *Fortuna* scholarship fund was set up in honor of Uncle Simon, which seemed ironic. But then what better way for Josiah to divert attention from his own people than to pretend to grieve over his brother's murder?

Lucy pulled her arm away. "Of course." She blinked fast.

"You're right. If you can find more lucrative investments to increase the scholarship, then by all means, have at it."

"Thanks. Dad's not up to visitors for very much time each day." In fact, it seemed as if he didn't want to see her at all. "I really do need the distraction." Understatement.

"Gotta run." Lucy nodded across the lobby to the burly man wearing a linen shirt flapping in the breeze. "Adolpho's here to pick me up for supper. I'll call you later." She tossed a wink over her shoulder, weaving around a picture-snapping tourist in a bright-colored caftan.

Chuck leaned forward, resting his elbows on his knees. "You're generous to help your father out."

Jolynn wished she could bottle his voice and sell it on the open market. Except he'd soothed that voice and those hands all over her by the water. In the end it hadn't meant a thing.

"It's important to keep my uncle's memory alive. Maybe you should apply for the scholarship."

"*Fortuna* employees can't apply."

"Oh, right, of course." She should have remembered that. Her brain was a mess.

She looked away to her cousin smiling up at her fiancé, teasing the top button on his *Fortuna* polo shirt with obvious ease and familiarity. How much did Lucy know about the family "business" and how deep in was Adolpho? She'd wondered about her cousin, about Bear before. How could they be a part of the business and not know?

Another reason to settle this part of her life. The whole notion that a person could "love the sinner but not the sin" mantra was a tough one for her, either way.

"Jolynn?" Charles's voice cut through her thoughts. "What really happened with that peeping Tom? What has security done about making sure it doesn't happen again?"

"I've got it under control. Honestly, the contessa down the hall was more freaked out by the noise." She really didn't want to talk about it, and it wasn't like he could do anything to help her on that score. "Isn't it about time for your shift?"

"Right." Charles pulled away and picked up his laptop. "Glad you've decided to forgive me."

He rose without another word and walked away. His long strides ate up the lobby at a slow loping pace. For a second she almost thought he had a slight limp, but as soon as the thought crossed her mind, it fell away to make way for another . . .

"Hey wait," she called after him. "I never said I forgave you."

Stopping, he smiled back over his shoulder. "You will."

She watched him stride away and wondered how he'd worn her down by saying basically nothing at all.

She kept him in sight all the way to the elevator, even going so far as to back inside. The door slid closed just as he stopped to talk to . . .

Livia Cicero?

★ ★ ★

Chuck charged into the small belowdecks cabin, pissed off, sexually frustrated, and yeah, pissed off all over again. He locked the door behind him before sweeping aside the striped privacy curtain.

"What the hell happened in Jolynn Taylor's room and why wasn't I notified?"

His brain had been on fire since the second he'd heard about the break-in at Jolynn's stateroom. Why hadn't anyone told him? As soon as he'd been able to cut short the conversation with Jolynn, he'd made tracks here, only half registering what Livia Cicero had said to him in the lobby on his way out.

Berg swung his feet from the top bunk and dropped to the floor smoothly. He had one earbud in, the other dangling. "Way to knock there, pal."

Too late, Chuck noticed Berg held a Sig Sauer in his hand. Shit. If Berg had been the enemy, Chuck would be a dead man.

So much for having his edge back.

"What happened in Jolynn's room this morning?" he repeated.

"Park yourself here for a minute and I'll tell you what I know." Berg held out a chair, waiting until finally Chuck sat, not even realizing until that moment how he scratched over the spot on his leg where a pin had been inserted.

Behind Berg, security cameras filled with images and readouts scrolled with data collections from *Fortuna* computers. "Apparently someone tried to break into her stateroom, came in over the balcony railing."

His hands fisted on his knees as he thought of her alone in her suite at the mercy of some faceless bastard. No wonder she'd been pale. "What happened?"

"She shouted her lungs out, pitched everything in sight at the intruder." Berg laughed low. "Her cousin was next door with her fiancé, and they scared off the guy in time."

Chuck wasn't smiling. Thank God, she'd defended herself and bought the time needed for help to arrive. Next time, she might not be as lucky, and it burned his gut to think about what could happen to her.

He rubbed his elbow over a faded scar. "You got anything in those readouts on the *Fortuna*'s scholarship fund?"

"Not right offhand, but I can run some scans, review what's on file, see if there are any red flags in the finances."

"It's a place to start." And the most important reason for coming to this room gelled in Chuck's mind now that he'd calmed down enough to think rationally. "What kind of extra surveillance goodies do you have tucked away there?"

Berg rubbed his mustache thoughtfully. "What did you have in mind?"

"I think it's time we kept a closer eye on Jolynn Taylor's stateroom."

SEVEN

The next morning, Jolynn soaked up some rays on the deck, her strapless wraparound dress baring her shoulders to the sun. Maybe not having an office wasn't such a bad thing if it meant she could hold all meetings poolside. And she'd chosen the smaller adult swimming pool. It was calmer with an Italian artist on the other side of the deck giving lessons. It was peaceful for the most part, interrupted only by the occasional waiter bringing lunch orders.

Sardinia had been left behind during the night as the cruise ship made its way to the next port of call, Sicily. Business meetings by the pool on a lazy summer day beat a stuffy Dallas office ten-to-one. Her father slept so many hours of the day, and when he was awake, he still insisted on business briefings, which didn't leave much time for visits with her.

When she saw him, he kept conversations superficial. Where had she gone at port calls? How was the *Fortuna*'s food?

God, didn't his brush with mortality make him realize they didn't have unlimited time to reconcile?

And while sometimes she wanted to confront him, she certainly didn't want to bring on another heart attack. There had to be a way. She just needed to be patient. The lingering taste of Charles only added to her determination to grab hold of her fate for a change, rather than letting the world drag her along.

She tossed the folder in the file case she'd started on the scholarship project across the iron table. "Bear, you can tell Dad I'm not so sure about the expense of a dozen Venus de Milo ice sculptures at the fund-raiser." Jolynn rolled her eyes at Lucy. "It's overkill, don't you think?"

Hebert Benoit waggled a finger in her face. "Respect your father, little girl."

She'd forgotten over the years how Hebert took such a special interest in the project. Hebert, her father, and her uncle had all been friends . . . in the beginning.

How then could Bear continue to work for Josiah knowing he'd been involved in the death? So many murky questions lurked in her dad's world.

Memories of the peeping Tom shadowed her mood as effectively as a cloud slipping over the sun.

They still hadn't found the guy who'd lurked on her balcony. But Adolpho had assured her the security had been beefed up in her room. Nothing creepy, though, he'd reassured her. Just alarm systems.

She shivered in spite of the sweltering Mediterranean heat beating down on their umbrella.

Lucy, her eyes tired from too much late-night partying with her fiancé, tapped Bear's arm. "Back to business so we can finish up and play. I'm not sure if we can cancel the order for the ice art this late. I can try, though."

Bear shoved to his feet. "I'll do my best to lobby for less glitz and more class, but I may not be your best help with the glamour angle." Winking, he stood, his burly chest stretching the *Fortuna* logo on his polo shirt. "Why don't you just let it go and play? We pull into port in a half hour. I hope you're not so jaded you can't appreciate Sicily."

Lucy squeezed her hand as Bear walked away toward a ship security employee. "Yes, do go enjoy yourself, really. You've helped tons already. Which I appreciate since it frees me up to make more wedding plans."

Wedding plans. Funny how she wasn't cringing over the upcoming zoo as much as she had been. "Good luck. Please go gently with the bridesmaid dress choices."

Lucy grinned. "You've put me in a powerful position. I know how fond you are of cotton candy pink. But you can rest easy for now."

"I'm still not sure I trust you, but I'll try." Jolynn tipped her face into the warming sun. Definitely a better locale for meetings and just what she needed to air out her tension today.

"Ooooh," Lucy whistled lowly, placing her glass back on the table, "look over there."

Jolynn pivoted in her pool chair to find Charles walking past a shuffle board game on the other side of the pool. He sure was worth every ear-piercing tone of that squeal of Lucy's.

Why did he have to look even more attractive, approachable? She realized she'd never seen him wearing anything other than his casino uniform. She didn't even have a clue as to his personal style until that moment. His scruffy, casual appeal surprised her. With his classic looks and bashful demeanor, she'd expected a more precise appearance, like a tweedy professor.

Instead, he wore jeans faded to a blue pale as the sky. The frayed right pocket hung loose. His wallet nestled in the left, beneath the ever-present backpack. The sleeves of his sun-washed linen button-down were cuffed below his elbows, the strong flex of forearms just barely visible. As he walked, his pant legs hitched up enough for her to see he wore brown boat shoes without socks.

What other surprises did Charles hold behind than handsome face?

Jolynn watched him move with athletic grace, taking the stairs to an upper deck. She should just seek him out. See what happened.

Social functions in Dallas had been a large part of the job at Hunt, Burroughs, and Murchison. Her choices for dates had usually gravitated toward individuals like her father. Such men would never be a true temptation to her heart since the last thing she wanted was a life on the edge.

Somehow, Charles had slipped past her defenses.

Hearing Lucy squeal again, Jolynn almost bolted from her seat until she recognized Adolpho Grassi with his arms wrapped around her cousin. The stab of jealousy for what the couple shared bothered her. She was happy with her life, damn it.

Lucy smiled up into the eyes of the man dwarfing her with his bulk. "Ready for lunch?"

"Yeah." He grinned right back down at her with equal adoration. "But we need to get moving, Luce. I only have a couple of hours before I start my shift."

Lucy turned pleading eyes to Jolynn. "Do you mind if we finish this some other time?"

"Sure, my brain's fried. You two go have fun."

"We will." Lucy leaned against her fiancé's chest. "The

Fortuna clothing shop is going to take care of measurements for his tux. Too cool, huh?"

Adolpho winced, a wry grin creasing his face. "Monkey suits? Yeah, great."

"Be nice." Lucy elbowed him in the stomach, before waving.

Jolynn watched the happy couple stroll away, which made her thoughts leap back to Charles. Why should she care how he spent his afternoon, damn it.

She snapped her file folder for the scholarship fund closed and slid it from the table, uncovering a computer thumb drive. Rather than bother with unlocking the combination, she simply tossed the thumb drive into her purse.

Lucy was right. She deserved a break, maybe even a day trip out to Sicily. And if she left the boat, she would be less tempted to hunt Charles down.

Time to hightail it off the boat right after she went to her suite to shower and change.

* * *

Chuck stepped into the narrow corridor, easing the door to Jolynn's suite closed behind him. His search of her quarters had uncovered some pretty high-tech surveillance gear, listening and visuals of everywhere except the bathroom, for God's sake. It had taken all his best angling and maneuvering to stay out of the camera's range. He seriously doubted that Jolynn had been flattening herself to walls by the door, commando crawling past the sofa, and walking across end tables in her bedroom.

The thought that someone had watched her changing, sleeping, vulnerable, had him resisting the urge to put his fist through the wall. Memories of his captivity dogged him, the constant guards and cameras. No privacy. Ever.

It was beyond stomaching to think that Josiah had been responsible for spying on his daughter in such a violating fashion, especially if she didn't know. And if it was someone else? Then that person was trying to get to Taylor through her. But to what end?

Neither answer made sense in regard to the terrorist chatter they'd intercepted.

Regardless, he'd made sure she was safe from spying eyes. Well, except for his own, but damn it, he was one of the good guys.

The average Joe spy wouldn't have been able to deactivate the listening device tucked in her kitchenette and the minicams focused on her sofa and bed without alerting the viewer. But then when it came to electronics, he wasn't the average Joe.

He cracked his knuckles, a rush still pumping through him at winning one for his team today. He'd rewired the suckers so they would loop old data back, which should give him a day or so to figure out what to do next before they learned their techno gear had been sabotaged.

Of course, that meant a return trip to her room, where he would be bombarded again with the scent of her perfume in the air, the silky feel of her shirts as he'd scanned her closet . . . He shook his head.

Now he should concentrate on work, knowing she was safe for the moment.

The elevator chimed.

Damn.

She was at the pool in a business meeting scheduled to last another ten minutes. Berg had been sure of that from a look-see at Lucy Taylor's planner in her computer. Odds were, it was the cleaning staff, and he could slip past unnoticed. Odds hadn't been in his favor since he'd met Jolynn.

His worst fear stepped through the elevator doors. Improvising, Chuck slid to the floor and leaned against the wall as if he'd been waiting for her.

He could hear Jolyyn humming just before she came into sight, head down as she strolled down the corridor, shuffling the file folder under her arm. She sifted through the contents in her sack of a purse. "Wallet, lipstick, silver token, disks, hair clamp. Wallet. Shoes." She frowned, staring at his feet. "Shoes?"

Her gaze traveled from his boat shoes up to his face. Eyes wary, she said, "You wanted to see me?"

Chuck pushed to his feet. He hated that he'd caused that defensiveness. She didn't deserve to be caught in the middle simply because he couldn't control his libido.

He shrugged. "Some crazy redhead says I owe her an apology. And while I sent a note, I thought perhaps more was warranted."

She nibbled her bottom lip. "That could be."

"I shouldn't have kissed you." He stared at her mouth and wanted to taste her all over again. The impromptu conversation was already barreling down a path he didn't want to travel.

"That's not exactly what I had in mind."

"I shouldn't have let things get out of control back in Genoa." He needed to give her a face-saving out. The truth seemed a pretty safe bet. "You're a beautiful, intriguing woman. I knew that was an emotional night, seeing your old man and all. You needed comfort, and I offered the wrong kind. My fault."

"What if I wanted the comfort?"

Chuck thunked the side of his head against the floral wallpaper. The truth wasn't working. Did this qualify as one of those extreme circumstances when he could justify inventing a cover story to save his hide?

He rolled his shoulders, popping joints echoing through the corridor. "I'm, uh, coming off a really bad breakup."

Lame, Tanaka. Couldn't he do any better than that? How would she react to the truth? That he'd gotten the shit kicked out of him by a sadistic bitch and henchman, and for the past two and a half years, his body had gone on deep freeze?

"I'm sorry to hear that. Was it serious?"

He ran a hand over his face, nodding as his Adam's apple bobbed in a long swallow. He wanted out now. He sucked at handling emotional issues these days and here stood proof positive.

"Is she a student, too?"

Chuck shook his head. "No, I took this job to get away, make a new start." That much was true, at least. "Uh, she tore out my heart and tap-danced all over it."

He winced at the cliché. But at least she'd bought into his reason for being outside her suite.

She squeezed his forearm. "Taking this job sounds like a smart move."

"I'm just not ready to open myself up to that kind of pain again." Her touch burned through his denim shirt. "I wouldn't want to run the risk of owing you another apology, so don't take this the wrong way. I really could use a friend."

"I understand."

"Thank you, Jolynn." Chuck shrugged his backpack onto his shoulder and shoved away from the wall. "Well, I'll see you around the casino."

He started down the hall.

"Charles. *Charles?*"

He stopped. His head fell forward. Something in her

tone—something real and genuine—reached inside him and squeezed. He was so not cut out for this kind of work. He had an inherent weakness when it came to women. Must have had something to do with the way he was taught to respect the nuns in the orphanage, knew they'd unselfishly dedicated their lives.

Except the way his body hummed for Jolynn right now was nothing like anything he'd felt around a nun.

* * *

Jolynn stared at his broad shoulders, the long column of his neck as he shook his head. He'd actually come here for her. And his apology had been so damn genuine, not just the words, but something deeper in his eyes.

She felt his contrition, a soothing balm to her raw nerves. Maybe she'd been thinking about it all the wrong way. Could she be looking at the first friend she'd ever had, other than Lucy?

Easing behind him, she rested her palm on his shoulders with small soothing circles. It took every ounce of willpower she possessed not to curve her fingers around his rippling muscles. She wanted to scratch her nails along the cotton fabric of his shirt.

Not friendly behavior at all.

He needed something different from her. She'd only begun to understand she might want something different from him. "Charles?"

"Yes?" His hoarse croak floated back to her.

"I've got too much to deal with here, and I'll be leaving at the end of the cruise. I don't need to plunge into a relationship. Maybe we have more in common than we thought. I could use a friend, too."

"Huh?"

"Yes." Jolynn smoothed her hand across his back. She understood betrayal. "And as your official friend, I know just the thing to help you forget all about her."

Flinching, Chuck turned. "What exactly did you have in mind?"

"I know this wonderful little out-of-the-way place in Sicily." She circled her tongue along her lips.

He exhaled. Hard.

"I used to go there when I came on this cruise during college vacations with my dad." Memories of those lonely visits threatened to stall her. "Anytime I'm feeling blue, I go there and satiate myself with all the cannoli I can eat."

"Cannoli?"

"Oh, yes. They're so good it's almost sinful. What do you say?"

"I say you make a very tempting offer."

"That's the spirit." She patted his cheek. "Just give me a minute to put these files away and we can leave. I'm so glad you stopped by to set things right between us."

Jolynn turned toward her door, only to just miss running into a tall, lanky man. Her stomach lurched. She hadn't realized how edgy she still was from the close call with the peeping Tom. Her mind raced back to the man on the balcony this morning and quickly realized this guy was taller, lankier. She must just be paranoid.

"Excuse me," the guy said with a distinctly Texas accent.

A familiar guy. She searched her memory and knew his voice sounded familiar. Someone from home?

Alarms blared louder in her head. She'd never thought to worry, but this was strange how she kept bumping into him. At least she had Charles with her.

He nodded crisply to her, to Charles, then circled past. Her eyes followed him to the next stateroom. The door flung open before he knocked and the singer, Livia Cicero, stepped out. Her exotic perfume swelled down the hall.

The lounge singer hooked arms with the Texas stranger and waved to Jolynn. "This is the new man in my life. His name is Rex. Isn't he yummy?"

The tips of Rex's ears turned red.

Livia hugged his arm closer to her side as she leaned into him even as she talked to Jolynn. "Come catch the show tonight. Keep him company while I sing and make the other women stay away. *Ciao!*"

As quick as she'd arrived, the woman sashayed off in a swirl of perfume and body-hugging turquoise silk.

Jolynn turned back to Charles, only to find his eyes lingering on the singer as she swished away. Jealousy surged through her. Unmistakable. Strong. And nothing a mere "friend" should be feeling.

Maybe the time had come to take a risk and follow up on her attraction to this man. She would show Charles Tomas that friends made the best lovers with no risk to the heart.

* * *

Jolynn strolled down the narrow side street in the seaside village. No matter how many times she came here, the view still took her breath away.

As did the man beside her.

Excitement tingled along her arms at the prospect of a whole afternoon with him. The world around her seemed brighter, more optimistic. She soaked in the differences in the locale around her as opposed to her flatlands Texas home with its high-tech steel city and wide-open ranches. Here everything was bordered by mountains or the sea. The shops and homes were packed together and crammed with history.

Arm swinging at her side, Jolynn kept the bag of pastries tight in her grip. Her other hand was tucked in the crook of Chuck's arm. She'd been surprised when he put it there, but he'd just shrugged and said something about not wanting to lose her in the crowd. He'd been distracted since they left the *Fortuna.*

Still, she wasn't arguing. Instead, she decided to just enjoy the day, her food, and the warm play of muscles under her fingertips. "History says that *cannolo*—that would be the singular of *cannoli* in case you didn't know—originated in medieval times when the Arabs brought sugarcane to Sicily. Prior to that, they only had honey as a sweetener."

"You don't say."

"I do say," she bantered back. "They rolled the dough around a piece of sugarcane and voilà. They were most popular in the spring."

"When sheep produced more milk for the ricotta filling." He angled past college students with ID packs dangling from around their necks.

"You do know about them then."

"A little bit. But I enjoy hearing you talk." Charles kept walking, staring ahead with his ear tilted toward her as if waiting to hear what she would say next.

He wasn't particularly chatty, she'd noticed. Her first friendship with a man was turning out to be about as successful as her romances, or lack thereof. Why was she so determined to try with this guy? Hadn't she been shoved away by him enough?

Then she remembered him sitting on her hall floor, worried because he'd kissed her.

Jolynn dangled the bagged treats under his nose as they passed a vendor selling Marsala wine. "There's nothing better than a good old-fashioned sugar high. You only had one at the café."

His mouth dimpled into a smile, a wicked glint shimmering in his eyes. "Nothing?"

The burn of her flush rivaled the fire smoldering low in the pit of her stomach. "Okay, there's almost nothing better." She cleared her throat. "So I hear."

Charles chuckled, dissolving the tension. "Come on, Red. Let's take that walk along the shore by the catacomb openings you wanted to see."

Touched that he remembered her request, Jolynn sprinted down the street, weaving between tourists until the crowd thinned. His gaze locked on her legs, and a rush of power shot through her.

He rubbed his neck as if he had a kink.

"You do that a lot." She slowed for him to catch up, arms extended for balance as she made her way down the rocky incline.

"Do what?" He held out a hand.

"Massage your neck, roll your shoulder as if you've got a kink." She jumped the last foot or so to the sandy shore, their cruise ship a mere speck docked down the coastline. A tunnel gaped in the cliff, water trickling out from the catacomb entrance.

"Only when you're around."

Jolynn halted, just in front of him, their gazes almost level. "I think maybe you might have paid me a compliment in there somewhere."

"Hey, Red, quit hogging the cannoli." He reached for the bag.

"If you think you can handle it." She grinned wickedly

and opened the sack. She dug through and pulled out two, passing one to Charles.

The jolt sparking up her arm at the brush of his hand felt anything but friendlike.

Jolynn slid her hand slowly away, seductively so before charging ahead. "Food lesson for you." She held up the bag. "A bit more on cannoli, plural. In most of Italy, the singular is cannolo, but here in Sicily, it's cannolu. And how appropriate that there's a difference, because to me, these are second to none."

He finished a bite and smiled. "You weren't lying. These are beyond better than the rest."

She eyed a family packing up in the distance nostalgically. "When I was a kid, my mom and dad used to bring me here . . . This was her favorite place to vacation." She stared ahead, keeping her eyes homed in on the water trickling from the tunnel into a little tide pool. "Dad would buy me two even though Mom said it was too much sugar for me. I would eat one, really slowly, then save the other for the next day so I could relive the outing all over again."

"How many times did you come here with your parents?" He followed her as she trekked farther and farther from civilization.

"Every summer until my mother died when I was seven. For a while, Dad wanted nothing to do with anything that reminded him of her." Even his child. "Then he threw himself into work."

"That had to be a difficult time for you to be alone." His low voice caressed the air.

His strides kept an even pace—slow, methodical, dependable. Like the man?

She kicked aside a small piece of driftwood as if striking back at an unfair world. "I barely remember my mother's voice, but cannoli remind me of her. She feels closer, more familiar." Uncomfortable with the sympathy she saw on his face, she stepped ahead. A gust of wind whipped a strand of hair across her eyes. "I don't want to talk about this anymore."

Reminiscing invariably brought pain. She dug into the bag and pulled out a pastry for herself. She took two bites fast and lost herself in the memory of her mother.

"Okay." He brushed aside the curling lock and took the pastry from her hand. "Do you always do that?"

"Do what?" She walked backward, chewing off another taste.

"Eat both ends and save the middle for that final bite."

Pausing, she stared at the pastry oozing filling out of both ends now. "Always. I love to save the best for last." She popped the rest into her mouth and licked her fingers. A breeze swirled around them, between them, linking them. "What about your family?"

He stared at her for so long she thought he wouldn't answer, then finally said, "I'm from Hawaii, my dad's relatives have lived there for as far back as we can trace. My parents are both dead now, though."

Her smile faded. "I'm so sorry. What happened?"

"My dad died when I was eight months old. My mom died when I was in second grade. There weren't any other relatives left alive so I grew up in an orphanage in Hawaii."

She backed against the rocky cliff, searching his eyes. "I'm so sorry."

"It was a good place." He toyed with a lock of her hair, the crisp air and his aftershave riding the wind. "I don't have any Oliver Twist horror stories to share about growing up there. The nuns treated us like the children they would never have."

Regardless of the rosy picture he tried to paint, she wasn't fooled. What child wouldn't grieve over having no parents? How could she have been so selfish as to forget the rest of the world had problems, too?

"I probably sound like a real whiner. At least I had my father. I know I should be thankful, but I just don't know how to . . ."

"What?"

"Be close to him. It's no secret he has, uh, questionable contacts." She tried to laugh. It didn't work. Her throat simply closed up, choking on the sound.

Charles wouldn't look her in the eye. Old feelings of frustration roared to the surface. Intellectually, she knew she wasn't like her father, but they bore the same blood, even the same name. How could she not be smeared with some of his guilt?

When Charles didn't say anything, the words just started falling from her mouth, "For the first twelve years of my life I really thought he gave simple boat tours for a living." Images of being Daddy's Punkin' teased her with thoughts of the early days, before her uncle had been murdered, before her world fell apart.

"You were just a kid."

"Old enough to understand the things I saw."

Charles's gaze snapped to her face.

She wanted to shock him, to let him know what kind of family she came from. Then he would run away, and she wouldn't be tempted to risk her already scarred heart. "Aren't you going to ask me?"

Sighing, Charles pressed his thumb and finger to his eyes. "What did you see?"

She shrugged. "Lots of questionable things, some more clear-cut than others . . ."

Memories of her father always left her hurting. So why couldn't she tell him everything? Share that unprovable secret? She ached to bury herself against Charles's chest for longer than some seaside moment-of-madness kiss.

But she didn't know how to ask. Her only dealings with men had involved distancing them with a sultry smile, a sensual facade to keep them on edge. When in doubt, go with what you know.

Her inner wild child flamed to life. Jolynn scooped the cream out of her other cannolo with her finger and slipped it in his mouth. His lips opened as if by instinct to receive her offering. She gently scored her nail over his tongue as she left the treat behind. His exhales grew heavier, warm whispers over her palm as erotic as any kiss.

He chewed while she traced the damp pad of her finger around his lips. Heat smoldered low in her stomach, flames radiating, higher, then lower, burning to the core of her.

"Jolynn . . . Lynnie. . . ." Charles's husky voice rasped against her ears, along her every simmering nerve. His eyes seared hers as he clasped her hand and kissed her finger before releasing it. "What am I going to do with you?"

Tears stung behind her eyes but she refused to let them loose. As if the sky cried for her, she heard the splatter of a single raindrop tap the muddy ground. Then another. The sporadic rhythm echoed the pounding of her heart.

He reached for her, and she sighed in expectation, her body hungry for comfort. He clasped her by the shoulders, his strong hands gripping her with a strength she welcomed.

But rather than the sexy, sleepy-eyed look and a softening of the mouth, she saw his lip tense into a tight line, his eyes razor sharp. She only had a second to wonder before . . .

He shoved her behind him.

Charles tugged the back of his loose shirt free. Smoothly, he pulled a gun from the waistband of his jeans.

Joy melted to confusion.

She realized the splattering sounds were gunshots from a silencer. Bullets pocked the ground around them, the cliff behind them.

Confusion shifted to horror.

Charles dropped to one knee and aimed with trained ease. His body transformed into a fluid, lethal line.

Horror became disillusionment.

He wasn't the man she knew, but she recognized him all too well. She'd spent her childhood surrounded by men like him.

Fearing for her life, not to mention her heart, Jolynn turned her back on Charles and ran.

Eight

★ ─────────────────────────────────────

Jolynn sprinted along the rocky cliff wall, farther and farther, the shoreline reaching closer. She splashed through the receding waves, frantic, desperately looking back over her shoulder, but her hair streaked in front of her eyes.

The stitch in her side, sob in her throat, stole her breath. Her frantic eyes searched for the safest path to run—a way to escape from the man shooting at them and the man she'd foolishly trusted. A simple blackjack dealer who just happened to carry a hefty gun tucked in his pants. She squelched the stab of pain that could well distract her. Get her killed.

She needed to get away from him, to find a police station. A few more steps. Ignore the pain. An impossible task.

Jumbled shouts and shots reminded her of the men behind her. She felt along the cliff wall, steadying herself. She hurt so much she wanted to run forever.

An arm locked around her waist. A body tackled her.

Jolynn screamed, her cry cut short by the steely forearm.

She didn't have time to brace her fall before her stomach hit the damp sand. Her arms slapped down, hard.

The bag slipped from her grasp. In her panic, she hadn't realized she still held it. Cannoli scattered across the foaming wave, rolling toward a bent casino ID.

Charles's ID.

His solid body pressed against hers, flattening her. Sand bit into her cheek, her clothes plastering to her body. A half-buried shell sliced into the vulnerable flesh between her ribs. She tried to shift free, but he pinned her arms. She stared at his beautiful hands—vise-gripped around her wrists.

"Jolynn," he growled in her ear, "I don't have time to argue with you. We need to get out of here—now. Do you hear me?"

She nodded, not trusting herself to speak. Words of recrimination clustered inside her. She burned to yell, screech, rage at him, but knew she couldn't afford the luxury. Had he come to work for her father or against her father? Regardless, she had no intention of doing anything he said.

"Okay, Red, when I get up, we'll run for it. On three. One—two—three." He rolled off and yanked her up by the arm.

Loading her anger into her fist, Jolynn punched him in the stomach. His grunt echoed in her ears as she took off running.

She clambered up a narrow path, not much but with a few footholds creating a ladder up alongside the opening to the catacomb. She would run all the way to Dallas if necessary to put miles between herself and the liar with an angel face.

His arm banded around her again. Charles hauled her up the embankment. His hard, impersonal touch bore no traces of the passionate man of the days prior, the tender friend of mere moments before. She searched behind them but saw no signs of the distant gunman who'd been shooting earlier.

The beach looked strangely peaceful, as if no one even noticed how close death had lurked.

Her arm wrenched in the socket as Charles tugged her along. Climbing relentlessly until civilization took hold again. People appeared here and there, a car driving past, a tourist snapping photos. Two teens with skimboards pointed at their soggy clothes and laughed.

Charles ignored them. His hand held firmly to her as he charged past cars and a van parked on a narrow side street. His gun was nowhere in sight, but she knew he had it within easy reach.

Was he going to steal a ride?

He pulled a set of keys from his pocket and thumbed the button. Lights lit up on a little Fiat behind the van. Hell. He had a car here. A car conveniently stashed on the off chance someone shot at him?

Her stomach lurched. A police station sounded so much better, especially since they were back on a public street now. What was he going to do? Kidnap her?

A pop whizzed by her ear. A back front tire on the van deflated. Oh God. The two or three bystanders scattered fast, ducking back into the safety of their homes. No help forthcoming from them.

Charles grabbed her arm and hauled her to his side. Gun raised, he squeezed off a shot. A man at the end of the back street clutched his knee and fell to the cobblestones—his gun skittering away. The reverberation of Charles's gunshot still vibrated into her, binding them with a nauseating link of violence.

He yanked open the Fiat's door and shoved her into the

driver's side. Pushing her the rest of the way inside, he slid in after. She angled over the gear shift and into her seat.

Charles untangled his legs from hers and jammed the key into the ignition. With a glance over his shoulder, he slammed into gear. They peeled away from the curb as a single bullet embedded itself in the rear window.

Bulletproof glass? On a Fiat?

Who was this man?

"Put on your seat belt—now." Charles's cold voice bore no resemblance to the speaker of heartfelt confidences.

Automatically, Jolynn obeyed, snapping the shoulder harness. He turned a sharp left onto the twisting main road.

He removed one of his hands from the wheel and sifted through the contents of the glove compartment. The car's weaving response launched Jolynn against the passenger door.

She grabbed for the steering wheel. "I don't know what's going on, but stop playing around and drive."

Charles abandoned his search in the glove compartment and shoved her aside. "For crying out loud, would you quit trying to kill us. I wear contacts and they fell out when we got tangled up back there."

His bare eyes glinted. He narrowly missed driving up a telephone pole.

Jolynn frantically inventoried the contents of the glove compartment. Tossing papers on the floor, she finally uncovered the small plastic case.

"Open it," he ordered, his strong square jaw tense.

She fumbled with the container, almost dropping it on the floor. Charles pulled his hands away and grasped for the lens case.

They swerved right. She screamed, clutching the steering wheel. "I would have appreciated a little warning."

A few muffled curses later, he slipped the contacts in place. Charles blinked fast. He pushed her hands aside and resumed control.

He cast a quick glance in her direction. "Thanks."

The nearly opaque brown of his unshielded eyes pierced her.

"Who are you?" Had she escaped one threat only to meet the same fate as her uncle?

He slowed the car to a more manageable speed, looking like a normal commuter tooling around the back roads of Sicily.

"Damn it, answer me." Rage coursed through her, this betrayal so much worse than her father's rejection the month before. She'd expected that. Charles had stolen something far more precious by the seaside cliff—hope.

"Talk to me." She thumped a fist against the scratchy upholstery. "I have a right to know. Do you plan to kill me, kidnap me, what?"

His hands clenched around the steering wheel as the little car whipped down a narrow road. The engine hummed with a precision and speed that were hardly hallmarks of the utilitarian base model of this vehicle.

Jolynn tugged his arm. Muscles flexed beneath her touch. How could she have ever thought him safe? "Hey, I already know you're not one for long speeches, but you're crazy if you think we're going to just pretend nothing happened."

His stony expression didn't alter. "I've left out a few details about my past."

"Drug dealer?"

"Absolutely not."

"Arms dealer?"

"If so, don't you think I would be decked out with more firepower?"

She considered how he carried himself, how he'd protected her. "CIA?"

"It's best you don't know the details."

Ah, so she'd gotten close with that last guess. Some reassurance at least that he wasn't the worst. But he was still tangled up in something horrible—and he'd lied.

However she looked at it—whomever he worked for, she'd been used.

None of this man's tenderness had been real. Jolynn remembered all she'd told him during their riverside walk. Of course, he'd only been interested in what she could relate about her father. Even his apology outside her stateroom had been a lie to wrangle his way into her confidence. She hurt. All the way to her toes, she ached with a pain that had nothing to do with her fall.

Pressing a finger against the fogged window, she wrote his given name, remembering her first night at the casino when she'd seen his name tag.

He downshifted around a corner, leaving the city behind, the countryside open ahead. "For what it's worth, my name really is Charles. You can call me Chuck."

She flattened her palm against the window and swiped away the scrawl. "Well, Chuck, I wish I could say it's nice to meet you."

"Give me the phone under the seat." His casual voice filled the car, bearing no more emotion than if he'd asked her to pass the butter. Of course he had a cell phone tucked away in his getaway car.

What else had he planted in her life without her knowing?

The old Jolynn roared to the surface, ready to fight. "Get it yourself, *Chuck*, you lying son of a bitch."

"That I am, Jolynn." A flutter of some emotion, weariness

perhaps, flickered through his eyes. "Now, let me have the phone anyway. I need to keep my hands on the wheel."

She wanted to argue, if for no other reason than to vent the emotions chugging through her, but bottom line, she didn't want to be in the middle of another shoot-out anytime soon. She reached under the seat, groping around for a moment before she found the slim device.

"Here . . ." Tossing it at him, she felt a grim satisfaction at his wince when it Frisbeed against his abs. The little girl inside her who threw rocks at statues wanted to hurl all her hurt at him.

"Thanks." He cast her a very unamused look before he punched numbers into the phone. "Four-six-nine. Alpha-Foxtrot." His clipped, professional tone cut the air. "I'm coming in."

The final confirmation of his deception slammed the door on her dreams. Jolynn wanted to kick herself for believing he was genuinely interested in her, that they might have something to offer each other. Worst of all, she still wanted him. And as much as she wanted to jump out of this car at the nearest corner, Chuck had kept her alive when someone out there was gunning for her. Someone who could still be looking for her.

For now, it appeared her best option was to stick close to him and pray like crazy a better option presented itself ASAP.

★ ★ ★

A cruise ship offered more places for a hired assassin to hide than a person would think.

Parked on a silver bar stool, he sipped his Peroni, eyeing the crowd over the top of the beer mug. Sure, the *Fortuna* left port and floated around. But with all the traffic going on and off this oversized party barge, it wasn't that tough to swap out one person for another as long as the people looked vaguely alike on the passport.

Everyone was more zeroed in on the beautiful people anyway. Like the jewel-draped contessa of who-the-hell-knew-where blowing on the dice for a different gigolo in each port. And the Italian torch singer laughing over lunch with her American flyboy.

But no sign of Jolynn and her new pal.

If all went according to plan, he wouldn't see their faces again. Ever.

He'd intended to take care of her later in the States, but then her trip presented too perfect an opportunity. And there would be less scrutiny here than in the United States. Although the parking lot carjacking attempt had been a bust. Breaking into her suite hadn't gone well, either. He'd intended for his underling to pitch her off the balcony, but instead merely stirred others on the hall into hysteria.

With luck, the local henchman he'd subcontracted to pop Jolynn during her sightseeing jaunt would eliminate the problem once and for all. Good God, the woman seemed to have nine lives.

It was a shame her fling with the blackjack dealer called for an additional death, but that could be turned into an advantage. It should be simple enough to toss around rumors of his having unpaid debts to loan sharks.

Problem solved. One more barrier out of the way to achieving his goal. Total control of the Taylor family and fortune. Thanks to the business being funneled through this cruise ship, that fortune was growing exponentially.

Speak of the devil, he saw one of the latest players in their exchange of information head for the slot machines.

Yes, things were moving along according to schedule. By

the time they reached their final destination in Spain, all the components would be in place for a top-dollar package.

An explosive package that would rock the world.

* * *

Chuck slammed on the brakes, the tiny village street narrow and packed with pedestrians. A battle raged inside him as fierce and tenacious as the one they'd just left behind. His worst fear had happened. He'd let Jolynn distract him, and she'd nearly lost her life for his screwup. While he'd stood there sucking on her finger like a lovesick puppy, his guard dropped.

Cranking a hard left around a corner, he narrowly missed an old man pushing a wheelbarrow full of produce. Jolynn braced her palms against the dash, silent for the half hour since they'd left the port city limits. He still couldn't be certain who the target had been. Was the attack an extension of the earlier attempt on Jolynn in the casino parking garage? Or had his cover been blown? What about the rest of his team back on the ship?

Regardless, his assumed identity was shot to hell. He seriously doubted he could convince anyone a blackjack dealer carried around a military-issue automatic and drove an armored car.

The disillusionment in her eyes when she'd stared at him . . . His hands shook. Now, he owed her.

He parked the Fiat on a side street in an older section of a remote little fishermen's village—with a safe house. He had addresses stored in his brain for one at every port of call along the way for this mission.

"This is it?" Jolynn asked, her voice full of skepticism.

He doubled-checked the address on the pastel pink

plaster and stone row house, age lines streaking downward with tiny cracks. "Yes, this is our stop."

She snorted. "I'll certainly think twice before advocating further government budget cuts. Do they make you guys type reports on a manual typewriter? Etch them on papyrus? I would wager you even boil the lead to make your own bullets."

Now probably wasn't the time to mention his techno background. "Glad to see you've recovered your sense of humor."

"Oh, I'm fine, invigorated. You sure know how to show a girl a good time." She swept her tangled hair back brusquely. "A walk by the water, pilfer some info about her crooked daddy, then treat her to a shoot-out and trip to CIA headquarters. What a great date you are."

He ignored the anger in her voice. If only he could ignore the pain in her green eyes as well. "I'm not CIA and this isn't headquarters for anything." He would feel his way through telling her more once he checked with the agents inside. "This is just a safe house. Of course, now that you've been here, it's no longer secure. Everything will be moved to another location shortly after we leave."

"If you're not CIA, you're obviously with some spooky agency. You wouldn't want this big bad Taylor selling you out to all her mob friends."

"Cut it out, Red." He scanned the area from the relative safety of his reinforced Fiat. "You aren't going to run from me again, are you?"

"I'm not particularly pleased to discover you've been lying since we met. But at least I know you're not a thug for hire planning to feed my toes to the fish or I would be dead already. Now that the gunfire has settled, it seems best to stay put with you. For now."

He knew her adrenaline rush would fade soon, and he needed to get her inside before that happened. Weakness would flood her in the wake of a day no one should have to experience. He shoved aside his own need to assess his actions, his guilt, fixating instead on taking care of her. "You do pack quite a wallop. I'll let you have that one. I figure it's your due for our . . . encounter."

"Encounter? You mean *kiss*. Toe-curling *assault* on my senses by a lying creep. If we're keeping score, then here." She kicked his shin, hard, the toe of her sandals digging deep.

"What the hell was that for?" Maybe she'd rallied a little too much.

"I still owed you for sucking on my finger."

"This car is wired for sound."

Her eyes widened in horror. He almost laughed. Hell, he needed a laugh, or a drink, or to be anywhere but in the middle of this mess of his own making.

"Really?" she squeaked, her hands dropping to her lap.

"No, but my shin feels better now." He smirked, knowing the grin would fire her, providing the extra push of energy to get through the rest of their ordeal.

"Can I believe anything you say?"

His smile faded. "Come on, Red." He shoved her cavernous purse toward her. "Don't forget the Black Hole of Calcutta."

After they left the car, Chuck slid his computerized security key into the lock and pushed through the front door, a hand between Jolynn's shoulder blades. Two layers of codes and deactivated alarms later, he guided her into the temporary office in the belly of the house. He scanned the room with a new perspective. He'd trusted military technology to keep him alive more than once. In fact, a tracking device

embedded in his shoulder had saved his ass when he'd been
taken captive in Turkey. He rolled his shoulder against the
phantom ache.

The stakes were higher now with Jolynn's life on the line.

Gripping her by the elbow, Chuck led her past the wall
sporting high-tech surveillance systems. An agent with the
National Security Agency wearing a ball cap was parked
behind one, and an Air Force Office of Special Investigations agent sat behind the other.

The ball cap–wearing agent—Mike Nuñez—spun his
chair around to face them. "The prodigal son turns up. From
the audio feed we got from your pals on the ship, it sounded
as if things got a little hairy out there for you. Glad to see
you're okay, Tanaka. Well, other than some mud."

Chuck looked down, only just realizing Jolynn's entire
torso was caked from when he'd tackled her. He glanced at
his clothes, only soiled along the knees and forearms.

What if he'd hurt her and in the adrenaline frenzy she
may not have felt the pain? "Jolynn?"

"I'm fine. And what's this about audio from while we
were at the water?" Her eyes crackled with renewed anger—
and fear.

Now wasn't the time to tell her how much of their conversations had been monitored by Berg back at the boat.

Nuñez pulled out a chair for her at the desk beside him.
"Are you sure? Let me get you something to drink before
we talk."

"Talk?" Jolynn's accusing gaze pinned him. "I don't
think so. I'm under no delusions that you sent this guy in to
check out hairnet violations among our cooking staff. Even
if I did know something, do you really think I would play
any part in your attempts to nail my father? If so, you can
all be my guests at a nice little river walk I'm planning for

revenge on pretty boy." Jolynn thumped Chuck on the chest and promptly winced.

"Damn. You *are* hurt." Chuck wrapped his fingers around her arm. "Where?"

"I'm fine." She flinched away from his touch.

"Apparently not."

She glared at him for a moment. "My ribs are a little sore from when you tackled me."

Panic knotted his gut. Chuck whipped her shirt up. Nuñez cleared his throat and tugged at the bill of his ball cap. Chuck pierced him with a stare until he turned away.

Chuck steadied his breathing and tried not to think about his knuckles grazing her gently rounded softness. He wanted her. With a throbbing ache he wanted to reaffirm life in the most basic way. He shrugged through a kink in his neck. It didn't help.

He studied the multihued purple, red, and yellow bruise spreading across her rib cage. Anger replaced frustrated passion.

Jolynn looked down at her bared skin, her eyes widening. The color left her face, and he caught her as her legs folded. He lowered her into a chair.

Her hand fluttered to her forehead. "I thought I was fine."

"Adrenaline fools us all sometimes." He knelt beside her and touched a hand to her ribs, prodding carefully. Her skin felt so soft, her ribs so fragile. "I think you should see a doctor. Who can we call? Hey? Nuñez?"

"Yeah? A doc. I'm on it."

Nuñez could always be counted on. Always. As an undercover NSA agent, he had been instrumental in the undercover op that had got Chuck out of Turkey in the first place two years ago. He'd become involved with a woman from the region during the case. She'd been sent into witness protection for a year before they got married. Nuñez had a few scores of his own to settle in bringing down the terrorist bastards pulling the strings.

The enormity of what he'd pulled Jolynn into threatened to swallow him whole. He didn't have the luxury of doubts about his edge or mojo any longer. He'd brought her into this. His own personal mission for vengeance had to be sidelined in the interest of keeping Jolynn Taylor alive.

She brushed Chuck aside. "Forget about finding a doc. I'll check in with the ship's physician."

He gripped his fingers around her upper arm. "The ship will have left by the time we get back." That part was a lie, but hopefully she was too disoriented to pick up on details like the passage of time. "And even if it hadn't, you need to stay here."

"Are you arresting me for something?" Her cool eyes locked in on his hand.

"Of course not."

"Then I'm out of here. I will catch up at the next port of call." She jerked away and stalked toward the door—a door she wouldn't be able to open even if she tried.

And even if she could pry the thing open? He had a fairly good idea of what waited for her beyond the secured exit.

He charged past an obviously curious Nuñez flattening his hand to the steel-enforced door just before Jolynn could try to twist the handle. "You need to be in protective custody until we have some answers. If you walk outside, you stand a good chance of being finished off by those guys in the truck back at the river."

She spun to face him. "They're after you, Chuck Whatever-Your-Last-Name-Is. Why would they want to kill me?"

"To get to your father." Chuck watched the pain stab

across her face and felt a moment's remorse for inflicting it. But he needed to use whatever methods of persuasion possible to convince her to remain in protective custody until he sifted through the facts. "Do you really think your father's going to be able to keep you safe this time? He can't even leave his room. I know his 'reach' is far, but there's no question his power is diminished now."

Jolynn rubbed her forehead, her brow furrowed. Was she weakening? He'd hurt her again, but he didn't have a choice.

He chose his next words with care, dealing the final blow. "Is it worth risking your life just to gain Daddy's approval?"

Her lips thinned, and Chuck knew he'd won. But at what cost?

NINE

Five minutes to go until her performance, Livia sipped her lukewarm lemon water, her standard drink to soothe her vocal cords prior to singing. Rex hadn't left her side all afternoon, and the constant need to resist the attraction was beginning to exhaust her. Soon, though, he would be seated in the audience and she could lose herself in the music.

From the tiny hall that led onto the stage, she studied the clusters of people drinking at tables, a larger crowd than last night. But so far, she didn't see any signs of Jolynn. She'd invited the woman at Rex's request. He'd merely said that he and Chuck needed to keep her in sight.

Was she a criminal? Or in danger? Either of which put both Chuck and Rex in the line of fire.

The specter of the unknown chilled her. Chuck had become her friend over the past couple of years, and she didn't want to see him hurt again. His recovery had been so difficult, he deserved to kick back. While she wasn't privy to details, the mission must be dangerous.

And while she was worried for Chuck, Rex was far more than a friend. Her gut clenched and she blurted out, "Are you sure you're safe?"

Rex's serious eyes turned toward her slowly, narrowing. He dipped his head toward her. "I'm not sure at all. You should quit and go home."

Leave him? Her stomach knotted tighter. "Then how will you explain your presence here? If you recall, you are here as my 'boyfriend.'"

"I'm finishing out the cruise to console myself after you bailed on me." He slid his hand up her spine, exposed by her backless dress. Inch by inch, he made his way upward until his fingers thrust in her hair. To anyone watching, they would look like lovers enjoying a close moment before she went onstage.

But no one was looking. Why did he have to confuse her so? She'd made the mistake before of believing in his kisses, in his touch, damn him.

Although two could play his game. And perhaps a little revenge might feel nice.

She leaned against him, batting her lashes as she stared up with her best "adoring" gaze. "One minute you want to spend time with me." She skimmed her fingers up to caress his bristly cheek. "The next you want me to leave. You're such a charmer."

His nostrils flared with awareness, inciting a wicked urge within her. She leaned even closer until her breasts pressed against his rock-hard chest, but what a double-edged sword that turned out to be. Her nipples tightened and she felt an answer from his as his rigid arousal between them grew harder, larger, pressed against her stomach. A tingle started low between her legs.

He'd always been attracted to her. That had never been in doubt. His heart just wasn't following his libido.

Right now, with her body on fire from wanting him, she couldn't recall why she hadn't just jumped into bed with him and to hell with the consequences.

★ ★ ★

Jolynn trailed Chuck into their room at the bed-and-breakfast—aka safe house—wearier and warier than she could ever remember feeling. Why the hell did they have to share a room? He'd vowed the rest of the place was taken up with techno gear and that the room sported a bed and a sofa.

Fat lot of comfort that was as she faced a night alone with him. He cradled a laptop computer under one arm and tossed a bag onto the wrought iron bed. A limp beige spread was draped unevenly across the saggy mattress. No hospital corners or mint on the pillow here. And sure enough, a saggy brown sofa stretched across the wall opposite the bed.

Her defenses were thin, about ready to shatter. Pretending to study the wooden beams on the angled ceiling, she looked upward to blink back her tears. Someone wanted to get to her father through her. She could be executed simply because of her last name. The only person standing between her and a faceless evil was a man she didn't know, couldn't trust.

Chuck looked past Jolynn at the cap-wearing guy. An agent? "Could you send up a strong pot of coffee before you head out?"

"You bet. We'll have some fresh clothes for you soon." The agent adjusted his hat, looking like an everyday touristy Joe, as if he hadn't spent the past hour grilling her about every detail of their crazy day. He'd told her he was with the NSA and showed her a badge, but hadn't shared a single thing about Chuck or what was going on. "Have a good night's sleep. We'll get you set up in better digs tomorrow."

As the door clicked behind him, Jolynn thought of the incongruity of their situation and nearly gagged on the well of hysteria. How could the two men discuss such sleeping arrangements while she waited for bullets to rip the air again? Could a day this horrible really be routine to them? Could she even trust Charles . . . uh, Chuck?

Chuck locked the door, leaving them alone in the stark little room that for most would have been a romantic getaway in a foreign country. What a joke.

She watched him prowl, check behind mirrors, in closets, around the bathroom. He stopped by the window and peered out, obviously doing his best to avoid her. He still moved with the same methodical grace she'd seen in him as a blackjack dealer. And his face that had seemed so handsome and refreshingly open now appeared harder, edgier.

Of course, he was still her every sexual fantasy rolled up into one man, from his body ripped with muscles, to the burnished tan of his skin. She could barely pull her eyes away from the strong lines of his face, the exotic tip of his mesmerizing eyes.

And right now, he barely seemed to know she existed.

God, she hated the silence laced with fear of the unknown. "Are you looking for our pals by the catacombs? We wouldn't want them to interrupt our little assignation."

If he heard the taunt in her voice, he ignored it. "Our people secured the space before we came. I'm just checking their handiwork. I have a bit of, uh, skill in the techno field." Chuck closed the slats on the wood shutters. The room

darkened to a gloomy cave lit only by a small lamp with a
stained glass shade. "Security on the street is tight, but we
still need to establish a few ground rules. Stay away from
the window. Don't answer the door, regardless. Don't touch
the phone—no calls in or out."

"Okay, buddy, enough tap-dancing around what you do.
I get that your pal is with the NSA. Is that what you do? If
not, what branch? You really can't expect me to just keep
going along with this on your say-so, while I'm kept in the
dark." Could he be CIA after all, in spite of what he'd said?
Didn't they take care of overseas cases? How did things get
handled when somebody was in a top, top, top secret job?

Without a doubt, these people had unlimited technologi-
cal resources at their fingertips—and they all spoke with
American accents.

"I work for the good guys."

"Oh, you're into politically correct terms. Sure, I'll call
a spy an agent if it makes you feel better." Why did he have
to be the one to watch over her? His presence only served
as an abrasive reminder of her gullibility.

"I work for the United States military," he said simply.

"The military?" She scrambled to keep up with this latest
surprise. "I guess I shouldn't be so shocked. They have
investigators and undercover guys like on that TV show,
right?"

"That's not exactly what I do, but basically, yes. And
there aren't as many walls between agencies as you would
think."

"You share information?"

"And toys."

"Ah," she said, a picture of how he worked beginning to
take shape in her mind, of how he'd been undercover as a

blackjack dealer, fooling her the entire time, damn him. "I must have missed the episode where military agents plaster a kiss down my n—"

"Jolynn."

"What?" She stomped her foot in frustration.

"Remember when we were in the car and I told you headquarters was listening to every word?"

"Yeah, you said you *lied*."

"Not this time." He tapped a finger along the edge of a framed reproduction of a Van Gogh self-portrait.

"Oh." Jolynn deflated.

How much of what they'd shared over the past days had been overheard? He made it all sound so low-key when she'd seen firsthand today how it was anything but.

And all these agencies had come together with all these "techno toys" because of her father.

She shivered. Brushing past him, she peeked through the blinds at the street below. The casual pace of the locals trekking home from work or sitting on the front stoop for a smoke seemed too innocent to harbor the kinds of threats she'd experienced in a single day. The familiar beauty of rural Sicily, complete with the air of history and decay, cautioned her. She knew all too well the darker underside of her father's world.

She'd protected herself the only way she knew how, by running to Dallas after college. Why had she been so stupid and returned? Her grip tightened until the wooden shutters dug into her palms.

"Jolynn, damn it, if you want to stay alive, you need to listen." Scowling, he crossed his arms over his chest, betraying no lingering signs of the gentle scholar. "Stay away from the window."

She let the wooden slat slip from her fingers. "Aren't you being a little melodramatic, *Chuck*?"

His eyes narrowed. "How do your ribs feel after that little party onshore, hosted by your dad's pals?"

Jolynn winced, more from his words than any ache in her side. "Okay, okay, I get your point."

"You were lucky—this time."

The air conditioner rumbled to life as she moved away from the window. Shivering, she rubbed her hands along her arms. The mud caked to her blouse prickled against her skin, an ever-present niggling reminder of how close she'd come to foolishly believing in Chuck Tomas—Tanaka. "I wish one of those two people downstairs would show up with our clothes."

"Go ahead and shower." He glanced up, as if only just realizing what he'd said. The air crackled in the silence following his loaded suggestion. "I have work to do."

Her eyes widened ingenuously. "Oh, did you forget something for math class?"

Chuck turned away and rested his laptop computer on one of the ladder-back chairs at the simple wooden table set for two. He grabbed the lace tablecloth and gathered up the romantic place settings into a clanking bundle. He set it in the corner, then opened his Pentium on the scratched tabletop. "I need to check in."

"I thought we already did that downstairs." She took in the carelessly discarded pieces of china and the single rose bud vase. The symbols of romance seemed to mock her from across the room.

"You gave them your version, now I need to fill in the blanks with mine." He kept his back to her as he knelt to plug in the computer.

"Does that include telling them how you used me? How you made me talk by flashing your dimples?"

Chuck glanced over his shoulder, then dropped his gaze to the cord in his hands. "Get your shower."

"Chatty as always, aren't you." Jolynn stared at his hunched shoulders, the three feet between them wider than the Mississippi. She should have been glad.

She stepped into the bathroom and nudged the door shut with her hip, wincing as the motion jarred her ribs. Her side hurt, even though the doctor they'd brought in assured her nothing was broken. Jolynn squashed the self-pity. Her father's rib cage had been cracked open, for heaven's sake, and she was whining over a few bruises.

How much did her father know about the afternoon's events? Was he worried? In spite of his cool treatment, she knew he would never tolerate someone threatening anything of his. And what if anger made his heart condition worse?

Why couldn't life be simple?

She hooked her toe in the back strap so she wouldn't have to bend over and eased off her sandals. She ached inside as well as out.

She shimmied her shorts off her hips and down her legs, the muddy cloth rasping along her calves on the way to the floor. She kicked them aside. Grasping the blouse at the bottom, she began to raise her arms. The cry of pain slipped past her lips before she could think to stifle the noise.

Chuck crashed through the door as the echo faded. Face-to-face with Jolynn, he exhaled, leaning against the wall. His guarded eyes traveled down and back up her half-clad body.

Standing in front of him wearing nothing but a muddy silk shirt and pink bikini underwear, Jolynn wondered how much more torment could be packed into a single day. She felt bone tired and soul weary.

Her knees buckled, and Chuck slid his hands under her arms. His gentle touch belied his reserved gaze, nudging aside the last brick in Jolynn's crumbling wall of self-control. He helped her sit just as the tears flooded down her face.

"I can't get my blouse over my head." She knew her voice sounded pitiful, and she simply didn't care.

For years, she had tried being strong and independent, yet her life was a mess. She'd finally trusted someone and almost ended up dead.

"Okay. Let's get you out of this." His controlled voice rumbled in the small bathroom. Chuck tugged the shirt on her uninjured side and helped slide her arm through. "Duck your head."

He slipped the cotton blouse free and let it fall down her other arm. Their breaths entwined as Jolynn sat, wearing nothing but a pink lace matching underwear set.

A part of her longed for Chuck to make a move, come on to her so she could label him as scum for taking advantage of their position. This would only offer more proof that he was the kind of man who would use her to get to her father.

Another option, that he might be too honorable to act on his impulses, unsettled her. She didn't want him to be a nice, decent guy after all. Then she would have to analyze her own feelings for him, and that scared her to her toenails because then he could hurt her. So much.

The most painful scenario of all seemed the most obvious answer. Without the glitter of her carefully constructed facade, he didn't want her.

All three choices sucked. She felt all of twelve years old again, gawky and unattractive, unwanted and unloved.

She tore her gaze from his, lifting a hand towel off the counter. She dabbed her flushed cheeks before pressing it against her chest while she waited for him to unhook her bra. He leaned forward, bringing her face level with his chest until she could smell him, feel his heat.

See his pupils widening with unmistakable desire. An answering heat seared her veins as she realized she hadn't imagined the attraction after all. He may have been lying about everything else, but not that.

Chuck reached behind her, his touch tingling along every nerve until her breasts tightened in response. He pulled away, and the straps of her bra loosened, slipping down her arms.

She pressed the towel closer to her chest, holding it firm in counterpressure against the latest ache—an intense longing to ditch her clothes and lose herself in out-of-control sex with this man. "I think I can manage from here."

He cleared his throat, stepping back. "Call out if you have trouble again."

"Just go away. I don't need your kind of help anymore."

★ ★ ★

Chuck eased the door closed and slumped against the wooden panel. He struggled to will away the throbbing drive coursing through him. His hands clenched in white-knuckled fists.

The angry bruise staining her skin below the ridiculous hand towel was a mere scrape compared to the horrors Chuck had seen during his years of undercover work. He could envision with graphic clarity the atrocities men and women inflicted with unthinking ease upon someone under their control. But that didn't ease the guilt he felt for putting the bruise on her perfect skin.

For a moment by the catacombs, he'd let his guard down, and damn it all, he knew better. While Jolynn was *not* the bitch who'd lured him in with sex, then tortured him for military secrets, she was a distraction all the same. Acknowledging his culpability in the events on the riverfront didn't bring him any peace. Maybe he didn't deserve it. One fact shone clear, and Chuck embraced it.

He would not fail again.

Resolute, he pushed away from the door and crossed the room, attempting to ignore the canopied bed dominating the honeymoon suite. He settled behind the computer and lost himself in routine. He clicked through codes and layers of encryption until he'd logged in to their security system on the *Fortuna*. He tried to tell himself he could keep her safe if he regained his control, his objectivity.

Work drew him in as he followed up with Berg on the encryption program he'd run on the odd series of repeating numbers that had generated from a few of the slot machines. Now if Berg could cross-check the timing on those patterns with old surveillance footage of the casino floor . . .

Chuck barely noticed Nuñez arrive with coffee, but consumed half a pot of the rich brown blend of Arabica and Robusta anyway. Even through his intense concentration, he registered the purity of the Italian brew as he e-mailed the first of his reports.

Absently, he reached to turn on another lamp, the meager light filtering through the shutters having faded with the crappy day. As he shifted back to the computer, his gaze locked on Jolynn silhouetted in the bathroom doorway.

"Hi." She tossed her damp hair over her shoulder.

Damn. "Hi."

Suggesting the shower, he'd imagined her returning enveloped in a voluminous terry cloth robe, her allure masked by yards of thick cotton to her ankles. Instead, the hem of her silky robe stopped midthigh, leaving a long expanse of leg bare. Her hair hung in a wet spiraling mass just past her shoulders. Water dulled the vibrant red to a deep crimson.

Jolynn, decked out in all her bold colors, clunky jewelry, and alluring body, was temptation enough. Jolynn, with her face scrubbed free and her toes curled against the hardwood floor, made the other vision pale to insignificance.

"Do you need me to brush your hair?" What the fuck? He hadn't meant to say that out loud. "Your side must make it tough to reach."

"I'd rather wake up with a tangled rat's nest. Thank you all the same, Tomas-Tanaka." She clutched the plunging vee of the robe closed, her eyes betraying not the least hint of forgiveness.

"You're welcome." He didn't bother to respond to her taunts. The last thing either of them needed was for him to add to the tension already tunneling through the room.

"Do you have to be the one to stay here with me?" She eased on to the corner of the bed, her mouth tight.

"Yes."

"Why?"

"Because."

"I hate it when you say that." She punched the mattress. "You spit the single word out like a wise old parent."

He shrugged. Jolynn was right. He'd never been one for lengthy speeches. Why waste the words? "I'm responsible for you. It's that simple. You can't just dial in a delivery order for the protective service of your choice."

"Thank you for explaining the complicated rules to simple little old me."

She batted her eyelashes and donned that vapid smile he'd already learned she used against dolts.

"Cut the airhead act," he snapped, frustrated with himself, with her, and with the whole damned mess. "I've seen your file all the way down to your college transcripts."

"That's right." She perched on the edge of the bed, her robe gaping as she leaned forward. "You know all about me now. But I don't know anything about you, do I, Secret Agent Man, College Student Chuck Tomas-Tanaka? You lie for a living." Anger radiated from her like an expanding storm cloud.

"Jolynn, I work for the air force, not the mob." He kept his voice calm in spite of his rising irritation with himself for botching his dealings with her. "I only did my job."

"The air force?" She blinked in surprise. "Okay, that's a surprise."

"How so?"

"I would have guessed army or marines because you're so . . . uh . . . pumped."

After the surgeries he'd endured to repair his broken bones, he'd worked out nonstop, needing every bit of muscle strength to accommodate for bone and joint weakness. And yeah, maybe he'd needed to let off some steam, punch back at a world that had dealt a near knockout blow to him. "If you're insinuating that the air force and navy guys can't kick butt in a PT test, you'd better keep that to yourself around my pals. Especially Vapor. He's this big-ass scary biker dude with a shaved bald head—"

But she wouldn't be meeting his friends. What the hell was he thinking? She stared back at him curiously, waiting.

He shook off the urge to just talk to her, to be with her

like they were an everyday couple getting away from it all in a sleepy little B and B. "It's been . . . a long day. Try to get some sleep."

"Fat chance," she mumbled, flicking the covers aside and easing under the cotton spread.

He prayed she would drift off soon. He watched her shift as she tried to face away from him, obviously trying to avoid him. Too bad he couldn't dodge the awareness of each breath she took. Flinching, she slid onto her back and stared at the ceiling.

"Chuck." Her voice eased across the room on a whispery breath. She turned her head on the pillow to look at him.

"What?"

Brow furrowed, she pressed a finger to her lips, then waved him toward her. Warily, Chuck stood. The rug over the hardwood floors cushioned his feet as he crossed to the bed, drawn almost against his will by this woman.

God, he straight up enjoyed her quick temper and warm heart, her shifting moods that she wore on her sleeve for all to see. She was a spark of vitality in the life he'd plodded through for the last two years. She rejuvenated something inside him that he'd thought had died. A youth. A high-spiritedness. It was impossible to be around Jolynn and not *feel*.

When she still didn't speak, he eased down on one knee. Damp spirals of red hair trailed over the edge of the mattress only a simple stroke away. Desire kicked through him with its now predictable force.

He leaned closer. Their cheeks almost touched. He couldn't actually see her face, just the pillow striped with her hair.

"What?" he whispered.

•

"You hurt me."

He knew she didn't mean the bruises.

If he stared in her eyes, he would find pain. So he didn't look, simply listened to her voice so soft only he could hear.

"When you kissed me that first time, that was just my body, something superficial. This time you took my confidences, my trust. Something so much more important than my body." Her chest rose and fell faster. "Chuck, how could you do that?"

He didn't move, didn't speak, just let the accusations roll over him like the warmth of her breath caressing his neck.

Chuck rocked back on his heels and returned her gaze, hoping she would see what he couldn't say. Neither moved, just stared, until her eyes grew glassy. She twitched as sleep seemed to grab hold. Mesmerized, Chuck watched her lids flutter closed until her breathing regulated.

He wasn't aware of the passage of time as he watched her, and he really didn't care. For so long he had tried to keep his guard in place around her, never allowing himself the unrestrained luxury of simply looking at her. With the room wired only for sound, he didn't have to worry about anyone observing his hungry gaze.

What was it about this woman that made her special? It wasn't as if he'd stayed celibate since he'd been rescued in Turkey. He'd had a couple of flings and even a for-real relationship shortly after he'd gotten out of the hospital. Except Annette Santos, who'd survived an attack by a serial killer, had demons of her own to work out. They'd been drawn by their common experience. But ultimately as Annette put her life back together, she'd bailed on him, calling him an "emotional cripple." Maybe she was right, because he truly hadn't given a damn when she walked away.

So here he was, still not so sure the past had cleared away but wanting Jolynn all the same. Why was he attracted to her in a way stronger than anything he'd ever experienced? Did the part of him that craved danger feel drawn to her?

His mind traveled a treacherous path of "what if." Of course, she wasn't a party to her father's dealings. Her relationship with Taylor was already strained. If pushed to the breaking point, she might even be freed of the old man's influence. Could there be a path through this mess, any possibility she would forgive—

Jolynn whimpered in her sleep, bringing all his protective instincts to the fore. She tossed, twisting in the sheets, restless, tiny moans escaping her lips as she frowned involuntarily, no doubt reliving the horrors of the day.

Been there. Done that. Bought the T-shirt. He shuffled aside more memories.

When her thrashing grew more fitful, he worried she might jar her ribs. Slowly, Chuck reached across and lifted the extra pillow, slipping it by her. She rolled onto her uninjured side, burrowing into the softness.

He drew back, pulling his hand away until Jolynn grabbed his wrist. Seeing she still slept, he didn't move for a moment. He tried to tug his arm free again, but she held tight.

Resigned to the inevitable and in many ways grateful to have no choice, Chuck slipped onto the bed beside her. He reclined with his back pressed to the carved headboard.

Jolynn abandoned the pillow and snuggled against him. Her arm curved around his leg. She sighed, her agitation ceasing.

Lifting a tendril, he tested the feel of it between his fingers before he laid it aside, smoothing his hand across her brow. He cleared away the rest of her curls and wished he could give her the apology she needed. But he would see to her protection. He owed her, and Chuck always paid his debts. His hand cupped around the base of her skull as he kept watch over her through the night.

TEN

★ ─────────────────────────────────────

She dreamed of him.

Jolynn held tightly to the dream, desperate to stay asleep where she could indulge herself. Where she could wrap her arms around Charles Tomas and pretend she didn't know his name was Chuck Tanaka. She could slide her hands up his shirt along the hard plane of his stomach, higher still until his pecs twitched beneath her sensitive fingertips.

The ache between her legs increased. She grazed her nails along his shoulders, down his back, hooking her leg over his to get closer. Hungrily, urgently, she rocked against the firm pressure of his thigh touching her moist core.

Overheating by the second, she rolled her shoulder to dislodge her robe. Air brushed along her bared breasts, teasing her nipples to hardened peaks. She arched her back, desperate for contact with his hard, warm body.

"Charles, I need more, now," she whispered as the thick coarseness of his hair slid between her fingers.

"Jolynn," he growled against her ear. "You have to stop."

God, her dreams were every bit as good as reality. She slid her hand between them and palmed the rigid length in his pants. This dream was getting even *better* than any reality she could remember.

Her hand worked the length of him, learning him, taking delight in the ragged groan that heated across her face. She kicked restlessly at the beddings, wanting to clear everything away so she would be all the more free to roll on the bed with him. Pleasure, release was so very close. Every nerve in her body tightened in anticipation as she rocked faster against the thick pressure of his thigh. Stroking him, stoking, she wanted him to come with her, in an explosive release they would repeat again more slowly the second time.

"Stop." His voice sliced through her dream, his fingers banding around her wrist.

Ice-cold reality splashed over her, jolting her awake. She blinked fast, her eyes adjusting to the murky shadows of the darkened room. Slowly, she became aware of her surroundings. Of the stark little room. Of Chuck beside her in bed.

Of her hand plastered against his crotch.

She snatched her hand away. His eyes stared back at her, stormy with restrained desire. Her chest was heaving, her body still achy with want. She curled her fingers against the urge to grab him by the shirt and finish out her dream for real.

"Chuck, I don't know—"

"*Shhh . . .*" He pressed a finger to her lips then pulled her robe back over her shoulders.

Damn, she hadn't even realized it had actually fallen aside and not just in her dreams. Heat flooded her as she thought of him seeing her, even in the shadowy darkness.

How could she be so angry with him and want him so

much at the same time? Her brain resented—hated—Chuck Tanaka for cruelly leading her on for the benefit of his investigation. But her body . . . Oh God, her body still wanted Charles Tomas, the enigmatic but tender student and everyday man.

Her hands fisted in his shirt, cotton warmed from his skin or hers. She wasn't sure. "I don't want this."

"I know. God, I know. Neither do I, but here we are all the same." He stared back at her with eyes as tortured as her insides.

For the first time since they'd stood by the entrance to the catacombs, maybe for the first time since she'd met him, she felt like she was seeing into his soul.

"What should we do?"

Shaking his head, he stroked back her hair, his hand not all that steady. "Go to sleep. For both of our sakes."

She forced her eyes closed, her body all too aware of him beside her, still holding her. And as she drifted off to sleep, she wondered why neither of them had even thought about leaving the bed.

* * *

A light tap jolted Chuck from his half-sleep power nap. Morning sunlight streamed through the slim parts in the shutters, casting bars of light across their twined bodies.

Their bodies. Jolynn, warm and soft curled against him. While he'd had his fair share of sex, he'd never slept with a woman before. Too intimate somehow, especially in light of how damn close he'd come to losing control with her last night.

Jolynn's whispered words echoed in his mind. *You took my confidences, my trust. Something so much more important than my body.*

God, there hadn't been any choice but to hold back, even when her hands and sweet body had been all over him during her dream. And yeah, he'd wanted to know more about that dream. He'd wanted more of her. But he couldn't betray her trust. Not again.

The knock sounded again, and he stiffened, already assessing his options for defense. He blinked to moisten his contacts, grateful for extended-wear lenses.

"Hey, wake up. Are you there, Chuckles?"

He heard Nuñez's voice and relaxed.

"I have your clothes. Open up, sleepy head."

"Hold on a minute." Chuck untangled his hand from Jolynn's hair and unwrapped her arm from his thigh. Inching away, he slipped the pillow into her embrace, waiting to move until she sighed and settled.

Chuck crossed to the door and peered through the peephole. He looked at Nuñez through the fishbowl glass, shaking his head at the distorted sight of the agent dressed as a local fisherman, adding a good ten years to his age through that crazy way he adjusted his features and stance. The guy always had enjoyed his undercover getups.

Chuck tugged the door open. "Nuñez, you've come up with some inventive disguises, but this makes the top ten."

Special Agent Mike Nuñez straightened his leather Greek fisherman's cap. "I'm simply an eccentric New Englander visiting my grandpa's roots. Sorry to interrupt."

He glanced at the hulking agent sitting in a chair against the corridor wall, then scowled at Nuñez. "You know as well as I, nothing happened here."

"No wonder you're so cranky." The guy was downright jovial since he'd tied the knot six months ago with a woman he met during the op in Turkey. Nuñez's wife, Anya, was every bit as much a victim of that sadistic bitch who'd kidnapped him—even if the bitch *was* Anya's mother. Now if they could just take care of the rest of the network. The hell spawn—Marta—had given up enough details when captured to keep herself alive but still they uncovered more layers to her dealings. She'd made a fortune kidnapping servicemen and stealing secrets from them. Those who agreed to cooperate were allowed to live and turned into spies. Those who didn't?

They were tortured until they died. Chuck was the only one to leave alive and with secrets intact—even if they'd had to carry him out on a stretcher.

"Lighten up, Chuck. I'm just teasing." He passed him one of the two sacks dangling from his wrist. "I brought you both some fresh clothes, some disguises I whipped up."

"Why do we need disguises, for God's sake? Just get us out of here," Chuck snapped.

"In case we need to move you after all. Always best to plan for every contingency. Since you don't speak fluent Italian, acting like tourists is your best bet." He held up the bag again.

Chuck stared at the sack as if it were a live snake.

"Nothing too outlandish, I promise. Just a pair of shorts and a shirt, a few items to make you both look like an average newlywed couple on vacation."

"I'll withhold comments until I see what's in there."

Nuñez passed him the waist holster for his 9 mm. "I thought you could use this."

Chuck grasped the gun, its familiar weight comforting. "Thanks. I don't mean to sound ungrateful. Put everything on the table if you don't mind. I'll change later." Raking his fingers through his shaggy hair, Chuck glanced at his ruined shoes. "I, uh, need to make sure she's safe."

"Take your shower. I'll watch over her. You saw the mountain out in the hall who just took over the next shift."

Nuñez's eyes burned with determination. "Jolynn will be fine."

Chuck snagged the bag on his way to the bathroom. "Her father's going to jail. I don't think she's going to be 'fine' about that."

* * *

Her father's going to jail.

The words pounded into Jolynn's brain as she curled under the thin bedspread. Still recovering from heart surgery, her father wouldn't be in any condition to withstand the stress of an arrest and trial. What would a stint in jail do to his health?

She swallowed back the bilious taste. Her own innate sense of justice told her she would condemn anyone else for such crimes, but every inch of her cried out for her daddy to be innocent.

Get real, Jolynn. You've known better for years.

She was such a mess, inside and out. Sore and exhausted and still aching to be with the man who'd haunted her dreams. Had she imagined everything last night, or had he really stroked back her hair and told her he wanted her, too, even though he knew it was wrong?

So very wrong.

A part of her hated him all the more for being honorable last night. If he'd been a jerk, she could have slugged him and kicked his sorry ass out of her bed. Now, she was still stuck in the purgatory of resenting Chuck and wanting Charles.

Jolynn pushed the pillow aside, groaning as every muscle in her body ached in protest.

"Morning after stinks, doesn't it?"

She startled more fully awake and sat up, spread clutched to her chest. She blinked, but the middle-aged guy dressed to look like the local fishermen she'd seen selling their catch on the street yesterday was still . . .

Wait. She narrowed her eyes. After a moment, she recognized the agent from the day before.

"Good morning, Agent Nuñez." Jolynn swung her legs over the side of the bed, unable to stifle the wince of discomfort. "Where's Chuck?"

She wondered why in spite of everything, she still sought the reassurance of his presence.

"Call me Mike." The agent nodded toward the bathroom, the shower hissing in the background. "He's cleaning up."

Guess I'm on my own again.

Mike shoved a hand in his pocket and withdrew a bottle of Extra Strength Tylenol with an American label. Snapping the cap, he selected two and extended his hand.

Jolynn tossed back the pills without water and prayed for their speedy effect. "Are you Chuck's partner?"

"Not really. I'm NSA. He's air force. We met on a job a couple of years ago. Situation called for us to work together again and here we are."

On the job. She shuddered.

Her father's going to jail. "I need to let my dad know I'm okay. He may be just another criminal to you people, but to me he's an old man with a heart condition."

"Hold on. You don't need to get defensive." Mike set aside the camera around his neck—although Jolynn imagined it wasn't a regular camera given all the toys around here. "I already figured that would worry you. One of our people will make sure your father believes you're okay, just enjoying some time to yourself. He doesn't know anything about Chuck, and we'd like to keep it that way. Chuck will just be calling into work sick."

"What if I want to go back to the ship?" She would never

see Chuck again. God, she didn't even know where he was really from.

"Surely you realize things have moved beyond that now."

"I'm not so sure I do understand." And she really didn't understand the swell of relief over hearing she wouldn't be saying good-bye to Chuck today. "For how long?"

"However long it takes. We can't let you endanger the safety of our other operatives. The best place for you is with Chuck. You would have died yesterday had you been with anyone else." Nuñez spread his arms. "Well, anyone other than Chuck or me, of course."

"Nuñez . . ."

Jolynn jerked toward Chuck's voice.

He stood in the open bathroom doorway, glaring. "This time you've gone too far."

Jolynn pivoted on the edge of the bed and gaped at Special Agent Chuck Tanaka wearing orange Bermuda shorts, a cabana shirt, and cheap flip-flops.

A much-needed laugh bubbled up inside her, rising until she couldn't contain herself. She held her aching side and let loose, tension flowing from her muscles. Giggles swept through her like a summer rain shower, cleansing away the tension of the past twenty-four hours. After the terror and disillusionment of the prior day, laughter felt good. She kept right on laughing until the sting of tears behind her eyes let her know how close she was to losing control.

Chuck scowled at his bare toes in the plastic aqua bargain-basement sandals.

Another laugh slipped free. "Ow!"

She touched her tender side.

"Serves you right," he snapped, although he couldn't hide the obvious concern in his eyes despite the words.

"Oh, it's worth it, down to the last chuckle. Chuckle . . .

Chuck, chuckles, like your pal said when you thought I was asleep."

His head whipped around, his eyes narrowed.

Her laughter faded.

Reality crept over her. Or maybe it had something to do with the somber expressions plastered on the two men's faces. This was big-time, serious stuff. Life-and-death stakes for them from here on out.

Yesterday, too, for that matter.

Chuck snatched the plastic bag dangling from the door-knob. "Wait until you see what Nuñez brought for you. He's already grinning like the Cheshire cat so I imagine it's going to be a winner."

"Thanks," she said curtly, sifting through the sack. "Wow, they've even included matching flip-flops. Your boss is some kind of big spender."

Digging farther, Jolynn nibbled her bottom lip. Nuñez was obviously out to cause trouble. Jolynn eased free a tiny wisp of floral cotton.

"Good thinking, Nuñez," he gloated. "She'll need a scarf to cover her hair."

Mike smiled. "Oh, that's not a scarf. It's her shirt."

"Shirt?" Chuck's smile flattened.

"A bandeau to match her sarong. I believe I have the terminology right for the garb. That's what my Anya calls them."

Jolynn sifted through the bag and pulled out another scrap of clothing not much larger than the first.

Chuck tugged the silky fabric from her hands. "Won't her bruised ribs show? And what the hell happened to keeping a low profile? There's no way she can fade into a crowd in this."

He held up the floral outfit, a piece in each hand.

Uh-oh. He did have a point. Ready to demand different clothes, she glanced at the silky wisps again and reconsidered. Perhaps resurrecting a bit of her Venus de Milo facade might not be such a bad idea.

She wanted him. He wanted her. If they spent more than a couple of days cooped up here, the attraction could easily fire out of control. So why not take a gamble where she would be the one in charge? She'd never wanted a man the way she wanted him, and with a ready-made time limit on the relationship, she wouldn't let it spiral out of control.

Nuñez waved aside Chuck's scowl. "Calm down. If we have to move you, the two of you will look like the rest of the tourists blowing through town. Throw a camera around your neck, wear a hat, have her put on big diva sunglasses, and play around with your accent. You'll be fine. I will make sure of it."

Clutching the clothes to her chest, she backed toward the bathroom. "Mike, if this is the way you treat your friends, remind me to stay on your good side."

Something flashed in his eyes, something dark replacing the warm and fuzzy guy who'd been chatting her up earlier. She saw the undercover facade peel away. She saw the kind of man Chuck worked with. The kind of people sent to take down her father.

Nuñez blinked and just that fast he was a regular fisherman again. "Just immerse yourself in the character you're playing. The rest will come."

Chuck quirked an eyebrow. "You've already made it rather difficult to fade into the background."

"Okay"—Nuñez shrugged—"these were the best I could do on short notice. Later this evening, I'll have something more practical to cover the body armor when we transfer you. Meanwhile, this will get you through the day in case you have to leave here and anyone sees you. Now, chill."

She forced a ragged breath to steady her pounding heart. Chuck had saved her out there on the water. She needed to remember that and hold on tight. Even if she resented needing his protection, she was dependant on him until . . . Hell, she wasn't sure when. The ship might not be safe. And Texas was a long way away.

She didn't want to fall victim to her father's business like her uncle had. She was here now, with Chuck, and while he might not be the Charles of her dreams, he was what she needed to keep her safe.

And on a deeper, more physical level as well.

She clutched her "tourist" garb to her chest. "I should go change."

"That's my cue." Nuñez adjusted his leather hat on the way to the door, his expression changing until he looked ten years older. He stopped half in, half out of the door. "Whatever will the two of you do alone in this room all day?"

* * *

By midafternoon, Jolynn stared down Chuck in an intense battle of wills. His expression gave no quarter as he sat a mere hand's reach away. Tension snapped between them so hot and tangible she could almost hear it crackle along the air.

Jolynn tilted her head back, her nostrils thinning as she weighed her options. Take him on? Or retreat, end it. God, how she hated to simply quit. Too many times in her life she'd simply folded to pressure, afraid to press her luck. She was just about to lose her nerve when . . . she saw the droplets of sweat bead on his forehead.

Her mouth curved in a smile of victory. "Hit me."

Chuck sailed the card across the scratched pine table. A nine. Damn.

"Busted." Jolynn scribbled the latest score on the notepad. Perspiration trickled down her spine.

"That's supposed to be the dealer's line." Chuck spread the cards facedown and mixed them around in a smooth card washing before gathering them up for a normal shuffle. He swiped a muscular forearm over his brow. "I wonder how much longer we'll have to wait for the air conditioner repairman?" He directed his voice to the bugged Van Gogh reproduction. "Did you catch that? We're melting in here."

The day spent with Chuck, both of them wearing next to no clothes, hadn't done much to improve her already irritable mood. When Chuck had suggested cards, putting a table between them had seemed like an inspired idea. Except it wasn't a very big table. Of course, a picnic table wouldn't be large enough. Jolynn brushed her fingers over her brow, the moisture caused by more than a broken air conditioner. Opening a window put them at risk, so they were stuck with a rickety old fan.

"Get ready for the next hand." Chuck resumed shuffling, although the cards, clammy with humidity, proved more sluggish than his normal handling. "Aw, to hell with it."

Chuck smacked down the deck. He whipped the cabana shirt over his head, muffling his voice until the shirt cleared his face. Was it her imagination, or had the table just shrunk?

She couldn't seem to look away from his sculpted chest. The man was totally ripped. As he tossed aside his shirt, each muscle flexed and moved. Sweat glistened on his skin, adding a sheen to an already smoking-hot, touch-me body.

The gun strapped to his waist cast a dark slash across his washboard abs. Her belly knotted. Then she realized how long she'd been staring. She glanced up quickly.

Chuck stared back. His chest rose and fell faster, his brown eyes turning smoky with an answering desire. She'd wanted to make the most of her time with him, and it appeared the time might have come. Still, making that first move was always a risk.

With a will of its own, her trembling hand reached across the small table. Her fingertips trailed a light path over his chest, snagging on the end of his silver chain before continuing downward. His muscles tensed in response, and she smiled, the age-old feeling of a primitive feminine power coursing through her.

The listening device offered her a degree of security in the exploration. Nothing further would happen between them with his NSA buddy in earshot and a guard in the hall.

Skimming her knuckles down the middle of his chest, she savored the texture of his damp, bristly hair. His heat simmered into her, bringing an answering flame that rivaled the sweltering room. She swirled small circles along his skin, lower and lower still until the table stopped her path. Leaning back, she brought her hand to her mouth, lightly tasting the salty flavor of him lingering on the pad of her finger.

His arm snaked across, gently imprisoning her wrist. He pressed a lingering kiss against her palm and replaced her hand on top of her cards. She couldn't move.

She didn't understand him. She certainly didn't need a man she couldn't trust. But after the past twenty-four hours had flayed her emotions raw, her body simply wouldn't listen to her head.

Chuck stared at their joined hands, his brow furrowing. What rattled around inside his mind beneath his lushly thick hair?

He scrubbed a hand over his jaw, then grabbed the pencil. After scratching a few words across the page, he pushed the pad across with one finger.

I never meant for you to get hurt.

He had heard her words the night before after all. She wanted to cry. If she looked at him, she knew she would.

Chuck retrieved the pad for another note, then passed it back. What else would he have to say? How much more could she take?

I'm sorry.

The words immobilized her in a way no lengthy speech could have. No one had apologized to her, ever. Not in any meaningful way. Even her father had sent her away without a word of explanation, much less apology.

Jolynn squeezed her eyes shut against the tears threatening to spill free. Eventually, the roaring in her ears dwindled, and she heard the rhythmic click of Chuck dealing the next round.

He dealt the hand with lightning speed in spite of the sticky cards, his gaze carefully avoiding hers. She reached for the pencil, and he nudged it just out of reach. She found his action almost more telling than words. He wasn't comfortable with emotional diatribes. That made his apology all the more touching.

"You're really good at that." Slightly breathless, she stumbled over her words. What happened now? She wasn't sure she could handle another night with so much need churning in their small room.

He tipped his cards by the corner for a peek. "Are you going to talk or play?"

Still a man of few words. Somehow understanding the bit of his personality that transcended any cover story reassured her. "Did they teach you about casinos in basic training or super spy school?"

Chuck paused, thumbing his cards.

Jolynn rested her chin on her palm, ignoring her hand on the table. "Is there some rule against you talking to me?"

He tapped the deck, his eyes growing pensive. "I picked up some tips here and there. My mom dated a blackjack dealer before she died. Not many kids get to play Go Fish with a professional cardsharp. And later on, the nuns at the orphanage enjoyed some poker to break up the monotony of too much Bingo." Suddenly, he bolted from his chair. "They really need to do something about the air conditioner."

Sweeping a broad path around Jolynn, Chuck crossed to the bedside table. He snatched the phone off the receiver, listened, then tapped the base.

His silence held a new air, a tension she might have missed days prior but understood all too well now.

"What—"

Chuck stopped beside Jolynn, pressing a finger to her lips for silence. He yanked his shirt back over his head. "Why don't you deal the next one," he said in a voice a touch louder than normal. "I need to make a quick trip to the head."

Chuck transformed back into the man by the river, the professional at the safe house. Every inch of him hummed with restrained energy, leashed power.

He wrapped his fingers around the grip of his gun and nudged the door open. Chuck pivoted to the doorway, body tight as if poised for a second confrontation. Peering out, he tensed.

Where was the guard? Jolynn hunched down in her seat. Chuck crooked his elbow, pulling his gun up and ready.

He took a deep breath and spun into the hall. His arm dropped to his side, and he stepped back into the room.

Jolynn relaxed, already growing weary with his cops and robbers drama. "Where's—"

Chuck shook his head. Jolynn frowned, looking past him.

Two pops echoed down the corridor. With a knowledge Jolynn wished she didn't possess, she recognized the sound from the shooting by the river. Another gunshot, closer. A scream. A shout of pain.

In a snap, Chuck locked the door and shoved a dresser in front. He spun back to her fast, dropped the floppy hat onto her head, and shoved her purse into her arms.

He held out his hand, brown eyes cold as stony onyx. "We're going out the window. Now."

Jolynn knew she only had a second to decide what to do. And the decision wasn't even tough. Someone had tried to break into her room. She'd been shot at on the beach. Her dad ran with a dangerous crowd. All that combined was more than enough reason for her to have some serious concerns for her safety.

She looked at the pad of paper still resting on the table. *I'm sorry.* The choice of who to stick with was a no-brainer.

Jolynn reached for Chuck, prepared to follow him out a second-story window.

ELEVEN

★ —————————————————————————

Focus narrowed, Chuck let training and instincts take over. He raced to the window to look out at the street below. The balcony was only one story up. Provided there weren't more goons waiting for them below, he could lower Jolynn down and jump.

Walking out the door didn't sound appealing. A look had shown him the guard lay slumped on the floor beside his chair. His eyes stared wide, unblinking, dead, a bullet hole in the middle of his forehead. God only knew what had happened to Nuñez and the OSI agent downstairs. A howling sense of fury raged through him along with a flashback to his time in captivity. For days, he'd sat beaten and half-conscious in his cell, listening to the screams of someone else a wall away, the captors shouting questions. It was almost worse when the noise stopped and he realized that faceless prisoner, a brother-in-arms he would never meet, was likely dead.

Cold sweat popped along his back. He couldn't think about those voices then or his friends downstairs now. He would call in the crisis as soon as he had Jolynn out.

A thump rattled the door. A boot most likely. He yanked Jolynn to the side because undoubtedly soon—

Bullets tore through the wood frame.

He threw back the shutters and yanked open the window. Fingers linked with hers, Chuck shoved her out onto the small Juliet balcony. "I'm right behind you. If we get separated, call the number inside the waistband of your skirt and ask for Rex."

The colonel would take care of her if worse came to worst. Chuck kept his 9 mm aimed at the door. The frame loosened, the dresser inching with every shove.

He turned to help Jolynn only to find she'd already swung a leg over the rail. Before he could so much as clasp her wrist, she launched herself toward the sidewalk.

Atta girl. Admiration for her spunk kicked through him as he grasped the rail. Up and over, he landed sure-footed beside her. Above, he heard the bedroom door crash in.

Hooking an arm around her waist, he hauled her through the walled courtyard and out onto the street. He snagged Jolynn's hat from her tight grip and clamped it over her bold red hair.

He eased his gun into the holster just before they rushed into a cluster of tourists scurrying away with wide eyes.

"Focus forward," he ducked toward her ear to whisper, pointing to a historic church with the pretended interest of a normal sightseer. "Don't look back and keep smiling like you're having fun."

Men in cop uniforms and dark suits flocked from three different side streets, rushing past toward the house.

She tugged his hand. "Shouldn't we talk to the cops?"

"Can't afford to trust them. We're on our own for now." He didn't know who'd compromised their locale and wasn't sure how far he could trust the other safe houses.

He weighed the option of stealing a car, which would then have cops everywhere on the lookout for that particular vehicle. Or he could risk retrieving the Fiat parked two more blocks away, tucked out of sight for just such an emergency. Hopefully, he would get a better sense when he scoured the area along the way.

But that would also necessitate leaving the safety of the crowd, making them easier to track.

He tugged her purse from her shoulder. "I need this for a second."

"Okay"—she passed it over—"but why?"

"*Shhh*, not now." He fished inside the bottomless pit, pushing aside her wallet, lip gloss, even a thumb drive for crying out loud before he finally found . . . the casino coin he'd given her the night they'd met. He surreptitiously dropped it in a fruit vendor's cart.

Her eyes went wide with realization, then disillusioned acceptance. Her eyes squeezed tight for a second with her sigh.

He tugged her along. "We don't have time for that now. Come on."

Gasping alongside him, Jolynn stumbled on a crack in the pavement. "Where are we going?"

Chuck lowered his mouth to hers. "Not now." He brushed his lips against hers before pulling back to flash a smile at a tourist next to them. "Newlyweds," Chuck said, putting on a thick Jersey accent. "Come on, babe."

"I'm right witcha, lover boy." Her Northern accent surprised him.

Her quick kiss scorched him.

He slipped an arm around Jolynn's shoulders, pulling her close to his side as he peeled away from the group and ducked into a side street. At the end of the road, the Fiat sat safe and sound under a portico covered in vines. He scanned the alleyway. Not deserted. Just everyday traffic. A lady hanging out her laundry. A man taking out trash who made him think of Nuñez. But he couldn't afford to let concerns distract him. Keeping Jolynn alive had to be his primary goal, double down, just as Nuñez would do if their positions were reversed.

Easing down the street cautiously, he watched, studied. The young couple pushing the baby carriage gave him pause until he saw an infant truly rested in the rickety pram.

Now or never.

He approached the car, tucking Jolynn beside him. "Hold on, babe," he said in his Jersey accent, "I've just gotta find de spare key."

He knelt beside the car, running his hand in the wheel well while checking the undercarriage for bombs. A quick search in the trunk and under the hood was all the time he could waste and as sure as he could be.

And to buy them more time to think, he rewired the GPS to send faulty coordinates.

As a last precaution, he said, "Stand over there while I back this baby out."

If the car blew when he started it, at least she would be alive. She could call Rex Scanlon.

He slid the key in the ignition . . . The Fiat's engine purred to life like a happy kitten. He threw open the passenger door and started down the road before Jolynn could finish buckling.

Jolynn panted, clasping her side. "Should we call your friend Rex?"

"Soon."

"Why not now?"

"Calling him from here is a last resort. How do I know which line is secure, who's listening? Someone sold us out back there, and until I know who, we're laying low."

He slammed the car in gear, flooring it out of the neighborhood and mapping out in his mind the best route to the nearest ferry to the mainland.

★ ★ ★

Alone on the *Fortuna*'s upper deck's jogging track, Rex Scanlon pounded out his seventh mile while staring over at the watery abyss. A handful of late-nighters milled about below, but he was alone up here with his rage. Waves slapped the side of the cruise ship, leaving Sicily behind for their next port of call, Olympia, Greece.

Departing without Chuck went against everything he believed in as a serviceman. As a commander.

He leaned into the hard night wind tearing across the Med, hammering his feet into the ground, punishing his body. He'd made Chuck take on this mission and now things had gone to hell. Chuck had already been through too much, had insisted his edge was gone. Why hadn't they—hadn't he—listened rather than being so damn sure this wounded captain just needed to get back in the game?

His breathing grew ragged and he knew his running form was falling apart. His concentration was screwed. But he couldn't make himself stop running, biting back the urge to growl out his frustration. After hours at the computers with Berg, contacting every intelligence ally agency, they still had nothing.

There were too many brick walls. He'd finally decided to come up here and air out his brain in hopes that he could make some sense out of who'd shot at Chuck by the water. And most puzzling, how he'd just fallen off the face of the earth after leaving the safe house.

A fluttery cloud of white snagged his attention and he almost stumbled. Slowing, he narrowed his focus . . . and found Livia leaning against the railing wearing a whispery white dress. Hell. How long had she been there? If she'd been an assassin, he would already be dead. And he wasn't any good to Chuck if he stopped breathing.

He leaned over to grab his knees, gasping. "What are you doing out here so late?"

"I just finished my last set." Her husky voice carried on the breeze.

"You shouldn't be walking around alone."

"I am not alone. You are here," she pointed out. "Where is our mutual friend? Because I'm not buying the story that he got fired."

And wasn't that the million-dollar question? He sank to the deck, sitting, tugging her to sit beside him. "I don't have any idea where he is." He forced his breathing to steady. "He and Jolynn Taylor got off the ship in Sicily and didn't get back on."

Livia's coal dark eyes went wide, a rail light glinting off her sleek black hair. "Then why hasn't there been an alert issued?"

Last scan of the ship showed there weren't any bugs up here, part of why he gravitated to the track. "We tapped into their computers. Messed with the manifests so it appears they decided not to come back on board. They're officially signed off rather than missing. We need the right people looking for them and not the wrong people finding them."

"I am so sorry." Her soft hand slid over his. "I know you must be frantic."

"He's your friend, too." He squeezed her fingers lightly, only just realizing he hadn't let go and no one was watching. They had no need to perform. Still, he didn't pull away.

"That he is." Her voice quivered.

She'd spent a lot of days visiting Chuck during his recovery. There had been a time when Rex wondered if a relationship was growing between the two. But he knew now, they were genuinely just good friends. His arm slid around her shoulders, and he pulled her to his side. Her soft curves fit too perfectly against him, kicking his heart rate back up as if he were tackling the eighth mile.

Her head fell to rest on his shoulder, the scent of Mediterranean herbs and flowers drifting upward. "How do you live this way? Always having to worry so intensely for the people you care about?"

"It comes with the territory," he answered without hesitation. "Am I supposed to say the job's too hard? Let somebody else make the sacrifice?"

Livia looked up at him, smiling, her lips full and tempting. "You are quite a man, Rex Scanlon. Your wife was a very lucky woman."

He thumbed her jaw. "That's up for debate but thanks."

She frowned suddenly.

His thumb slowed at her chin. "What's wrong?"

"That is the first time I mentioned your Heather and you didn't wince."

The creamy softness of her skin, the sincere desire in Livia's eyes, was all he could see at the moment.

"Honest to God, I'm not thinking about her right now. I'm just thinking about how glad I am to have you here even though you should really be anywhere else. Somewhere safer."

"Ah, Rex, I think we've been here before."

He knew she didn't mean the boat, but rather a return to their old attraction. It hadn't ended well for them last time, but for the life of him, right now he couldn't remember why. Cradling the back of her head in his palm, he kissed her. Or she kissed him. Either way, her lips were moving under his, her breasts pressing against his chest, so perfect and soft he'd been certain his memory of touching her must have been faulty.

He was the forty-four-year-old father of two college-aged sons who would be horrified to hear their old man was making out with a twenty-nine-year-old pop star. And somehow none of that felt wrong or strange, because it was Livia in his arms. Livia's hands skimming up and down his back, plunging into his hair.

His mouth trailed over the perfect shell of her ear, down her neck, and as much as he wanted to take this further, he knew he couldn't afford to stay up here any longer. Work waited below. A missing brother-in-arms. And a mission going nowhere fast to figure out how the hell this ship was being used in a terrorist plot to set off a dirty nuke in the United States. He'd been so intent on studying those boarding the ship, he hadn't for a moment considered one of his own wouldn't get back on.

With more than a little regret, he eased away from her. "You have to know how much I want to finish this . . ."

She gripped his shoulders, fingernails digging half moons into his flesh through his shirt. "Find Chuck. We can deal with these . . . feelings . . . between us once you have done that."

Livia's eyes were filled with complete confidence. He wanted to believe her. He wanted to believe in his gut instinct to trust Chuck could kick the crap out of anything that came his way. That somewhere out there on that island of Sicily, Chuck was holed up keeping Jolynn Taylor safe.

* * *

Safely aboard the ferry from Palermo, Sicily, to Salerno on Italy's mainland, Jolynn tried to ignore how their microscopic cabin put them in such close confines.

Chuck hadn't wanted to be out in the open in the mass seating for the ten-hour crossing. He'd paid cash for the closet-sized space with only bunk beds with mud brown coverlets and a tiny private bath. A small fan attached high in a corner blew halfhearted gusts into the stuffy space.

Just outside the cabin, a handful of men spoke in rapid-fire Italian as they walked past on their way to the snack bar or observation deck. But from their raised voices and laughter, they seemed everyday passengers—not killers searching for Americans on the lam.

For the most part, she tried not to move, staying curled up in the corner of the tiny bunk beside the brass portal. But the choppy sea splashed against the glass. Every roll of the boat jostled her closer to him on the other end of the bottom bunk. Tantalizing swipes of his leg brushing hers sent her overrevved nerves tingling again.

She tugged her sarong over her knees and searched Chuck's tense face in the dim light of the single bulb overhead. A string hanging from that fixture swayed like a pendulum. "Does anyone know where we are? Some of your people, I mean? I didn't miss how you threw that coin out."

"Listening device." He shrugged unapologetically. "I would prefer no one knows where we are. Not yet, and not until I can assess our situation."

The drive across Sicily had been tense but blessedly uneventful. Still she couldn't miss the tension in Chuck's muscled shoulders as he kept his ear toward the door, his gun in his hand resting on his knee.

"What's the next plan? Another safe house once we reach Salerno?"

She needed details, some sense of ownership in their plans. Had she forsaken all control by running off with him? By placing herself completely in his hands? But then again, she'd never seen a man with such supremely capable hands, whether he was dealing blackjack, aiming a weapon, or stroking a touch along her skin. Her gaze landed back on his broad palms now, remembering them sliding over her skin the night before.

Chuck scrubbed his thumb back and forth along the grip of his 9 mm. "I'm looking outside the agency for somewhere to regroup." The ferry's motor whined almost as loudly as the sound of gurgling water as they chugged through the night. "For now, if there's a missing persons' report out, I want the local authorities to assume the goons at the safe house took us. The goons who tried to kill us will think we're back with my people or in another secured location. Hopefully, they'll run circles around each other. Meanwhile, that should buy us some time to slip away until I figure out who the good guys are."

The quiet serenity of the cabin echoed with adrenaline letdown after chaos. It appeared they were safe, for a moment at least.

Chuck had saved her life, twice, fighting odds that no gambler in Taylor's casino would have taken.

"Jolynn, I . . ." He studied his hand resting on his knee, weapon held and ready.

She clasped his free hand resting on the thin mattress, twining her fingers through his, owing him so much more than that simple touch, but not sure what else to offer.

She waited, afraid if she started talking, he would shut down, become the man back at the bed-and-breakfast who grunted answers. There wasn't a notepad in sight to carry him through.

"I'm well trained and I have technical skills that most can't even dream of."

No great revelation there. Still, she waited. There had to be a point, if she just listened closely enough. She needed to make some sense of what had happened today with the attack on them. And while he was at it, maybe he could explain why he'd felt the need to get so close to her when she didn't know a damn thing about her father's operation. In fact, she'd made it a point to know as little as possible about his life.

"If I'm good, it's because I don't think like other people anymore. I don't . . . feel things the way other people do." Setting his gun aside carefully on top of her purse on the floor, he shifted to face her fully. He seemed so intense, so focused, as if the words required more concentration than when he'd saved them by the catacombs. "That's also what makes me rotten at relationships."

She bristled, all the tension of the day firing to life and igniting the fuel of her fear. "Is this a brush-off? One of those 'I'm not ready to commit' discussions? If so, you can save it. Just because I'm ready to trust you with my safety and maybe even my body doesn't mean I'm at all interested in risking my heart."

He cocked an eyebrow, before rolling a kink out of his shoulder. "What I'm trying to say is I owe you an apology. Not a couple of words on paper, but the real thing." He picked up a lock of her hair and rubbed it between his fingers. "I'm sorry you got hurt. I'm sorry you're in danger because I couldn't keep my head on straight around you. I'm truly sorry."

He blamed himself for this? Because he was genuinely attracted to her? He'd apologized before, but this was something different, intense, personal. He was acknowledging they had something between them, something unique. Something powerful.

Something she craved every bit as much as he did.

"I appreciate that you're being honest with me. God, I really do. And we both know I all but made a fool out of myself over how much I wanted"—*still want, crave, burn to have*—"you. But things have gotten extremely complicated. What the hell do we do now?"

"This." Leaning forward, he cupped her face in his hands and slanted his mouth across hers. He kissed her, deep and hard with all the unrestrained intensity she'd glimpsed in him on those rare occasions when he'd let her look.

Initially, she stiffened, all her reservations regarding his assumed identity flickering through her brain. Yet her reasons for turning away from him seemed unimportant in light of their brushes with death. She knew all about "Protector Syndrome," the rescued falling for the rescuer, and she simply didn't care.

His words at the bed-and-breakfast echoed through her head. He worked for the military, not the mob. While dangerous and apparently in some kind of dark ops capacity, his world had purpose. Honor.

She'd felt the razor edge of that dangerous world today, and their near brush with death made her all the more aware of the rasp of his beard against her cheek, the gentle caress of his calloused hands along the small of her back bared by her sarong. His musky scent mingled with hers in a primal perfume that made her ache for a deeper connection.

Rather than questioning the "whys" and "wherefores," she should lose herself in this moment as she'd planned. A very real danger lurked outside that door. She might never have this chance again.

Wrapping her arms around his waist, she slipped her hands inside his shirt. She kneaded the muscles bulging under her touch, a testimony to the strength that had saved them both. His skin felt heated, vibrant, and alive. He pulled her closer, his tongue plundering, caressing, affirming life—his, hers, theirs entwined.

His fingers tangled in her hair, loosening the braid. He grabbed a fistful of curls unraveling from her braid. He pulled his mouth from hers and buried his face in her hair, inhaling deeply. She reveled in his groan.

Greedily, his lips moved to her neck, and she threw back her head, offering him freer access. A moan traveled up the length of her arched throat, begging for release just as her body begged for relief.

Chuck's hands slid lower, curving around her hips, his fingers sinking in with sensual surety and want as he reclined her back on the narrow bunk. Hungry and needy, she wriggled closer, couldn't get close enough until he blanketed her with his body. Jolynn looped her arms around his waist. His thigh nestled between her legs, against the apex of her thighs, searing her with his heat.

His hand tucked under her bandeau and loosened the knot. Anticipation burned over skin already eager for his touch. Air whispered over her nipples, her breasts tightening in response just as his mouth closed over a peak.

The moist, tugging sensation jolted through her in waves of warm, liquid fire. The intensity rippled on top of taut emotions, almost more than she could bear.

He transferred his attention to her other breast. She brushed her fingers over his bristly shorn hair, urging his head closer. She inched forward and rocked her hips against his, desperate for relief and wanting, needing, this man to be the one to initiate her.

Other men had tried. Once she'd left her wild teen years behind, she'd indulged in more mature affairs, brief and unsatisfying encounters that made her wonder if she just didn't have a passionate nature. She was quickly changing her mind on that.

While assuredly this was just a physical reaction, she didn't care. Hadn't she told him the body didn't matter, only her soul? Well, he couldn't have her soul, but she wanted him to have her body, wanted to take his in return.

A moan slipped past his lips. "Jolynn . . . Lynnie . . ." He traced the shell of her ear. "I want you so damn bad, but this isn't the place or the time."

"What's wrong with here and now? No one can see, and God, I need you to take the edge off." She cupped his face, pulling it to hers.

He returned her kiss, then drew back, skimming his lips over hers. "As incredible as this feels, I need to be sure you're not going to be sorry later. The adrenaline is kicking in overtime, and we're both reacting to the afternoon's events."

"Last time I checked, I'm an adult. So unless you think you're only reacting to the adrenaline . . ."

Groaning, he scooped her bandeau from the floor. "I would laugh if I weren't hurting so bad. I've wanted you since the first time I saw you. I'll probably have to apologize again afterward. But I'm not strong enough to turn you away anymore."

Relief tumbled through her. She couldn't stand another rejection. Couldn't stifle another moment of her need for him.

She pressed a lingering kiss to the patch of skin exposed by the vee of his shirt. "Good. Then there's nothing holding us back."

TWELVE

Jolynn's lips on his chest sent a bolt of longing straight through to his groin. Reservations and worries scattered. They had a window of time here on this ferry to explore whatever insanity had taken hold of them both from the first second they'd laid eyes on each other back in the *Fortuna*'s casino.

Right now, he wasn't undercover and she wasn't the crook's daughter. They could be Chuck and Jolynn. They could be together.

Her fingers flew down the buttons of his shirt, her mouth following each revealed patch of skin until she grazed the fly of his shorts. The brush of her wrist against his straining hard-on had him gritting his teeth to hold back. She unzipped his pants and freed him from his boxers before he could blink. Her soft hand working up and down the rigid length of him threatened to finish him off right there.

But he didn't want this to end so fast. They had hours before they docked, and he intended to make the most of every minute they spent behind a locked door he'd barricaded with a metal table. So he ground his teeth, reined in the throbbing need to pump his hips along with the stroke of her fingers until he spilled himself onto her stomach. He wanted—*had*—to be inside her.

The swaying light overhead cast a warm glow over the dusky rose of her nipples, still tight and damp from his mouth minutes earlier. It was clear she wanted this every bit as much as he did.

His hand fell to the knot in her sarong, tied at her hip. A deft flick later and the length of fabric loosened. Inch by inch, he tugged the silk between them, the softness of the skirt replaced by her infinitely softer skin. Finally, she was naked other than her panties. The narrow bunk limited his access, not to mention made it damn near impossible to look his fill. And God, how he wanted to see her.

He slid from on top of her to kneel beside the bed. She rolled to her side, reaching for him, cupping the length of him framed by the open fly of his shorts. Her little purr of pleasure, her obvious desire for him, cranked the heat so high the fan couldn't begin to ease the steam rising.

"Patience . . ." His whisper warmed along the creamy skin of her stomach, his thumbs hooking in her underwear.

He pressed a kiss first to her bruised ribs, then along her stomach, enjoying the way her hands moved restlessly over his shoulders, in his hair. Skimming her panties down, down, down her endlessly long legs, he followed the path of his hands with his mouth. She moaned when he rasped his unshaven cheek along her thigh. She sighed when he kissed behind her knee.

And when he worked his way back up the inside of her leg, she went very still, her breath coming faster until he nuzzled, urging her to open for him. One of her feet slipped to the floor as she continued to lie back on the bunk.

Yes. Every nerve ending inside him shouted in unison as he caught the scent of her. Lapped at the essence of her. His tongue flicked at the little bundle of nerves swollen and taut as her nipples, letting him know she was every bit as hot for this as he was.

Her head thrashed against the pillow, her red hair spilling over the side and onto the floor. A flush started over her skin, broadcasting how close completion lurked . . . He flicked his tongue faster, harder, while he explored her slickness with one finger, then two.

Her nails bit into his arms, deeper. With her hands and her scent all over him, he could just as easily come undone right now, too. While continuing to sip, nuzzle, suckle along her heated core, he reached for his pants, dipping into the pocket, searching for his wallet and the one thing he'd made damn sure not to be without since the first time he'd put his lips on Jolynn's.

He fumbled through until he finally found one of the condoms he'd stored away. Three seconds later, he'd sheathed himself. Anticipation seared his veins, his brain, his ability to think about anything but kissing his way up her stomach, higher still until he stretched on top of her.

Her eyes were glazed and dilated and completely fixed on his face. Without a word, he thrust inside her. Her back bowed upward, a sigh of pleasure filling the cabin as she squeezed around him, tighter, pulsing again and again until her breathy gasps turned into a moan.

Slanting his mouth over hers, he caught her next shout of release and moved inside her, driving her to a second release that clamped a silken vise around him. To hell with holding back, he let go and rode the orgasm right along with her. Her legs locked around his hips, her heels digging into his ass, and their sweat-slicked bodies rocked against each other in time with the roll of the ferry along the waves.

By the time the last aftershock rocked through him, he
realized his fist was knotted in her hair. Probably too tightly.
And he had to be heavy on top of her because he could
barely find the strength to lift himself off her.

Sated, he flipped to his back, holding her to him the entire
time until her limp body draped over his. The tired little fan
overhead circulated air over their bare skin—not that he'd
ever managed to get his pants down, only open. He stroked
back her hair as she buried her face in his neck. Having her
here in his arms felt so damn right, that for the first time in
years, he closed his eyes and fell deeply, dreamlessly, asleep.

* * *

The shower stall in the ferry cabin wasn't big, but Jolynn
figured they didn't need much room anyway when they were
plastered against each other. The last ripples of her release
shimmered through her as her leg slid down his and back
to the floor again. Water sloshed down their bodies, swirling
into the drain. Anyone with hearing would buy into their
story about being newlyweds. She'd given up trying to stay
quiet two orgasms ago.

Chuck eased from inside her and slowly turned her mus-
cleless body around, adjusting the showerhead over her hair.
Before she could ask, she smelled the shampoo in the air
and his fingers started the most delicious massage along her
scalp. She didn't even consider protesting. They'd explored
every inch of each other's bodies over the past five hours.

And with that thought came a chilling memory, of the
moment she'd felt the ridges on his shoulders, seen the scars
on his thighs. She had to ask. . . . And he had to know she
would . . .

"What happened to your back? The scars?"

His hands in her hair hesitated for a second before he

lifted the long mass up to the water. "An overseas op didn't go as planned. I spent some time as a prisoner. The people who had me weren't very . . . hospitable."

The water might as well have turned to ice. Her body chilled from the inside out. She hadn't guessed, even knowing he was in the military. "You were a POW? In the Middle East?"

His hands curled around her shoulders. "You should realize by now that I don't participate in your standard sorts of military missions. Much of what I do is secret, under the public radar."

His words stirred a whole black abyss of possibilities. Her world had been plenty dark growing up. She knew what sorts of horrors amoral people could inflict on another. And if he was out there fighting an undercover war, those he engaged would have no rules or any sort of accountability.

Even knowing what she did, having seen the brutal world they lived in, her stomach still rolled at what must have happened to leave such deep scars on his body.

She started to turn, to wrap her arms around him and hold him safe and alive right there. But he stopped her. His grip on her shoulders tightened and she realized he didn't want her comfort.

So she said simply, "I'm so very sorry."

Without answering, he lathered her hair again, his thick strong body pressed to hers in the tiny cubicle. The tension in his knotted muscles relayed too painfully well what it had cost him to share even that much with her. The enormity of what he did in his secret ops military world seeped through her. Men like him didn't exist in her world, not the shady one she'd grown up in, and definitely not in her corporate button-up life in Dallas.

He was a special breed.

Her forehead fell to rest on the tile, her eyes burning, flooding, overflowing with the pain he seemed unable to express and she couldn't escape. Tears mingled with the water streaking down her face as she stood silently while he finished washing her hair.

★ ★ ★

An hour after the ferry docked in Salerno, Jolynn tilted her face into the muggy midday wind whipping through the Fiat's open windows as they drove deeper into rural Italy. About twenty miles ago, he'd let her roll them down, which she took to be a good sign.

Thank goodness they'd been able to bring the car. She understood they had to stay alive but stealing a car didn't feel right. He'd swapped license plates twice already—just stealing those made her feel weird enough—and fueled the car once. He had money, a false passport. She had no idea how much longer he intended to keep this up. At some point he should check in, right?

But he wasn't talking much. In fact, he'd clammed up right after she'd asked him about the scars. She hadn't realized at first how he'd shut down. He'd distracted her by making love again in the narrow bunk until they'd both been too exhausted to stay awake.

At least she assumed he'd slept.

She glanced over at his set face with harsh angles and dark circles under his eyes. "Road trips are becoming quite a habit for us."

"Uh-huh." Chuck nodded, staring straight ahead at the rural highway as they passed the precise rows and rows of a vineyard.

"That's my guy. Mr. Conversation." She watched the breeze ruffle his hair.

She wanted to crawl across the seat and give him a kiss guaranteed to knock his flip-flops off. He definitely stored some mighty strong passions behind his analytical facade.

It was only physical. Wasn't it? Their out-of-control, mind-blowing, rock-her-world sex on the ferry didn't have to change a thing.

Yeah, right. Fat chance. "Are you certain we aren't being followed?"

Chuck grunted, gripping the steering wheel as their little car ate up the miles. Green farmland stretched ahead for miles, broken only by the occasional villa.

"What does that mean?" She imitated his grunt.

"Yes. I'm sure."

And men claimed women were moody. "I hate it when you give me those cryptic answers that explain nothing." She tried to console herself with the fact that his methodical side would keep them alive.

He didn't look away from the road. "I guess it's just a habit I have when I'm thinking."

"You must do a lot of thinking."

"Yeah."

"Chuck!"

"Sorry." His face dimpled with a half grin, but he still didn't say anything more.

The enforced inactivity in the car left her restless. Or maybe it was the man himself who made her feel like her skin was suddenly too tight for her body. Jolynn drummed her fingers against the armrest, while trying to determine exactly where they were—as if that might give her some control over her life. A truck rumbled past in the other lane. A lopsided barn rested on a hill alongside ancient trees and one corner of castle remains.

Having exhausted all the scenery outside the car, she

studied the man beside her. His looks had somehow shifted over the past days, beyond the simple alterations to his clothing. The quiet scholar had transformed into someone more aloof.

The mixture of both men created a fascinating picture. She knew she wanted him, probably would have every inch of him once they got to wherever they were going. Why didn't that make her feel better?

"Chuck." Her voice cracked, so she tried again. "Where are we going?"

"To a friend's cottage."

She groaned at his clipped, cryptic answer and abandoned her quest for conversation.

* * *

A half hour later, the car slowed as Chuck turned onto a dusty, unpaved road. The Fiat shimmied, ambling over the rutted path. The canopy of olive trees parted, unveiling a small cottage. A porch as large as the main structure encircled the one-story stone structure.

Chuck parked the car in back, not that anyone could see the house from the road. An overgrown vineyard provided a thick wall between them and anyone who might actually venture this far out.

"Stay in the car while I take a quick look around." He slid from the car, his hand resting on his weapon. The area looked deserted, but he wasn't taking anything for granted.

Livia had offered to let him use the rustic retreat once, back when he'd been recovering from his injuries, working his ass off to walk without crutches or braces. He'd hit another low point after he and Annette broke up. Life had been a roller coaster during his recovery. Livia had said her mother used the place for a creative retreat, that it rejuvenated the soul. The slow pace of the country and the mellow Italian sun had pulled him out of his slump.

While he'd been forced to drive for a while, the place was a godsend. Out of the way. Anyone after him would have no reason to look for him here. And once Livia knew he was gone, she would put two and two together and tell the colonel exactly where to look.

His cursory search showed everything was just as it had been when he left last time. No unexpected visitors. Just privacy and a little dust.

He opened the door and reached behind to lift out the sacks of groceries and supplies they'd bought earlier in a small town he'd felt reasonably sure was safe. He'd used cash and kept it quick. "We're all clear."

Jolynn's footsteps crunched along leaves and gravel as she followed him. He had to give her credit. She hadn't complained, and she'd sure held her own when they'd hauled ass over the balcony at the safe house—a safe house that wasn't so safe after all. He admired her grit. She'd known when to take care of herself and when to follow rather than insisting on charging out solo. Even his pal Livia hadn't always known where to draw that line.

He climbed the stone steps without speaking. He'd faced some hefty ghosts during his time here, finally dealing with the crap that had happened to him during his captivity. But he'd left here ready to put on his uniform again. He'd come to peace with the fact he wouldn't fly anymore. Wouldn't be in the thick of things with his crew in the dark ops squadron.

Yet here he was again.

He passed her the bag. "I thought you might want a little privacy to shower and change after our drive today."

And no way could he let himself think of how they'd showered together earlier, how with a few simple words she'd peeled back any protective barriers he'd built over what happened to him in Turkey.

Turning away fast, but not quick enough to miss the confusion in her eyes, he charged back outside to attend to the business of securing the perimeter in case someone did find them. For years working in air force top secret tests, he'd had the most advanced technology at his fingertips. Right now, however, he was stuck with a MacGyver approach from things at his disposal and a couple of items purchased when they bought clothes.

Emptied cans to hang from the bushes to rattle—a technique used back in the Vietnam era.

Trip wires rigged to a flare.

And a simple baby alarm for a door worked just as well for adults needing a little advance warning if someone made it undetected as far as the cottage.

An hour later, Chuck eased himself onto the front porch step, the wooden planks digging splinters into the flesh below the hem of his Bermuda shorts.

The freshly fueled generator hummed in the distance. Trip wires along the perimeter of the cabin reassured him. If someone beat the odds and found them, they wouldn't slip past without warning. Meanwhile, the safety measures would buy him time to sort through the facts.

Time. Spent alone with Jolynn.

He tried not to think about her a few feet away inside the cottage. Bathing. How many more times would he have to suffer images of her naked and writhing in his arms?

Looking down at his hands dangling between his knees, he could still feel the imprint of her breasts burning into his palms. Desire for her rocked through him, shaking his concentration when he'd needed every scrap to keep himself from flying apart.

He zeroed in his focus on the mission rather than the woman. Professional instincts told him to keep her in hiding and wait for Scanlon to find them. He wasn't exactly AWOL.

She would never know how much it cost him, facing the ghosts rattling around in the old cabin. And the timing couldn't have sucked more after their little shower chat on the ferry. Maybe he would sit out here awhile longer. Chuck stared down the empty lane. The canopy of ancient olive trees was heavy with the humidity of summer heat.

Jolynn wanted him to talk, but after the concentrated hell of having to keep his mouth shut during weeks of torture, sometimes he wondered if talking would ever come easily to him again.

"Chuck?"

A gentle hand smoothed his wind-tousled hair. He glanced over his shoulder at Jolynn. Hollow inside, he looked away before she might see shadows in his eyes.

She settled beside him as his gaze swept the trees.

Jolynn nudged his shoulder with hers. "Nice little place you have here."

"The cabin would probably fit in the pool on your father's cruise ship."

"Only if you stuck a Venus de Milo statue on the roof." Her eyes twinkled jewel tone green. She held out a large-toothed comb. "Do you mind? My side's kinda sore and the reach makes it worse."

Brush her hair? Sounded like heaven and hell to him, but she hadn't really left him any choice. Not if she was hurting. "Scoot down a step."

She eased forward, dusting the step before sitting. He slid behind her, bracketing her body with his knees. When she leaned back, Chuck almost groaned out loud at the feel of her, the scent. Maybe they should just have sex again so he wouldn't have to talk.

But she'd asked him to brush her hair.

Might as well get to it. He cradled a lock and slowly worked the snarl from its spiraling length. Hands that held a gun with ease felt awkward combing the long hair. He tested the silky strand between two fingers and raised it to his face, inhaling the floral shampoo they'd bought at the little village store.

"Chuck?" Her husky voice flowed over him.

"Yeah?"

"Was it true, what you said?"

His hands paused. No way in hell did he want to return to their discussion about his time in captivity. He'd already explained why he had the scars. God, he definitely didn't want to hash through the details of how he got them or all the surgeries it had taken to piece him back together again. If his shaking hands right now were any indication, the shrink he'd been forced to see hadn't finished his job putting his brain in order again.

Not sure how to answer her, he simply said, "Is what true?"

"What you said about how your parents died. About growing up in an orphanage in Hawaii. Was that a part of your cover story, too?"

Prime example of Jolynn lowering his defenses and leading him into revealing too much.

"Chuck, are you listening?"

"Yeah, I'm just surprised." Surprised and relieved. "Of all the questions you could ask, why that one? Why now?"

She tipped her face to look at him. "I'm having a hard time separating Charles Tomas from Chuck Tanaka."

"Every bit I told you about my parents, including the part

about growing up in an orphanage in Hawaii, is true." Chuck worked through a snarl at the base of her skull. "My father did die before I was one and my mother died when I was in the second grade, but she dumped me in an orphanage when I was in kindergarten so she could run off with her blackjack-dealing boyfriend."

He yanked the comb the rest of the way through.

"Ouch!" Jolynn leaned forward, ducking her head out of his reach. "If you don't want to talk about it, just say so while I still have hair left."

"Sorry." The word grew easier every time he said it. Chuck gripped her shoulders with gentle hands and pulled her back into the embrace of his knees. He didn't want to think about why touching her made him feel better.

Jolynn smoothed a hand along his leg. "It must have been hard for you, growing up alone."

Chuck grunted as he brushed her hair. "I told you before. The nuns were good people. No rulers or knuckle rapping. It was a solid, safe place to grow up. And I guess you could say I had a home full of brothers and sisters. Squadron life felt like a natural fit after the way I'd grown up, the people, the uniforms."

She tilted her head and empathy flickered in her eyes. "Somehow I don't think it's quite that simple."

"I have to admit I didn't join the military with that intent or insight by any means. I took an ROTC scholarship because it was the only way I could get a degree. Then I realized I'd dumb lucked into the perfect career, the perfect life for myself."

"What exactly is it you do in the military?"

He settled on the standard answer he'd been allowed to roll out in the past, part truth, the rest hidden. "I'm an avia-tor, a navigator actually. I worked in the military testing world, like a test pilot, creating and fine-tuning all the latest gadgets. Or rather I used to fly before . . . Body can't cooperate with that now because of a busted eardrum. So now I'm just a regular techno computer guy." His chest went tight. "Moving on to your next question . . ."

Her head lolled against his knee, and she pressed a soft kiss on it before speaking. "So Chuck Tanaka is the name you were born with then."

"Uh-huh," he agreed, thankful as hell she'd let the other subject go. "But the nuns gave us all new middle names to give us a grounding and reminder of our lives with them."

"And you are?"

"Charles Gabriel Tanaka." He felt her smile against his skin. "They liked the angels."

"That was nice for you and whoever got Michael and Raphael." She wrapped her arm around his leg and rubbed his shin absently. Or on purpose? "But I feel a little sorry for whoever got stuck with the fourth archangel, Uriel."

Chuck smiled down at her in spite of his crappy mood as she dispersed the ghosts with her laugh. "Pretty impressive. Not many people could come up with all four names."

"I spent a lot of years in parochial school." Jolynn traced patterns on his calf with her fingers.

He struggled to control his breathing. Her bare arm hooked around his legs. Caresses turned to a firmer touch, more deliberate, and he realized she had more than talking on her mind. Maybe she'd even used the question about his childhood to show him she wasn't going to push on the other topic. Maybe she understood his need to leave that part of his past alone. He'd done as much as he could to come to grips with what had happened, with all he'd lost. He just wanted to move on.

And right now, moving on by losing himself in sex with the hottest woman he'd ever met sounded like a damn fine idea.

Except this time, he wanted to take it slow. To see every nuance of her arousal played out on her face, on her bared flesh.

A rush of adrenaline rivaling any burst from the past few days powered through him. He lifted the veil of her hair and exposed the vulnerable patch of skin. Ravenous with a hunger he suspected he could never fill, Chuck pressed a kiss to her scented flesh. Her heartbeat throbbed beneath his lips, and her body stilled. The pulsing against his mouth increased.

He traced the outline of her face with the backs of his fingers, trailing from her forehead, over her delicate ears, along her jaw, and meeting at her chin. Her skin felt so soft against his roughened calluses.

Chuck circled the pad of one finger around her parted lips, before tapping her upturned nose. Her breathy gasps flowed over his palm in waves of heat that permeated his skin and coiled within him. Chuck brushed the fingers of both hands across her eyes, closing her lids with gentle strokes.

Skimming his hands down her arms and back up, he nudged aside the dress, baring her shoulder. Her head fell back and her cheek brushed against his as he feathered kisses against the softest skin ever made, skin that tempted him to explore every inch.

He absorbed the feel of her, like a dried-up river soaking the rain after a drought. He cupped her breasts through the cotton fabric. Memories from the ferry exploded through his senses. As his thumbs stroked, he could feel her cresting, and he yearned to toss away her clothes.

Her gentle moan provided all the encouragement he needed.

His hands met at the tiny buttons along the front. Her lids fluttered open, unveiling mossy green eyes darkening with desire. She shifted in his embrace until she leaned against his leg. Her hair brushed over his knee. Already he could imagine it tangled around him in the big brass bed inside.

She gripped the front of his shirt with a typical bravado he recognized as signature Jolynn, and tugged him toward her.

THIRTEEN

Jolynn clenched his shirt in her fist and jerked him toward her. She was taking charge this time.

She stopped a hair shy of contact, puffing a breath over his cheek. His pupils dilated in response. He moved closer. She inched back, pressing her fingers to his lips.

"Red?"

"Chuck, I want you."

"Good, because I want you, too." He angled his face to kiss her.

She leaned her head back. "I know you do." She could feel his desire throbbing against her stomach, but she didn't trust that his logical mind wouldn't scavenge some last-minute excuse to remain honorable. "Are you done ignoring me today?"

"I just brushed your hair and spilled my guts, for crying out loud, woman."

Refusing to let him dodge the real question, she held his eyes with hers. "I'm talking about the moody silent treatment you gave me in the car and the way you shrugged me off once we got here."

"I was securing the perimeter. I was keeping you safe, damn it." Chuck kissed her hard and fierce, scorching her with a heat that surprised her.

Had he been holding back before, even in his kisses? His hands fisted in her wet hair, his body tense and urgent against her.

He ended the kiss abruptly and pinned her with his eyes. "You have every reason to question me based on how I kept the truth from you in the beginning." He brushed her hair away from her face with unsteady hands. "But I only did what I had to in order to keep you safe. Is that so hard to understand?"

The sad reality of it all swept over her. "You were just doing your job."

He muttered a curse. "You're more than that to me."

"Am I?" How much did she want to be?

Stubbornly, she pushed aside the thought before it led her to places where she could be hurt.

His hands tightened, almost painfully. "You can't begin to imagine the pure evil I've seen. The thought that any of it might touch you scares the hell out of me. Since the moment we tangled on the floor of the casino, you've tied me into so many knots I can't think straight. If I can't think, *you die.*" His eyes burned like twin molten hot flames. "Can I make it any clearer than that?"

Awed into silence by his heated speech, she merely shook her head. If that's what happened from his storing words, she could only imagine what a flow of emotions from Chuck would entail. What would it feel like to have such strength, such power wash over her?

The composed man faded, and she saw his very human need, not just a physical need, but a yearning for her.

She pressed a kiss to his lips, his beautiful eyes, over his jaw, and journeyed back to his mouth. Without breaking contact, he backed her up the steps as their kisses grew more frenzied. His tongue delved deeper as they pushed through the front door of the one-room cottage.

The place was small, but quaint and surprisingly well equipped. His legs tangling with hers, he kept dance-walking with her, past the kitchenette, farther by the leather sofa in front of a stone fireplace, an old upright piano against the only full wall, and finally, finally to the wide brass bed. He lowered her onto the gold-and-white woven spread, the mattress giving as he joined her.

Chuck slanted his mouth over hers, stealing her breath as his hands slid between their bodies. His calloused fingers snagged along her skin. He released two more buttons on her dress. The bodice slid free, hooking on her elbows as she struggled with his clothes.

She fumbled with the buttons down his cabana shirt. Whipping the shirt down his arms, she flung it on the floor. His silver chain glinted in the light streaming through the windows. She touched a tentative hand to defined muscles dusted with dark hair.

Chuck unstrapped the holster and set the gun on the back of the piano. The sight of the weapon chilled her, threatening her with thoughts of the outside world.

He pulled her close, melding the heat of their bare skin. Her breasts, already sensitive, tingled meeting his bristly chest. She arched into his touch.

"Your ribs," Chuck groaned as he moved his mouth to her neck. "Need to be careful," he said as the protector-warrior peeked through his passion.

"Forget about being careful."

Chuck dropped to his knees, his hands skimming across

her bruised side before his lips followed. His healing touch was so whisper soft she wouldn't have felt it except for the jolt of electricity shimmering up her spine.

He finished unbuttoning the front of the dress, nudging aside the sleeves and bunching it down and off her body. Kneeling at the foot of the bed, he paused, just staring at her in nothing but her underwear.

The longer he gazed, the more she ached for his touch. Her breasts pebbled inside the satin of her bra, her panties growing damp with her desire.

The intense flame of his eyes devoured her, flickering over her body. Jolynn stretched along the bed, enjoying the way his eyes lingered on her breasts. Growing up, she'd walked past all those busty statues that littered her life, and sometimes standing by those double-D stone goddesses, she'd even felt self-conscious of her barely A cups. But right now, she felt her body was one hundred percent as worshipped as any stone goddess.

She hooked her finger in the waistband of his shorts . . . and unsnapped. A quick swipe of her hand freed the zipper as well.

Her eyes locked on the thick length of him straining from his boxers, and yeah, she couldn't help the shiver of appreciation that rippled through her. She knew well what pleasure his body could bring her. She gazed up to find him watching her with a very self-satisfied grin on his face.

"Thanks, Red."

She rolled her eyes at his audacity. "You're welcome."

She slid her hand inside and wrapped her fingers around his heat and stroked the grin right off his face. Chuck closed his eyes, his head falling forward, his breathing ragged.

By the time she'd finished her sentence, he already stood by the bed again. He tossed his gun and a box of condoms on the table before he flung the rest of his clothes away with uncustomary negligence.

Smiling, she noted the strange combination beside the bed. Her Chuck, always protecting her in some form or another.

She stared into the eyes of Chuck, valiant warrior and passionate man. However, Chuck, angel protector and gentle scholar, was every bit as real. Mortality had smacked her in the face more than once over the past days, throughout her life for that matter. She wasn't going to pass up even a minute's chance to be with this man she'd already fallen halfway in love with.

Jolynn hooked her thumbs in her panties and slid them free. She linked her fingers with his and tugged him back down to rest over her. She sank into the bed, anchored by his warm weight.

"Jolynn." Chuck whispered her name on a groan as he rolled to his side without releasing her.

They lay side by side on the mattress, so much wider than the little bunk on the ferry. She traced the outline of each muscle clearly defined across his chest, taking wicked pleasure in the reflexive twitches at her touch. She refused to skirt past the scars. Those were a part of him, too, although she would respect his obvious wish not to talk about them.

The setting sun streaked through the window, casting shadows along the cut of his defined muscles flexing under burnished skin. He kissed, licked, nipped first one breast, then the other, laving equal attention. She threaded her fingers through his coarse dark hair, urging him closer. Wanting more. Wanting everything.

Drawing her into his mouth, he sent sparks of pleasure deep inside her, gathering between her legs. As if following her thought, his hand slid low between them. He massaged the heel of his hand against her. Her fingers tightened against his shoulders in synch with the clenching inside her. She writhed, seeking relief. So close, release tormented, waiting, ready for her to plunge over if only she would let herself.

"Chuck."

"Hmmm?"

"No more. Hurry."

He pressed a soft kiss to her lips and turned to the bedside table, tearing open the box. Jolynn stroked her hands over his shoulders until he faced her again.

Shifting her to her back, he molded his full length to hers, the blanket of his body a sensual, welcome weight. He held his full bulk off her. The muscles of his forearms bulged. But she wanted him, all of him.

Jolynn hugged her arms around his waist, nestling against his hips until he began to fill her, the prodding sensation foreign, yet wonderful. Almost painful, yet so right to be with this man. Chuck moaned into her mouth, his tongue dancing a mimic of his body.

She hooked her ankles around his legs and urged him closer. Smiling up at him, she brushed her fingers against the somber furrows in his forehead.

An added edge of tenderness tempered his urgency. Chuck lowered to his elbows, sinking farther within her tight passage, stretching her. He combed his fingers through her still damp hair and tugged her lip between his teeth, her body writhing beneath him. Damn his torturous patience.

She arched her hips against his, encouraging him to move faster, harder, and unwind the coil inside her. Chuck thrust deeply, firmly.

He coupled powerful strokes with gentle touches, and something about this coming together was more intense, more personal with those shared confidences between them that said she was more than a mission to him. The feelings growing between them were special, shared.

The power, the intensity surged through her, and she pushed, rolling him to his back. Straddling his hips, she rode him, milked the angle of his erection pressing all the deeper. Her head flung back, and *yeesss*, he seemed to hear her unspoken need as his hands took advantage of the freer access to her breasts. The way he cradled, fondled, plucked, doubled the tension inside her as he continued to thrust, fill, rock against her. Flames of blue and red intensity entwined throughout her, singeing every corner of her with showering sparks until her fingers twisted in the bedspread.

Her head flung back with the power of her release rolling through her, over her until she shouted in pleasure. The force of her voice ripped free without worry of anyone overhearing, doubled the bliss pumping through her. He tensed beneath her, his hoarse shout of fulfillment sending another shimmer shooting through her until she shuddered in the aftermath, collapsing on top of him in a depleted heap.

* * *

Chuck felt her body relax on top of him. Looking at his hands clenched around fistfuls of her hair, he wondered how one man could feel so complete and so damned confused at the same time. He buried his face in her fiery mane and delayed confronting his conscience a moment longer.

She felt so good, so right. Already he dreamed of the next time he would watch her face as he eased inside her.

The breeze from the open window cooled his heated skin, and he pulled away. Chuck stretched the length of the bed and tucked her against his chest. He smoothed her hair away from her face. He wasn't good with flowery speeches, but women wanted to be held afterward, right? He could offer her that much, found he even wanted to.

Resting her head on his shoulder, she hooked a finger along the links in his silver chain. "Where did you get this?"

He watched her hands move and remembered the feel of them on him. "One of the nuns gave it to me when I left."

"I should have guessed." She quirked an auburn eyebrow. "And?"

"Saint Christopher is supposed to protect travelers. Since I'd accepted the ROTC scholarship, Sister Mary Esther told me the medal would protect me in my military journeys."

"It hasn't let you down yet." She dropped the chain.

There'd been moments back in Turkey where he'd thought he'd been forgotten. Forsaken. Left to die. But looking back now, on the other side of hell, he suspected he'd had some help even then.

"I'm still here, so I guess not." Chuck pulled her closer, fitting her to his side. The medal had been taken from him when he was captured. He'd thought it was gone forever, but when authorities had been searching through Marta Surac's residences, it had been uncovered. Somehow Nuñez made the connection and returned it to him—a miracle in and of itself. "Why don't you try to get some sleep?"

"What about you?" Her husky voice swirled over his chest. "I know you were only pretending to sleep on the ferry. You must be exhausted."

"A little, yeah." He rubbed his hand over her back, the silk of her skin stealing up his arm and flooding through him. "Don't worry about staying awake, too, though. I've got security and warning devices in place. We can afford to relax our guard for a little while and recharge."

For now, he trusted the systems he'd set up along the perimeter. He could afford to soak up this moment with

Jolynn, this rare time when he felt relaxed enough . . . to . . .
sleep . . .

* * *

Some people feared the dark. Chuck Tanaka embraced those
increasingly rare opaque moments when no one touched
him. No one beat him.

He rolled from his back to his side on concrete as cold
and unforgiving as his captors. The chain on his ankle
shackle rattled in time with the muted music thrumming
above him from the bar. A groan slipped between his
cracked lips and echoed in the damp cement cell, which
reeked of cigar smoke wafting from the guard outside his
door.

Which battered part of his body summoned the sound?
Who the hell knew? He'd gone past pain two days into
captivity.

Now he focused on one thing. Keeping his brain locked
away from the sadistic bastards who'd been working him
over.

And the she-demon. She worried him more than those
two goons. She utilized mind games with a skill that scared
the crap out of him. Early in his "stay" he'd heard screams
from the next room. The only screams lately had been
his own.

He didn't expect to live. Even if somehow beyond the
odds he was rescued, he could feel himself bleeding out
inside. Still he fought the Grim Reaper to give the tracking
chip a chance to work, to lead someone here to break up this
twisted woman's operation.

The device would continue to transmit even if he died,
but the reading would show he wasn't alive, rendering their
search less urgent. Someone else could be taken. If by

chance, he could hang on long enough to tell them what he'd seen . . .

His focus faded. He grazed his fingers along the back of his shoulder, where the flight surgeon had embedded the tracking device. How much abuse could the microchip withstand? What a way to field-test the thing. The bitch's clowns had put it through every pace with their fists.

He couldn't keep on with his nonanswer policy. He needed something else to help him hang on.

Try to think. Work up plausible misinformation in advance. Pray the chip kept working.

He heard the tap, tap, tap of high heels advancing in the hall. Bile burned his raw throat. Light flooded his cell.

Chuck pushed against the cement floor and forced his body into an upright position, keeping his eyes off the battery they'd placed in the corner yesterday as taunting evidence of how far they were willing to go. He sagged back against the wall, but by God, he was sitting.

The door creaked wider to reveal the nameless woman. His devil sure as shit did wear Prada. His eyes traveled from her shoes up her legs to her smile. "I have your Jolynn, you know . . ."

* * *

Chuck bolted upright in his bed.

Sweat soaked his body from his nightmare. His brain was screaming with the image of his she-devil captor taunting him, claiming she had Jolynn.

Impossible.

Scrubbing his hand over his face, he pried his eyes open and looked around the one-room cottage. How long had he slept? He flung his arm wide and encountered cool sheets.

Oh God, where is she?

He rolled out of bed and to his feet. Chuck grabbed his gun off the piano and sprinted across the room toward the front door.

Marta Surac was in a high-security prison for the rest of her life. Most of her contacts had abandoned her like rats from a sinking ship. And the rest, she'd sold out to save herself from a firing squad.

So why then was he right back here on this side of the world cleaning up the mess from all the secrets she'd pried out of captured and tortured members of the military? Did she still pull strings? Did she have unshared contacts?

Mike Nuñez was married to Marta's illegitimate daughter. Were they all wrong to assume he hated the woman every bit as much as they did? He could have sworn Nuñez wanted her dead because of the way she'd used her own daughter to gain power through sex.

Damn it, Nuñez wouldn't have sold him out. He was sure of it. Nuñez could very well be dead now, a possibility he'd avoided thinking about and now brought bile up his throat.

Just as he yanked open the front door, Jolynn came out of the bathroom. He sagged against the leather sofa, swamped by feelings too profound to be labeled as simple relief.

Jolynn sauntered past and perched with a hip resting against the counter. Her red hair hung in a snarled mass just past her shoulders. Bare legs seemed to stretch for miles below his cabana shirt, which she wore with sensual elegance.

So much more beautiful than even the first time he'd seen her all decked out in the casino.

"I've made breakfast even though it's already past lunchtime." She motioned to the two place settings at the bar stools in front of the counter with small glasses of orange juice and a boxed pastry.

"Are you okay?" he asked, unable to shake the chill of his dream.

"My ribs are fine. We slept together. And while it was amazing, we didn't swing from a trapeze." She brushed her body against his, the pastries and orange juice between them. "Yes, I'm fine. Thanks for asking."

Chuck set the gun aside and looped his arms around her waist, kissing her hard and fast and hoping that the taste of her, the scent of her, the feel of her body would calm the roaring in his head.

He gave himself only a moment to feel her, to reassure himself before he pulled back, uncomfortable with the intensity. "I need to check outside, just to make sure everything is still secure." He cupped her hips and pulled her against him. "Then we can finish this."

She lifted the pastry box and ran it under his nose. "Food first. I'm starving."

"Go ahead and start without me. I don't know how long I'll be." Chuck unfolded a pair of jean shorts and a T-shirt to wear. When he tugged his head free through the cotton shirt, he found her gaze searing over him.

Jolynn washed down her breakfast with a large swallow of juice. She flicked her tongue across her top lip. He almost flung his clothes off again.

"Chuck?"

"What?" He sat on the edge of the bed to lace his new tennis shoes. He needed to distance himself from her and regain his concentration. Chuck mentally reviewed the series of warning devices placed around the cabin.

"Won't someone come looking for us here?"

"Eventually."

"And that will be a good thing or bad thing?"

"Good." That would mean Livia had figured out he must

have gone to her cabin. Sending a message through to her would have been too risky, especially when he didn't know if he could trust lines going onto the ship.

She twisted her hand in his T-shirt, yanking him toward her. "You're doing it again."

"Huh?"

"Slipping away from me with cryptic answers."

"Sorry." He scrubbed a hand along his jaw and tried to decide how much she needed to know. "Truly, I have this under control."

For now.

He checked his clip and headed for the door.

FOURTEEN

Jolynn fanned her face with a paper plate. How much longer would Chuck need for his security check? She stood by the window and watched him bob and weave from sight, threading around trees. She knew their time at the cottage was temporary. He would have to reconnect with the outside world soon.

She wandered across the room, wondering again how he'd known about this place. Her fingers trailed across the back of the leather sofa, skimmed over the ivory keys of the old upright piano. The notes came through surprisingly clear for such an antique. She tested the run of the keyboard, settling into a few measures of "Ave Maria." She wasn't a gifted musician by any stretch, but she'd taken and passed the requisite music classes at boarding school. The nuns at her place had been a little less generous with their warm fuzzies than Chuck's nuns.

But then she'd excelled at pushing the envelope by her teenage years.

Yet with all the experience she logged along the way, nothing had come close to touching her the way Chuck had. Through the night, she'd held him close while he'd slept with his head pillowed on her breasts, their bodies uncovered in the muggy heat. She'd memorized his face, the tiny creases that dented into dimples when he smiled. Something he rarely did.

She'd studied his scars more closely, figuring out which ones must have come from his time as a prisoner and which appeared surgical. Looking at his legs, she'd cried, realizing he must have steel rods in place. Even his toes were a little crooked. How many bones had been broken?

How much was still broken inside? Because there was no way a person could go through something like that and returned unaffected.

Still, he'd put his life back together, gone back to the same job that had nearly killed him. The cut of his muscles had broadcast strength, even relaxed in sleep. Those same powerful arms had cradled her tenderly against his chest.

He thought himself cool, unemotional, her logical scholar and agent. But she saw beyond the shield to a strong man, honorable, possessing a touch that had skimmed over her body with a gentleness she'd never imagined existed in a man.

His hands renewed, rather than destroyed.

While she saw the emotional depths in Chuck, would he make his way through the tangle to find peace for himself?

Tugging the hem of his cabana shirt, she wondered what would happen next. The thoughts crowded in her brain, too much to consider all at once. She settled onto the piano bench. Thumbing through the sheet music stacked neatly on top, she looked for something to play to pass the time until Chuck returned.

Some of the pieces had been marked up with directions and personal messages. Curious, she pulled the whole stack from the top and fanned through for more hints about the owner of this place Chuck knew so well.

At the very bottom, she found a music score book with what appeared to be original compositions. The pages had yellowed with age, some of the notes penciled on the bar graphs having faded. She rested her right hand on the keys and starting plucking out the core tune . . . a ballad, given the tempo instructions.

Slowly, the song took shape, coming faster from her fingers as she recognized the familiar melody. Shock raised the hair on her arms. She yanked her hand back and searched the book frantically for the end of the song where the composer had signed . . . *Livia Cicero*.

* * *

"How do you know Livia Cicero?"

Jolynn's question blindsided Chuck as he walked through the cottage door. He closed the door carefully, weighing her words and wondering what the hell had tipped her off. Could he have been talking in his sleep? Details of this op were top secret and he wasn't at liberty to satisfy her curiosity.

Reaching for the small bottled orange juice, he stalled for time to gather his thoughts. The question was so out of the blue, she must know something, but how much of the operation had she figured out?

"Why do you ask?" He knocked back a swig of the OJ, eyeing her reaction.

Her arms were crossed over her chest defensively. Closed off and angry. "This place must belong to Livia Cicero. A studio of some sort. Her name is signed all over the sheet music." She jabbed a thumb toward the upright piano. "Are you and she having an affair?"

"God, no!" he blurted out, shocked—and relieved. Here he'd been pinging off the walls thinking she'd uncovered his whole reason for being in Europe and she was just jealous.

Slumping onto the arm of the leather sofa, she scratched behind her ear, her body language opening somewhat, but not much. Her green eyes were still wary. "That sounded sincere enough."

"Because it's the truth." He set aside his drink and reached for her, squeezing her shoulders. "In case you haven't noticed, you're all the woman I can handle right now."

Still, she didn't smile, just stared at him, waiting, her eyes demanding more of an explanation.

He circled past and sat on the sofa, elbows on his knees. "Livia and I met when I was recovering from my injuries. She'd been wounded in an explosion during a USO tour. She paid some goodwill visits to recovering troops while she herself was recovering and deciding what to do about her career."

"I remember her accident. A couple of years ago, in Turkey." Her eyes widened with shock as she turned toward him. "And you were there? That was tied into your capture?"

While the details weren't out there in the news, parts of the mission weren't classified any longer. "My unit launched a rescue operation to locate me. They used the cover of the USO tour to slip into the country. I'm alive today because of that undercover. And later, in part because of Livia, too. Yes, we became friends. Close friends when I needed one.

She let me use this place once when I needed to get away, sort some things out in my head." He held up his hand before she could even ask. "But I was here alone. I care about her, but not that way. And she's in love with someone else."

Jolynn's forehead furrowed as she put all the pieces together. "The military colonel with her on the cruise . . ." She clapped a hand over her eyes. "He's not there as just her boyfriend, is he? You're all a part of the operation to investigate my father."

He scrubbed a hand along his jaw, knowing there wasn't anything he could say to reassure her. "Well, Jolynn—"

She shook her head. "Never mind. You probably couldn't tell me anyway, but I know I'm right. Whatever you're investigating must be something huge to involve so many people. You need to go back."

"No. I don't." He linked his fingers with hers and tugged her until she tumbled from the arm of the sofa into his lap. "As you said, there are lots of people handling this. They'll do fine without me while I keep you tucked away here."

"While you keep me from blabbing, you mean." She shoved at his chest. "Screw me silly so I'm too lovesick to ask questions. I should have known better."

His arms tightened around her. "That's not true and you know it."

"Chuck, people have been lying to me my whole life. You seem to forget who my father is. I saw my first murder when I was twelve years old."

Everything went still inside him. A murder? "Do you want to run that by me again?"

She sat stiffly in his arms, but at least she wasn't running away. "I was home on break from school, waiting for my dad. Two of his henchmen shot my uncle behind the ear. Execution style. My father may not have been holding the gun. Hell, he wasn't even there, but that wouldn't have happened on his property without his say-so."

His hands fisted until the circulation slowed. No adult should witness something like that, much less a child. He wanted to pull her in tighter and wipe away the images from her mind.

However, he knew from experience, nothing could stamp out the horror. The best he could do was share it, let her talk and maybe dull the sharper edges in the process. "Did you confront anyone about what you saw?"

"I was labeled a hysterical teenager." She gathered her hair over her shoulder, looping it into a loose knot that trailed down her chest. "My nanny and my father threatened a lot worse than boarding school. Since I wasn't interested in a stint in a psychiatric ward, I opted to keep my mouth shut. As a reward, they sent my cousin Lucy to join me in boarding school."

"The director of operations on the *Fortuna*."

"That's the one." She sagged back against his chest, caught in her memories. "We had one helluva good old time. Since we both knew Dad didn't want us back home, that made us pretty much invincible at school. When we got in trouble, Dad greased some palms, bribed my way back in. So I stuck it to his checkbook every chance I could with drinking and men." She stared up at him as if defying him to judge her. "And I do mean *men*."

All too clearly he could envision the disillusioned teen lashing out at the world, lashing out at a crook of a father who'd shattered her innocence. Chuck couldn't change the past, but he could be here now, listening, accepting.

When he didn't speak, she looked away, fidgeting with her hair draped over her shoulder. "One Christmas break from college when I was particularly pissed over his lack of attention, I chose Dad's accountant. He'd eyed me often enough. There's no need to dwell on the gory details. He possessed the finesse of a Mack truck. Things got rough."

His muscles tensed and a black fog of anger threatened the edges of his concentration as he saw where this was headed.

"Lucy heard me . . . call out just in time. She persuaded him to leave—pulled a gun on him actually, told him she knew how to use it." A small smile chased away some of the shadows in her eyes. "After that, I decided I didn't much care about having my father's attention and went my own way."

Chuck forced his breathing to stay steady, not to let his own simmering rage show through. "Well, Red, for what it's worth, you have my attention and it has nothing to do with your father."

Her hand slid up to his neck. Did she realize she was rubbing along the kink he never quite seemed to get rid of? "I'm a big fan of your attention."

He dipped his head, skimming his mouth over hers. This didn't seem the time for a big clench, but he needed to connect with her, let her know men—*he*—wasn't like those other guys who'd let her down.

And in order to prove that, to keep her safe, he would have to return to civilization and take down her father, once and for all.

* * *

Building a dirty nuke wasn't simple, but it was lucrative. And the *Fortuna* offered the perfect setup to transfer the bomb's blueprint into the appropriate hands.

Hands behind his back, he wandered through the casino's main floor. The roulette wheel spun and clicked like a clock counting down the time until he pulled everything together. Chimes and bells, shouts and groans filled the air as thickly as the perfume from the overscented, overprivileged women littering this place. Cleavage spilled out of low-cut designer dresses that probably cost as much as the high-roller chips they wagered and lost without a thought. Diamonds and other precious stones flashed in the lights that stayed on round the clock to keep bettors from realizing just how long they'd been throwing money away.

Smiling, nodding politely at the customers, he didn't give a damn that they saw only his uniform, his position as an employee hired to serve. That anonymity would work in his favor in the end.

No one needed to know his role. His ego didn't require stroking. He just needed cash. His parents may have been idiots enough to gamble away every euro they ever made, but he was smarter than that. Better yet, he would use their vice to his advantage.

Those slot machines were gold mines. Not because of the winnings they churned out—chump change in comparison to what he would rake in with this job. No, the true value was in the data linking, all the equipment intertwined into one system, so much information flowing through the transmission cables. It was easy to hide tidbits of his own here and there, nobody the wiser.

A familiar voice—Lucy's—drifted over the regular chaos that came with a casino in full swing.

Lucy perched on a high bar stool at a tiny round acrylic table, leaning toward Livia Cicero. "I can hardly believe your contract with us will be finished after this cruise. Are you sure we can't persuade you to stay on for another month?"

The Italian diva stirred her lemon water with the little straw, her red sequined dress glittering under the multiple chandeliers. "After my accident, my voice, my energy, just isn't what it used to be."

"I'm so sorry to hear that. It's a loss to your fans everywhere." And clearly Lucy was one. She'd about popped the eardrums of everyone around her squealing once she heard they'd landed Cicero for a six-month contract. "I realize we were lucky to get you this long."

"My pleasure. The *Fortuna* had treated me well," she answered diplomatically, and neatly dodging the not too subtle hint for her to stick around longer.

It was no secret Cicero's voice had never fully returned to normal after her accident. The huskiness itself was sexy as far as he was concerned. But then he wasn't big into music. He slowed his perusal of the casino floor to catch more of their conversation. Up until a couple of weeks ago, the singer had intended to stick around. Something had changed that.

Lucy spun a drink napkin round and round on the table nervously. "I would like to send you an invitation to my wedding. I know you probably can't come, but . . ."

"You have my address. It is always an honor to be invited to share in someone's special day." Livia smiled politely, her lips full and red, the kind that would look perfect going down on a guy.

Wedding . . . it was always about the wedding. At least that kept Lucy distracted. Just the way he wanted her. He stopped beside her table. "Hey, baby."

Predictably, Lucy squealed, jumping up from her seat and throwing her arms around his neck. "Adolpho, what perfect timing. You'll never believe who may be able to come to our wedding . . ."

While Lucy rambled on, he stared over her shoulder at Livia Cicero's plump red lips. Too bad she would be leaving so soon, because he really couldn't afford the time right now to indulge in that little fantasy piece of ass.

His eyes skated to the slot machine closest to the roulette wheel. Right on schedule, his courier slid in the card, looking to the rest of the room like an ordinary gambler.

Adolpho could almost see the information uplinking off that card picked up in Greece. Another little piece of the puzzle went in place, bringing him that much closer to the end of the cruise and the start of a major international terrorist incident.

* * *

The damn car wouldn't start and the sun was setting fast.

And her nerves were ramping up just as quickly. Jolynn studied the Fiat's engine for at least the third time, still unable to figure out why the thing wouldn't crank. They'd charged and recharged the battery, only to have it drain in a second, almost like the thing was draining juice.

Chuck grew edgier by the minute, and after their day of already intense sharing, she needed a return to lighter territory before her nerves snapped. She wanted a chance to enjoy the passion they'd just begun to explore.

"Pass me the wrench, will you?" Jolynn called from under the open hood. She tweaked the fuel line, her wrist bumping—oil spurted upward, damn it—just grazing the side of her face as she jerked away.

Chuck slid from underneath the vehicle, oil splattered on the middle of the *I Love Italy* T-shirt he'd bought from a vendor on their way here. "What did you do to my car, Red?"

"I didn't break anything." She tilted her head to the side. "I thought this was supposed to be top of the line."

"What can I say? Government budget cutbacks are a bitch." His eyes sparkled in the dim light they'd rigged to hang outside once they realized they wouldn't finish before dark.

Their time here away from the world was coming to an end. In her head, she acknowledged it. Her heart screamed for more time.

He wiped the tip of her nose, then rubbed the grease between two fingers. "My God, you're beautiful."

Her ribs went tight and she fought the urge to get sappy, overly emotional, to throw herself in his arms and be a drama queen selfishly demanding more time. "Well, apparently judging by the way you've checked out this engine, you could have fixed my car that night in the garage."

His smile dimmed. "I won't apologize for that one. I thought there was someone stalking you that night."

She shivered at the threat she hadn't even known existed then. How many more hidden dangers lurked there when they returned?

They would have to face all of that soon enough. For now, for their last minutes here, she wanted his smile back.

"When was your first time, Chuck?"

His eyebrows shot up toward his hairline. "Excuse me?"

"When was your first time?" Did he have some James Bond list of conquests, Jolynn the latest in a long line of brainless bimbos? She squelched the thought. While she may not completely understand Chuck, she knew him better than that.

"Uh, well," he began, rolling a kink out of one shoulder, "what exactly do you want to know?"

"Well, you could start with *when*."

He scratched his head.

"Where?"

He cleared his throat.

"Who taught you?"

He blushed.

"Oh yeah, and the make and model."

Chuck frowned. "Make and model?"

"Sure." She grinned wickedly. "The level of difficulty with that first engine is important."

"Engine?" He leaned closer, crowding her under the hood.

"Uh-huh." She toyed with the neck of his T-shirt, leaving a tiny grease stain along the collar. "When did you first start working on cars?"

"You want to know when I started working on cars?"

She blinked fast with overplayed innocence. "What did you think I meant, Chuck?"

His eyes turned lazy again. "I can see I'll have to watch myself around you."

He inched closer, pressing a lingering, open kiss to her mouth, before slinging an arm around her shoulders. "An old Buick sedan, twenty-one years ago. The nuns' car broke down and they were short of money from taking care of us. They'd gotten desperate and tried to fix the car themselves. They'd spread the engine in pieces on a blanket on the lawn, and I wandered over." His eyes roved the engine they'd been poring over all afternoon. "I sat on the ground beside them and looked through the repair book, looked at the parts scattered across the blanket, and I just knew. The pieces fit together in my mind."

His face cleared and he bent back over the engine, apparently on the trail of something . . .

Watching him now, she could envision that little boy, too, and God, she embraced that picture as it made him more human to her. She needed this to be about more than just rescuing her, taking down her dad.

She stared up at the night sky, blinking back the watery

sting. Or at least trying to. It seemed the stars blurred and turned colors seen through the prism of tears. The colors turned brighter, exploding into an umbrella of sparks like the best fireworks ever, and she realized—

"Shit." Chuck straightened from under the hood. "We've got company. Somebody's tripped one of the warning flares I rigged at the top of the road."

FIFTEEN

Flare splitting the darkening sky, Chuck reached for his gun in his waistband and shoved Jolynn behind him. "Go back to the cottage."

"No. I want to help." She picked up a wrench—his own personal warrior goddess in blue jeans and a tourist T-shirt.

Fear churned in the pit of his stomach. Didn't she know better than to risk her life with cold-blooded killers hunting her down? "You're wasting time. And if I have to use a nerve pinch on your neck to make you pass out, that will waste even more time. But I'll do it, because you are not coming with me."

Still, she hesitated, the sparks overhead illuminating the indecision on her face.

"Damn it, Jolynn, you're a hindrance if I have to watch out for you. Go. Inside."

Her mouth went tight but she stopped arguing. He hauled her close to his side, shielding her as they raced to the front of the cottage, scanning the grounds, searching every olive tree and not finding a thing out of the ordinary.

At the base of the stone steps, he growled low in her ear, "Look in the piano bench. There's an extra gun stashed there." He'd been planning to give it to her when they left, and now regretted he hadn't done it sooner to make sure she knew how to use it. "A Glock. Do you know how to shoot?"

"Are you kidding?" She kissed his cheek hard and fast. "I'm from Texas. It's a matter of pride."

"Fair enough. Don't be afraid to use it."

There wasn't time for anything more. Even though he wanted to give her a dozen other reminders to stay away from windows and to lock doors. Hell, he'd like her hidden in a bunker. But his best bet was intercepting the threat before it got anywhere near her.

The second he heard the door close behind her, he narrowed his focus to the trees, the drive. A soft breeze ruffled the leaves on the trees, showering a handful of olives to the ground as the flare whistled back to earth. Damn it, if he'd gotten the car running sooner, he would have had her out of here. Why hadn't he realized sooner that when he'd rerouted the GPS tracker to send off incorrect coordinates, he'd created a power surge that wrecked the battery?

The battery, for God's sake. So damn simple. Once he disconnected the GPS altogether, he'd already drained the emergency charger. But a few hours with the battery attached to the generator, and they would be out of here.

He prayed he wasn't too late.

As he ducked under branches and wove around gnarled old trunks, his feet smashed unripened fruit that had fallen prematurely to the ground. His weapon drawn and ready, he neared the top of the road where he'd set a trip wire to the flare. A rustle sounded in the leaves ahead of him. His heart drummed in his ears, his muscles tensed for action. He eased around the fat tree.

The trip wire snared a spindly leg, a wild goat thrashing.

Chuck sagged back against the trunk. Relief seared his brain. The worst hadn't happened. They hadn't been found. Jolynn wouldn't be stuck in that cabin with a Glock he hoped she could fire as well as she claimed.

Adrenaline buzzed through his veins as he carefully approached the goat and slashed the wire free. Standing, he eyed the cabin, a sanctuary that was safe for a little longer. He had one night left here. One night left with the woman who'd turned his world upside down, the woman he'd come to care about far more than he should have. Because judging by the way his heart pounded with more than fear for her safety, Chuck knew it was going to hurt a helluva lot more than rehab to walk away from her when this op was over.

* * *

In the belly of the *Fortuna*, Colonel Rex Scanlon leaned over Berg's shoulder, staring at the computer readouts spitting from the row of computers. "That can't be right."

Berg shook his head, dark circles under his eyes from working twenty-four/seven for days in the windowless cabin on a section of the deck most passengers avoided like the plague. The noise of the engine room chugged on one side of them while the roll of the ship was more obvious. "I've checked and double-checked. That GPS tracker was dead-on in Sicily for days. Then it blipped for a second today, just after sunset, showing up on the Italian mainland before shutting off altogether. So Chuck is either in Sicily or roaming around somewhere on the Italian boot."

In the corner, Nuñez propped his feet on the bottom bunk, cradling his arm still in the sling from the bullet he'd taken back at the safe house. "I think he's screwing with us. I would have bet good money he ditched the car. Now I'm guessing he is just making us think the car was somewhere else. He could have headed to the mainland to evade the threat, then tucked the GPS on a random vehicle in case someone else was trying to track him."

Rex propped a shoulder against the top bunk. "So he could use the better-equipped vehicle and didn't have to risk stealing a car. If anyone could make that happen, it would be Chuck."

Nuñez flexed his hand poking from his sling. "I'm just glad it looks like our guy's alive after all. Things were hairy back there at the safe house. I never saw the ambush coming . . ."

Heavy silence settled in the room, interrupted only by the thumping of the engine next door. The thought of Chuck out there . . . Rex bit back the doubts. He had to trust his instincts, and his gut had told him Chuck was ready for this.

Berg cleared his throat. "Well, we're not any closer to finding him since we don't know which coordinates, if any of them, are correct."

"The guy's good." Nuñez swung his feet to the limited floor space. "Hey, do you think with all that gear there, you could safely rig up an untraceable phone call home to my wife?"

Berg adjusted his headset. "I'll see what I can do for you, my friend."

Nuñez's wedded bliss was no secret—and neither was David Berg's messy divorce. All the same, Dave didn't snap back with a jaded response like he would have a year ago. Maybe things were better for the guy?

He was certainly holding up his end here on the job.

In the last week, they'd gained physical access to the data cables streaming information from the four slot machines they'd tagged from Chuck's insights on those repeated codes. When surveillance footage showed the repeat travelers Livia noted using those machines again, finally they knew where to narrow their search. Given cell phone chatter picked up from known terrorist cells about moving the plans for the dirty nuke through the Med, this felt like the time and the place.

The means.

Unless someone was yanking their chain with a diversionary tactic.

Biting back a curse, he decided to take his crummy mood outside. "I need to air out my brain. I'll be back when I have something of worth to offer here."

Rex slipped out the door and into the narrow corridor that echoed with the *thump, thump, thump* of the engine room. Pretty much the same sound as his raging headache. He rounded a corner and damn near plowed over a woman in red.

Livia, leaning against the wall, obviously waiting for him.

His headache increased.

He kept his trips to check in with Berg to a minimum, not wanting to draw undue attention to the room. So how had she found him? "What the hell are you doing here?"

Livia arched away from the wall, scarlet sequined dress stretching over her breasts. "I watch you more than you would think, Colonel." She tapped his chest, her little black silk bag dangling from her wrist. "We're supposed to be an item, remember?"

"I'm not likely to forget." Especially with her supple body an inch away from his fingers, which were just aching to snap open the halter top of her gown, a surefire cure for his headache and anything else plaguing him. "But we're not in front of an audience now."

Although they were in a hall too damn public for what he wanted to do with her. They'd settled into a friendship of sorts again during their time together on the boat, but he couldn't forget how badly things had ended between them before. She'd insisted she couldn't be in a relationship with him because of his feelings for Heather, even years after she'd died. Just thinking about how damn unfair and random life could be made him edgy.

"What's this about?"

Bravado seeped from her along with her smile as she dropped back. "I'm here looking for you because it's been a depressing afternoon. I wanted to see you, which is selfish, I know. You have bigger worries."

She started to turn away, reminding him he was being a selfish ass. No surprise there. But she deserved better, and he would damn well scavenge it up for her sake.

He caught her hand, turning her back to face him, her fingers impossibly soft and cool. "Upsetting because . . ."

She stroked her throat, her silk bag trailing between her breasts. "My contract singing for the *Fortuna* is up. I knew this was a short-term deal, even more so once I contacted you about . . ." She glanced around the hall, cutting herself short. The corridor was deserted but she seemed to realize it was still best to guard their words. "And after you're through, it's not like they will want to keep me on, even if I did sign another contract, which I won't. My voice just won't hold up to another round. Performing again was . . . magnificent . . . but it is over. A lot of things will be over once we dock."

The grief in her eyes stabbed clean through him.

"A lot of things?" His hand still holding hers, he drew

her closer, her breasts a deep breath away from skimming him.

She pressed a hand to his chest, sketching a fingernail down the buttons on his simple white shirt. "While I was talking to Lucy about my contract, her wedding plans came up and it made me weepy, okay?" Her hand closed on a fistful of cotton in the center of his chest. "We're playing this love game and sometimes it hurts because of the way I feel about you."

The intensity of her words caught him off guard. "Livia, you may have forgotten a tiny detail here. You were the one who dumped me."

She thumped her fisted hand against him. "Because you didn't love me enough."

"That's bullshit," he said bluntly, but honestly.

This woman had torn him up inside, driven him to the edge of sanity, and still he wanted her. More every second as she stood there in her do-me dress, trying to coerce words from him he'd already done his damnedest to express.

She rolled her eyes and stomped her foot, every bit the diva who had blasted through his grief two years ago. "You are not very much of a romantic."

Desire flamed through him as fiery as her fighting words. "You want romance? Lady, I'll give you romance."

He slid one arm around her shoulders and the other under her legs. He scooped her up before she could finish a yelp. His world was going to shit on this op, but with Livia in his arms, at least this day would end a whole lot better than it had started.

Her arms locked around his neck, her little purse swishing against his back. "What are you doing?"

Charging up the stairs, he angled sideways. "Carrying you to my cabin. Got a problem with that?"

Her fingers slid up into his hair. "Only that you're not walking fast enough."

He ignored the gasp of a prim buttoned-up couple as they reached his floor, a giggle from two women stepping from their suite. A waiter carrying a room service tray stepped out of their way with a discreet smile and finally—thank God—finally, Rex entered his room. He booted the door closed behind him.

Wriggling in his arms for the first time, Livia shimmied out of his grasp. Her dark eyes locked on him for two more gusty breaths before she pulled his face to hers. Her lips parted, and he drank in the familiarity of her. He knew her, with such a core-deep recognition it rocked the deck under his feet.

She kissed with a passion and innocence that had always surprised him, touching him somewhere deep inside that only one other woman had ever reached.

Then Livia turned into liquid fire against him. Her hands were all over him, tearing at his clothes. And he didn't need any further encouragement. After holding back for so damned long when it came to Livia, the force of his desire for her slammed through him.

"The bed," he growled. "Now."

She raked her fingernails lightly down his back, cupping his ass. "The door. Right now."

Yeah, no wonder he was crazy about this woman. The Italian-English barrier didn't come into play when they spoke the same language. Here. Now. Against the door.

A possessive growl rumbling from deep inside him, he slid his hands up her body, over the curves of her high soft breasts. Farther still, he reached behind her neck and released the halter clasp free. The top of her dress rolled down and bared creamy flesh he'd only dreamed about.

The reality beat fantasies, hands down.

And speaking of hands down, hers freed his buttons and opened his pants before he even realized he was still staring at her. She smiled at him with a timeless feminine power as she stroked down the length of him. He throbbed in her fist, ached all the way to his teeth to be inside her.

Then he realized . . . "Condom. We need one and I'm not packing."

"Then what good luck of the drawing that I am." She dangled the little black bag in front of his face.

Staring at the bag and her audacious smile, he was so stunned he didn't even bother correcting her "luck of the draw" phrasing. Because holy hell, he hadn't seduced her. She'd seduced him. Which was a hundred percent all right with him right now.

Stroking along her hip and around, he reached behind her to tug the zipper down until her sequined dress slithered to the floor. Her signature scent drifted up like incense as he unveiled her. She wore a crimson red thong and simple strappy flats, a reminder that she couldn't wear heels since her accident.

His chest clenched tight. She'd come so close to dying on his watch two years ago. He skimmed along the puckered skin where her leg had been set, stitched.

"Livia . . ." he groaned.

"Shhh . . ." she whispered against his collarbone, kicking aside the last of his clothes, rolling the condom down his hard-on. "Forget about the past. This is all about celebrating how very alive you make me feel."

Her words stirred him and made him wish he was more of a poetic guy, the kind who could give her all that romance his beautiful diva craved. But for some reason, she wanted him anyway.

He clasped her hands and stretched them over her head against the door, positioning himself between her legs, against her. She grazed her foot up his leg and he lifted her until she hooked her heels around his waist, the perfect angle for him to drive home inside her.

His head fell to rest against the door, his teeth clenched in restraint as the moist heat of her squeezed him like a silken glove. So damn perfect he almost came undone right now but he wanted more than that from her. He wanted more than a quickie against a door.

Holding her to him, staying inside her, he walked toward the bed. Every step, each roll of his hips against her, drew a moan of pleasure from her mouth. She bit her lip, her eyes closing and her head lolling as she rocked against him. He lowered her to his double bed, covering her with his body, plunging fully inside her. Her jet-black hair splashed back against the stark white pillow as she thrashed in obvious pleasure, mumbling gaspy phrases in Italian that he could swear would stay burned in his memory so he could translate them later.

But at this moment, the power, the rightness of being with her, of watching her face as she flew apart in his arms, swept him right over the edge of release with her.

He had been fighting his feelings for Livia Cicero for two years, certain he couldn't let go of the past enough to step into the future.

Cradling Livia in his arms, he realized how very wrong he had been.

* * *

Jolynn lay sprawled on top of Chuck. His chest heaved with deep breaths under her breasts.

Her side ached, but she didn't care. She wouldn't wish

away the pain. When her ribs healed, Chuck would be long gone from her life.

Their skin melded, warm and moist from the exertion in summer heat. She blew light swirls of air between their bodies, bringing a smile to his face while he kept his eyes closed. "Sorry there's no air conditioner here. The generator's not powerful enough to sustain it."

"It doesn't matter." The cottage was special to her because of what they'd shared. "The safe house was warmer and much less private."

Jolynn flinched as the words fell from her mouth. She'd done it again, shoved the real world into the middle of the room like a flashing neon Venus de Milo. Since the incident with the flare, he'd distanced himself from her.

She wanted the sharing back, sharing more than their bodies. One minute he was everything she wanted in a man, the next he drifted away from her, leaving her heart colder than before.

"Hello? Chuck?" She bracketed his face with her hands until he opened his eyes and looked back at her. "Where are you?"

"Sorry." He cupped her face. "I'm reorganizing some things in my head. Sifting through the past few days. Trying to make the picture fit so I can be sure you're safe."

But if they left, he would be in more danger protecting her. "Why would anyone want me dead?"

Chuck quirked a brow. "Why did they kill your uncle?"

She couldn't suppress the shudder at his words. She tried to roll off him. He cupped her neck, pressing her head into his shoulder.

Chuck stayed silent, his fingers digging a rhythmic massage into her tensed shoulders. Everyone assumed she had it all, the pampered daughter of a rich man, no matter how hard she'd tried to carve out an image for herself as a dedicated number cruncher. An uneasy thought settled over her as she realized she hadn't let anyone close enough to listen until Chuck.

"They hurt him, Chuck—my uncle Simon, who tossed me in the air and pulled my pigtails. He let me pester him when he worked on cars." Her eyes stung at the memory, the grief she hadn't ever dared let past the horror. "They put a twenty-two behind his ear and murdered him."

The metallic taste of fear and disillusionment burned her mouth. She trembled, waiting for the nausea to abate. "Sometimes I feel like my life ended that day as well. Does that make sense?"

"Yes, it does." His chest rose and fell rapidly under her cheek.

"Now, they want to do to me what they did to my uncle. I didn't do anything wrong. I don't have mysterious unpaid debts or seedy connections, so they just want to get to my father through me." She tilted her head, forcing him to look at her. "Am I right?"

He stared at her without answering, his eyes glistening icy blue. "Probably."

Jolynn sagged against him, resting her forehead on his. Chuck didn't deserve to die for knowing her.

"Just because they want to hurt you doesn't mean it's going to happen." He gripped her shoulders. "I won't let them."

Why didn't he understand she feared his death even more than her own?

Chuck lifted her off him and sat up, the determined agent returning. "Damn it, listen to me. You don't seem to realize how good I am at my job. You'll be sunning by the pool in Dallas before the week's out. No one will hurt you again."

But if she were in Dallas, that would mean saying good-bye to Chuck. The thought chilled her quiet for so long she realized he'd fallen asleep, his breathing evening out to a low snore.

Careful not to wake him, she eased off him and padded across the wood floor to the kitchen, needing distance to gather her tangled thoughts and ease the building headache. She grabbed her purse off the counter and fished through it, searching for the aspirin he'd given her after she'd bruised her ribs.

Reality invaded her like an insidious disease. The clock had run out. Her time with Chuck was over. The longer he stayed with her, the greater the danger because of her family, her blood connection that couldn't be ignored or erased. She'd been greedy here at the cottage.

The cruise ship, Dallas, everything about her past life felt so distant. Could it have been only a few days ago that she'd discussed Lucy and Adolpho's wedding plans? And the fundraiser, too, scheduled the day after the ship docked in Genoa again. How could time have become so distorted?

Would Chuck just walk away when they returned?

Her heart squeezed at the possibility. But more than that, she knew she came with a lot of baggage. Would her family history be a problem for him? For his job that she didn't know all that much about to start with?

She sifted through her purse, pausing to flip the thumb drive over and over in her hand. Viewing her life from Chuck's perspective, she saw herself for what she was. The daughter of a mobster. Corruption under glitz. She massaged the minidrive in her hand like worry beads, flipping it over and over.

A minidrive from accounting. Her ears roared with the sounds of her heart pounding.

Had Lucy noticed the thumb drive was missing, and how much information did it hold? Once they figured out she'd taken it, no way in hell would they let her fade into the background. An all-out search was probably already under way for her and Chuck.

Undoubtedly, the next flare wouldn't be set off by a goat. Chuck was in more danger than even she'd realized.

Jolynn thought about that young boy dumped by his mother in an orphanage. He'd braved the world with nothing more than a saint's medallion from a nun for protection. Maybe someone should protect him for a change.

With potential evidence in her hand, she could do the honorable thing and prove to herself she wasn't one damn bit like her father. She needed to figure out a way to confront her father—while making sure Chuck was out of the picture.

Sixteen

★ ─────────────────────────────────

The telephone rang by Livia's bed, jarring her from the best sleep of her life after the best *sex* of her life.

She slapped at the end table, desperate to silence the damn thing before it disturbed Rex—and their time together. She swept the phone from the table. Yet the ringing continued and continued, *mio Dio*.

Again the blaring noise kept on until she realized it was not a normal ring, but a buzz from Rex's bedside table. His personal cell? Or a BlackBerry? Her naked leg between his, she toed his calf until he stirred. The intimacy of the moment wrapped around her, being together, their bodies spooned into a perfect fit.

Rex mumbled in his sleep as he rolled toward the side of the bed. Then his muscles tensed, rippling down his back as he jolted awake.

"Shit." He sat up sharply, snatching his BlackBerry up and glancing at the faceplate quickly. "Colonel Scanlon here. Speak to me, Berg."

As he sat on the edge of the mattress naked, elbows on his knees, his face went devoid of expression. He mostly listened, interspersing the occasional "affirmative" and "roger."

Livia burrowed deeper into the sheets, her body languorous from loving. Good thing she had not known how powerful it could be with Rex or she never would have made it through the past two years with her sanity intact.

But now she did know. In full detail. Twice in the last three hours. Moonlight streaked through the portal across Rex's nakedness. Everything from the defined muscles roping his lean body to the hint of silver at his temples declared him a one hundred percent honed, seasoned *male*. There was something infinitely attractive about a man who knew his way around a woman's body well with confidence, but none of the arrogance that too often came with youth. He was everything she'd dreamed of, everything she'd hoped for.

And everything she'd feared because now, more than ever, she knew she could not let him go. Her heart and body would belong only to him for the rest of her life. Melodramatic? Perhaps. But she'd long ago given up denying her flamboyant Italian nature. Tonight, she wanted to embrace every bit of the volatile, all-encompassing love she felt for Rex.

After what they'd shared, she wouldn't be so foolish as to walk away again. She would give him his space now to complete his mission, but afterward? Her body tingled with excitement and a hint of apprehension. Stakes were high with her heart on the line.

"Roger that, Berg. I'll be down in fifteen minutes." Rex ended the call.

He turned to her apologetically. "As much as I would like to stay with you 'til morning, I have to go."

"I understand." She tucked the sheet under her arms. "Work phones . . . or would that be work calls?" She deliberately tangled the American idiom to tease a smile from him. Unsuccessfully.

He gathered his clothes tossed haphazardly around the cabin. "Local authorities have just made an arrest based on suspicious cell phone chatter my guys picked up."

Livia crawled to the edge of the bed. "Can you tell me who?"

"It won't be a secret given the guy's pretty high profile around here. Head of security for the *Fortuna*, Adolpho Grassi. He was just taken into custody. He's being loaded onto a police vessel now to be transported back to Italy." He pulled on his trousers and reached for his button-down shirt.

"That's it? The investigation is over?" Maybe her future with Rex loomed sooner than she'd expected.

"If he talks. It appears he has been allowing passengers of questionable backgrounds on the ship, allowing new passengers to board by swapping identities with someone who left the ship. All very shady stuff, especially in light of the pattern you noticed of those three people returning again and again, cruise after cruise."

"Adolpho? Lucy Taylor must be devastated." She tugged the comforter closer to ease the chill seeping into her bones. She'd known this was dangerous. But to learn the person in charge of protecting the passengers had been endangering them all? It was too much to take in.

Dropping to the edge of the bed, his shoes in hand, he scowled. "I'm worried about you. What if I asked you to step away, leave, say you're sick? I'll have a helicopter here to transport you before you can say 'ante up.' "

She could see from his intensity that he could and would make it happen. Nothing was impossible for him. But he

needed to direct that drive elsewhere, and he needed to let
go of the fear that every woman in his life could die as his
Heather had. "Thank you, but no. My leaving might arouse
suspicion and endanger the rest of your case. Just because
you have Grassi does not mean you are ending your undercover plan. Am I right?"

His jaw flexed with clenched teeth before he finally nodded tightly. "Just because I agree doesn't mean I'm happy."

"Then after your work, come back here and I will make
you happy." She stretched provocatively while gliding a hand
down his chest, then stopped shy of his belt, patting his taut
abs lightly.

"Do you think you could put a sweater on?"

She sidled against him, savoring the bristle of his cotton
shirt against her breasts. "That sounds too stuffy. How about
when you're through with business, you come over here and
make love to me again, and then again for the next fifty
years."

His head snapped back. She bit her lip. This wasn't the
right time at all, but blast her impulsiveness, the words had
just fallen out.

Rex exhaled. Hard. "Lady, you are giving me whiplash."
He studied her with puzzled eyes. "Last time I checked, you
dumped me because you said what I have to offer isn't good
enough."

The hurt in his voice surprised her. She'd only thought of
her own breaking heart at losing him, never once realizing he
might be aching every bit as much for her. "I said I thought
you were still in love with your dead wife." And she was beginning to realize how very honorable it was for a man to give
his heart that deeply. "But now that time has passed, I think
perhaps you have room to care for someone just as much."

"What makes you say that now?"

She considered his question carefully, suspecting a lot could ride on her answer. Perhaps their whole future. Her confession had been so impetuous, she hadn't thought out the why of it all. So what had nudged the notion to life?

The answer flowered in her mind, bright, beautiful, and taking root more firmly by the moment. "Because I can see in your eyes now that you love me, too."

"Oh, you can, can you?" He combed her hair from her face with his long, oh-so-capable fingers.

"Are you denying it?" She leaned into his chest with more confidence on the outside than the inside. A nervous flutter started in her tummy.

He stayed silent, his throat moving with a long swallow as he continued to brush back her hair again and again as if memorizing the feel of her.

The more she looked into his eyes, his soul, the more she understood. Now her stomach fluttered from sympathy for him. "It's okay if you're still a little scared. Loving me is a risk. Loving anyone is a risk. But I intend to show you how very worth it I am."

"I believe you." He cradled the back of her head, her hair gathered in his hands. "And I do love you, Livia. God, do I ever love you. So damn much it scares me with how important you are to me."

She saw his sincerity, but also saw his fear. This wasn't easy for him, loving her. Not today. And probably not for a long while.

When she'd first met him, she would have been frustrated by his reservation. Perhaps she'd even misread him before, allowing jealousy to taint her perceptions. And if so, she had not deserved his love back then.

Now, however, she saw a man with a love in his eyes so powerful it humbled her. "You are something special, Rex Scanlon." She angled forward to kiss him, unable to miss how his hand trembled as he cupped her waist. She stroked his bristly, strong chin, his face, teasing his bottom lip and hoping to tease a smile from her somber man as well. "I think I will make quite a splash as a colonel's wife."

Chuckling softly, he smiled against her mouth. "I do believe you will."

And that simply, her future fused with his. After all the drama of their courtship, she appreciated the ease with which they'd both finally accepted their life together. A huge part of that existence, of the man, included his call to military service. "Now go to work. Make this Grassi talk so we can get on with our lives."

"I will," he vowed. "And maybe we'll have some luck locating Chuck, too. My guys are following up on a lead."

She straightened quickly. "What? Can you tell me where has he been hiding since we lost him in Sicily?"

"Actually, we got a blip. I'm thinking he may have left the island."

Left Sicily for the mainland? Her surprise quickly turned to possibility. And why not? She had been so focused on thinking of him stranded and hiding that she hadn't considered how resourceful Chuck could be. The man was a survivor.

If he had gone to the mainland . . .

An image of her cottage retreat filled her mind, the very place she'd loaned to Chuck for a week a year ago.

Livia ran to catch Rex at the door, her feet tangling in the sheet. She grabbed his arm urgently. "Oh *mio Dio*! I think I know where he is. Oh God, Rex, I'm almost certain I know where Chuck's been hiding."

* * *

The Fiat purred like a healthy kitten. Chuck would have preferred a sleek tiger with more kick in the engine, but at least he had the vehicle running again. Jolynn settled in safely beside him. The sunrise cast a crimson haze over her face like some kind of mood lighting from a vintage movie. Without question, he wished they were riding off into the sunset together.

But he couldn't delay checking in with the ship any longer.

Hopefully he would receive the all clear to bring Jolynn in, tuck her somewhere safer. If not? Then he would have to come up with another plan. And he would, damn it.

Both hands on the wheel, he steered around potholes on the narrow road. A split rail fence bordered the rolling green dips and swells leading to the nearest seaside village. "How are you doing over there, Red? Need to stop for something to eat?"

She cocked her head to the side. "Why do you call me that?"

"Huh?"

"Red." Her fingernail scratched along a split in the dashboard. "And why do you call me Lynnie?"

"All right," he said, confused, but then who knew what went on in a woman's mind? Certainly not him. "If you don't care for nicknames, then I'm cool with that."

"I'm not even sure you notice you're doing it. You call me Red when we're laughing. You call me Lynnie when we're making love." She clutched her oversized purse to her chest. "You only call me Jolynn when you're angry or frustrated. The other times, you leave off Jo. It's as if you want to slice away that part of me which reminds you of my father."

"You're being ridiculous." Wasn't she? He eased up on the gas, coasting downhill toward the town's edge. Built into a mountain, the village wrapped around a medieval church with the steeple poking far above everything.

"Am I?" Her voice went ragged. "What do you think is going to happen with us when I see my father?"

What would *happen*? Why the hell was she even asking that? He could untangle glitches in high-tech test programs but didn't have a clue what went on in this woman's brain. "That's not a problem since you won't be seeing him."

"You don't have the right to decide that for me. If I want to get out of the car right now and walk to his house, there's legally nothing you can do to stop me."

She was right, but still . . .

"And that's what you want?" Shock rippled through him. "You've spent most of your adult life keeping him at arm's length. Can you honestly say you still want to have contact with him after everything he's put you through?"

"He's my father. I have to do this. You don't need to understand or agree."

"You've got to be joking." He glanced over at her, dumbfounded.

She shrugged. "I tried to stay away from him for years. But then I heard about his heart attack . . . Good or bad, he's my blood."

"So was your uncle and look how well that played out for him." He couldn't hold the sarcasm from his voice, but damn it, she needed to understand how dangerous this line of thought could be.

"Don't you think I know that?" She pounded the worn leather seat with her fists. "Relationships are complicated. When I heard my father might die, something shifted inside me. I knew I couldn't just walk away from him any longer.

Chuck, I need to see my father and make peace with him. And I need to do it alone."

"Fine, damn it." Chuck straightened, pushing the words through gritted teeth. "You can see him whenever you want. I understand they have liberal visitation at the pen. Drop in as often as you like during his twenty-to-life stint at your local correctional facility."

She winced as if slapped. Then her face shuttered away emotion. "Chuck, we slept together a few times and fixed a car together. That's it. The sex was good and you're an interesting guy, but don't go ruining it by trying to turn it into something more. Just take me back to the boat. I'll arrange for a *Fortuna* vehicle to transport me to my father's house."

This was it. She was, no shit, dumping him to return to that viper's nest she called a family.

Why did civilians always think everything would be okay, that they would be okay, somehow exempt from the risks right in front of them? Criminals didn't have a conscience. Her *father* didn't have a conscience.

Frustrated as hell, he knew he wasn't going to make any more headway with her on the subject. And God forbid he should slip up and call her Red or Lynnie.

Maybe an update from Berg would make her realize how imperative it was that she stay away from the ship and anything to do with her father. Now that they were clear of the cottage and in a town of sorts, he figured he could risk a call in to the ship. He needed to make contact. Too much time had passed and Livia must not have guessed his locale.

He thumbed the secure code for Berg's line, as secure as any communication could be these days. Techies like himself were cracking the newest safeguards daily.

After one ring, the other side picked up. *"Ciao! Buen giorno!"*

Berg's Italian sucked, thickly laced with a Southern accent. But his familiar voice was a welcome sound.

"Four-six-nine. Alpha-Foxtrot." Chuck recited his code to verify without question he was on the line and not compromised. "Need an update, my friend."

"God, Chuck," Berg barked into the phone, "it's good to hear your voice. We thought you might be dead. Sure wish you could have given us some word sooner."

"What happened to Nuñez?" Chuck gripped the phone so tight it cut into his flesh. He'd functioned okay, but the chance Nuñez had been taken or killed had never been far from his mind, messing with his head.

"He's asleep on the top bunk right now. Snoring, too, I might add. Bullet winged his arm, but he's already bragging about how he'll work that into a disguise. And how's Jolynn Taylor?"

"She's fine." Still doing her best to pretend to ignore him even as she listened in to his every word.

"Thank, God. Where is she?"

"Secured." He wasn't trusting the phone lines with everything, especially when it came to her safety. "Now, catch me up on what's been happening since I left."

Only a few days during what felt like months of living. Jolynn should have been readying herself for that damned fund-raiser and her friend's wedding, rather than hiding out from gunmen and terrorists.

"After Nuñez reported about how things went rogue at the safe house, we assumed you were taken by whoever shot up the place."

"Keep talking." He didn't want to risk any longer than need be on this phone. "I—and a half-dozen other agencies—have been chasing your GPS all over Sicily, until you blipped on the mainland last night. The colonel's lady thinks she knows where you are."

"Where I *was*." He'd been right to be careful, to fall off the map if all those groups had been on the lookout. No question, not everyone's motives would have been pure. He palmed the steering wheel, taking a tight turn down a one-way road along a canal leading to the medieval church. "Who leaked our location at the safe house?"

"The OSI agent who was working with Nuñez. She started up an affair with a guy who works for a local security firm . . . pillow talk . . . blah, blah, blah. Same old shit that has taken people down for centuries, people who can't keep their pants zipped."

Local security firm. The pieces closed together, jagged edges sliding into a seamless fit. Danger had been hovering closer to Jolynn than he'd imagined. "And that security guy must be tied to Adolpho Grassi."

"The security guy *is* Adolpho Grassi. Italian authorities have him in custody. He's on a police boat back to the mainland. Straight up, he started spilling his guts in hopes of cutting a deal. Said he never intended anyone to get hurt. That he just needed Jolynn Taylor to quit nosing in the ship's finances and go home. He set up the attempt to attack her in the parking lot, the peeping Tom incident outside her room, the shooting by the water. It wasn't until the safe house that things got out of control for his goons."

It all made sense, especially if Grassi wanted to keep his connection to Taylor's business tight through marrying Lucy. Jolynn coming back into the picture pushed Lucy out of the favored position. "Seems like things have tied up neatly."

"We're all hoping they'll get more out of him once he's in an official interrogation. But all signs point to him being tied up in however that data is being shuffled through the slot machines," Berg said. "How did you make the connection so quick?"

"He's also tight with the director of operations at Taylor's, Lucy Taylor." Jolynn's cousin. She would have all the more reason now to want to return to her family. Damn it. "Lucy's engaged to the guy."

"She and her uncle—the big man himself, Josiah Taylor—have taken a helicopter back to Taylor's estate in Genoa. Poor kid, finding out about her fiancé this way."

Lucy Taylor's bad taste in men almost got Jolynn killed. Chuck found his sympathy level for Lucy was low. A warning bell clanged in his mind. He was losing his objectivity. He didn't want justice. He wanted revenge.

He tried again to lose himself in the routine of work. "Any idea on a motive? Ideological or financial?"

"We're guessing it must be the latter. Probably hoped he could also tap into the family fortune by tapping her and use those connections to tap into bigger dollars. Strangest part is, there isn't one single shred of evidence linking Josiah Taylor to any of this. The guy's coming back squeaky clean. Not that I'm complaining since we've got Grassi. It's a rare gem to get our hands on such a weak link in a terrorist plot."

Chuck eyed Jolynn, who'd given up looking out the window and was studying him with open curiosity.

"At any rate," Berg continued, "with Grassi in custody, we're hopeful the rest will unravel quickly and we'll stop the flow of information. The brass supports your decision at the safe house. You protected her, kept her out of the fray, and stirred things up enough we were able to skim some crap off the top. We've upped surveillance on the ship. Good work, my brother. Congratulations, you can come in whenever you're ready."

Congratulations? Instead of victory, Chuck felt his gut fill with dread. He'd been expecting to hear a litany of reasons he could give Jolynn to stay tucked away safely with him. And instead, he'd gotten an all clear that the threats to her had passed. His mission had refocused on tracing the transfer of terrorist data. He not only could walk away from Jolynn, but he had to for the sake of the operation.

But he would be damned before he would simply drop her off at the ship to make her own way home. He would drive through the gates of hell, right up to Josiah Taylor's front doorstep and confront the devil himself. Because the time had come for someone to look that old man in the eye and let him know the consequences of hurting Jolynn.

* * *

Her elbow rested in the open window. She kept her face averted. The wind tangled through her curls as she absorbed the enormity of what had happened. Her cousin's fiancé had been stealing from the *Fortuna*, laundering money for heaven only knew what kind of lowlifes. Lucy would be crushed.

And Chuck's investigation appeared to be complete. She didn't need to hide out any longer.

They'd spent the day charging up the Italian coast, racing back to Genoa. The ship would be docking soon. Her father would return to his monstrosity of a mansion. Lucy would, too, for that matter. Tomorrow, the scholarship fund-raiser would go off without a hitch.

There was nothing holding them together. She twisted her fingers in her purse straps. "I want to thank you for all you've done for me. I know I gave you a lot of hell in the beginning, but you really put your life on the line for me and I won't forget that."

She wouldn't forget *him*. Ever. He'd changed her life and perspective in just a few short days.

His jaw went tight in an understated sign of stress, like how he rolled his shoulder and cricked his neck. She was beginning to recognize so many nuances about this man.

"Jolynn, I know we were careful with birth control, but nothing is foolproof."

She hadn't even considered . . . An image glittered to life in her mind of a chubby-cheeked cherub with a precious thatch of dark hair. Her hand fluttered toward her stomach, stopping shy of actual contact. "The timing's not right. I don't think—"

"Regardless," he cut her off short, "if you find out you're pregnant, I expect you to tell me."

"You know I wo—"

"I don't want to assume anything. You tell me. Even if you don't want it, I do."

She gasped that he would even have to wonder. But then how much did he really know about her? "Chuck—"

"No kid of mine is ever going to grow up without at least one of his or her parents."

"But—"

He charged ahead right over her. "You're probably thinking I don't have the kind of job suited to family life. But I wouldn't hesitate to change jobs if that's what it took."

There was so much about this man to respect, to love. His honor was shredding her to pieces here, and above all, she couldn't afford to break down now. "I would tell you, but I would keep it."

She wanted to say more, to tell him how much he meant to her, how she would give anything to have his child. But if she said any of those things, walking away would be all

the harder, and she had to do this. She had to find closure
with her father and his world.

And no matter how much it broke her heart to say good-
bye, she refused to let Chuck step into the cross fire for her
again.

★ ★ ★

Driving through the scrolled security gates, Chuck steered
the Fiat up the winding driveway to the Taylor estate.

While called a villa, the Italianate-style country home
was quite clearly a mansion, newly built with an amalgama-
tion of all bells and whistles from ornate bracket-corbels to
balconies with renaissance balustrading. And if that wasn't
enough, it sported a domed cupola in the center large enough
to display its own Sistine Chapel mural.

And statues. Good God, there were a lot of Grecian and
Romanesque stone statues with fountains around the estate
with sculptured hedge gardens just like Jolynn had described.
He'd seen CIA satellite images of the property, but none of
them did the place justice.

Jolynn sighed. "Gaudy, isn't it?"

Diplomacy kept him quiet.

He considered just kissing the hell out of her. She didn't
look overly emphatic about wanting to leave. Instincts prickled along his spine. Why was she pushing him away? Why
not just continue their affair and see where it led?

Could she really love her father that much? Chuck
wouldn't give up a cold for his mother, who'd dumped him
at the orphanage.

He started to ask her again, but she was already half out
of the car. Chuck slid out from behind the wheel. He looked
over the roof of the Fiat and . . . Damn.

Josiah Taylor stood at the top of the marble steps. Still gaunt from his heart attack, Taylor leaned heavily on a carved cane. There could be no doubting the relationship between father and daughter. Taylor's red hair, dulled to auburn with streaks of silver, still looked disturbingly like Jolynn's. Both shared a long-legged, lean grace. Even at half power, Taylor generated a sense of authority, a somber force.

His custom-fitted suit shouted of wealth. His brown eyes, hard and focused, glinted with a fierce, streetwise determination. He reminded Chuck of the house. Purchased heritage.

Old Man Taylor and Chuck locked eyes. Josiah was no fool. Chuck suppressed the inclination to crick his neck to the side, roll the ache out of his shoulder that had never quite left since his captor had carved the tracking device out of his back.

Chuck noted the defiance mingled with vulnerability in Jolynn's stance and remembered her confrontation with her father in the hospital. He wouldn't leave her to face rejection alone. He could see this through for her.

A selfish part of him hoped Taylor would turn her away, and Jolynn would come back to him. Safe, away from this place and this man forever.

He jogged around the car and stopped her before she could climb the steps. Tipping her chin with a knuckle, he kept his voice low. "Do you remember what I said to you by the shore that first night?"

She smiled faintly. "You'll need to be a bit more specific."

Chuck caressed his thumb along her chin. "Anyone who doesn't want you is a fool."

Her knuckles grazed his hair softly as she sealed her mouth to his for not nearly long enough and turned to her father.

Watching her leave him, he felt a twist in his gut that made the day his mother left seem like a mere case of indigestion. Chuck studied Josiah Taylor, a man who'd made a fortune saying to hell with the rules. Josiah adjusted his cane and extended a hand to his daughter. Jolynn climbed the marble stairs and stepped into her father's embrace as if she'd done it a thousand times. The old man folded his arm around her shoulders.

"Daddy." Jolynn's muffled voice drifted on the muggy summer breeze.

"Welcome home, Punkin'."

The front door swung open, and Lucy eased forward a step, eyes red-rimmed. Chuck gritted his teeth, having no sympathy for her. The woman had put Jolynn in danger owing to her abysmal choice in lovers.

Lucy inched closer to Jolynn. "Jo?"

Jolynn spun to face her, holding still for a moment before folding Lucy in a hug.

Taylor held the door wide. "Punkin', why don't you and Lucy go on inside? Hebert's around here somewhere. He's been worried about you."

And she left, just that fast, and without a backward glance, she went inside with her cousin. The front door eased closed behind the two women.

"Tomas," Josiah's voice boomed through the air, "or whatever your name is."

Chuck stood tall, staring the man down without a wince. "Tanaka. My name is Captain Charles Tanaka of the United States Air Force."

Josiah leaned heavily on his cane. "I wish you'd kept her with you."

Taylor's words damn near kicked the ground out from under him. "What did you say?"

"You heard me, boy."

Chuck's ears roared with anger. All the built-up frustration since Jolynn had told him she wanted to go back to her father boiled up inside him. "You son of a bitch. Don't you think you've hurt her enough? What was the big welcome-home-baby hug all about if you didn't want her?"

Taylor leaned on his cane, studying Chuck through calculating narrowed lids. "She's not safe here. She's never been safe. I protected Jolynn the best I could by getting her away from my world, and you stupid fool, you brought her back."

The roaring in Chuck's ears eased as the words seeped in deep enough to trigger his reason. Something was going on here, something they'd all missed or overlooked.

Taylor gestured toward the house with his cane. "But what's done is done. Let's make the best of it. Come on inside, boy. I have a little something to give you."

SEVENTEEN

Jolynn had expected it to hurt. She wasn't prepared for this. She'd always thought ramblings of broken hearts and wounded souls were mere melodrama. Now, she changed her mind. She didn't want to be honorable and keep him safe.

She wanted Chuck.

The ache was too deep for tears. Hitching her purse onto her shoulder, she followed Lucy up all forty-two steps to the second floor. Each time her foot hit a marble stair, the echo bounced around the palatial entryway like a racquet-ball whacked by Goliath. And of course, there was the requisite freaking huge statue in the middle of the landing. Clearing the last step, she approached her childhood room with dread.

As a kid visiting Italy, she'd always felt overwhelmed by the spacious suite, like being smothered by a feather pillow too large for her head. Her father had hired an interior decorator to create a showplace little girl's room in cotton candy pink. Jolynn hadn't wanted to hurt his feelings, so she'd never told him she'd wanted a Disney princess bedspread from Sears. Then over the years . . . nothing changed.

It seemed so insignificant now. Especially in light of the pain and betrayal her cousin was going through. Better to help Lucy through her loss than think about her own. One saving grace—if she could call it that—of losing Chuck was that it sure put her father's lack of love into perspective. She'd spent five minutes in this house and she'd known she would trade all future Christmases with the de Milo statues for a year with the man she loved.

Lucy pressed two wadded tissues to the corners of her eyes as she sank into the ruffled seat in front of the dressing table. "I can't believe you're even willing to talk to me after what Adolpho did."

"It's not your fault. You're as much his victim as I am. I'm just sorry you got hurt." Setting her purse on the raspberry carpet, she curled up in the window seat and hugged a frilly throw pillow. "Lord have mercy, our judgment in men could use some help."

"At least yours wasn't arrested." Lucy blinked fast, with none of her usual confidence or exuberance. "You always could one-up me, Jo."

"You're joking, right?"

"How could you have not known? I've been like a poor relation for as long as I can remember," she said bitterly. "Your dad only paid for my school because of you. He gave me a job. You have an inheritance."

"Which I won't touch." Shocked by her cousin's feelings, she tried to reconcile Lucy's image of their childhood with her own very different impression.

"You have the choice."

"I never knew you felt this way."

"Well, I did." She scraped back her strawberry blond hair, staring in the gilded mirror. "I still do sometimes, like now."

"I'm sorry." She wanted to reach out, but worried that might make things worse.

Her cousin turned to her, green eyes red and swollen. "What do we do now?"

For years she had turned to Lucy. Now Lucy looked to her. When had she become the stronger friend, the one to offer comfort? Since knowing Chuck. Being with him, seeing herself through his eyes and his unflinching worldview gave her a newfound confidence that went far deeper than the old bravado she'd used like a sorry shield against the world.

She slid from the window seat and hugged her cousin without reservation. "We do what any self-respecting woman does when she's having man troubles. We'll eat our body weight in chocolate."

Lucy's giggle mingled with a snort, and Jolynn joined right in. Yeah, the laughs bordered on hysteria, but it felt good to let off some steam.

Jolynn gasped through the watery laughter. "I'll be back in a minute with something good and two forks."

Easing back down the curving staircase, she gripped the handrail. Her gaze swept down into the cavernous entryway. The little cottage she'd shared with Chuck could fit inside with a simple plunk. She would do almost anything to spend forever in that small house with him.

Anything except endanger his life.

What would he think when he found the thumb drive she'd left in his car? She trusted he would make sure the information landed in the right hands. If she turned a blind eye to her father's illegal dealings, then she was just as guilty.

Chuck's offer to sweep her away from all of this had sounded so beautiful she'd feared she might cave and accept. But she'd learned more than a little about honor from Chuck. So she'd left him standing by the Fiat instead of climbing into the front seat and suggesting they just take to the road. Together. And forget the rest of the world.

An impossible dream.

Jolynn paused in front of her father's study. His hug had felt so familiar, even after all the years apart. Now that Chuck was gone, she needed to confront the old man. She loved her father, but she wouldn't condone his actions if he had any part in Grassi's dealings.

No matter what Lucy's fiancé had confessed to, Jolynn found it tough to believe her father could be innocent in all this.

Outside the study door, she heard Chuck's voice, and her fingers clenched around the brass lion's head knob. Was he still here?

Not giving herself time to think about how hard it would be to walk away from him a second time, she swung the door wide just as her father passed a large envelope to Chuck.

★ ★ ★

Chuck stared at the envelope in Taylor's outstretched hand, an envelope full of evidence nailing Simon Taylor's killers. God, it had shocked him when the old crook had actually offered to help him close the case. Yet his mind pounded in protest.

Taylor's arm didn't waver in spite of his obviously failing

health. He stood behind his mahogany desk shiny with panels and scrolled carvings as over the top as the rest of this place. Rows of books with uncreased spines lined the wall behind him.

Would pursuing the information in that envelope help Jolynn? Or would it put her at risk, stirring up enemies? For one very dark instant, he felt himself slip inside Josiah Taylor's skin. Chuck didn't like the ease with which it fit.

He would do *anything* to keep her alive.

Taylor rattled the envelope, his other hand resting on a gold gilded globe. "Take it, Tanaka. This information cost me a bundle eighteen years ago. It's finally time to use it. Even I know this is the only way now."

"Chuck?"

Jolynn's voice thudded into Chuck's gut more firmly than a fist, sucker punching him at his lowest moment. Turning, Chuck found her framed in the double doorway.

"Daddy, what's going on?" She stepped deeper inside, no makeup, still wearing the jeans and tourist T-shirt he'd bought for her. Her long hair tumbled down her back, and to him she'd never looked more beautiful.

"Nothing much." Taylor stared at Chuck as if daring him to contradict. "I'm just helping your pal out a bit with his investigation."

Chuck pivoted back to Taylor. What was the old mobster's game? Could he even be trusted?

Of course not.

Jolynn moved between them. "Would you two stop this stare-down game? I'm a big girl now, in case you haven't noticed."

Taylor dropped the envelope, the papers smacking the mahogany desk mere inches from his reach.

"Punkin', he and I both want the same thing. To keep you safe. Why shouldn't this young man and I work together?"

"To keep me safe?" Her laugh was anything but humorous. "Then you should have chosen a different line of work, old man."

Chuck studied Taylor warily. Would he push Jolynn away again under the guise of protecting her? Jolynn deserved better. She needed her father to quit dragging her through life backward by her hair if she ever wanted to move forward. Why couldn't Taylor see that his form of protection was hurting her?

Selfish logic told him that if Taylor rejected Jolynn, Chuck could have her. Thoughts of grabbing happiness with her and honor be damned tempted him. He almost caved. Almost. If she found her peace right now, then maybe she would walk out the door with him today.

"Tell her," Chuck demanded, already knowing what the old bastard would say, sensing what the envelope held and what it meant. "Tell her what happened to her uncle, to your brother. It's time."

Jolynn paled as she glanced between the two men, her brow furrowing. "Chuck? Daddy?"

Chuck gritted his teeth. "Tell her about why you sent her away and I'll take your damned envelope."

The color leeched from Taylor's face until Chuck feared he'd pushed the ailing man into another heart attack.

"All right, boy." Taylor straightened, inhaled a shuddering breath, and turned to his daughter. "Simon died because I wanted out of the 'organization.' I wanted to run a legit operation, and I refused to look the other way for those who didn't. They killed my brother to shut me up. If I didn't cooperate, they would have come for you next. For eighteen years, I've kept my mouth shut." His gaze flickered to the pack of papers, then back to Jolynn. "I sent you away to keep you safe."

Jolynn stood frozen as the statues on her father's front lawn. Not a smile in sight. Could she find any kind of peace in this new revelation? Someone ought to gain something from this miserable day.

Taylor turned to Chuck and nudged the envelope forward. "They took more than my brother. They robbed me of my daughter. Make them pay."

Jolynn stared at the envelope as if it were a snake, then turned accusing eyes on her father. "Daddy, are you crazy?"

Taylor frowned. "Jolynn Marie."

She didn't even flinch. "Daddy, you made your choices, choices not to go to the police sooner, not to tell me the truth once I was old enough to understand. I love you. And I forgive you."

She glanced at Chuck, and he thought about how unresolved garbage could rot a person's insides.

"But if you're playing some game here and Chuck gets hurt. . . ." Her face paled under her freckles. "What good will it do Uncle Simon if Chuck dies? Huh? Did you ever think of that?"

Why was she defending him when not a half hour earlier she'd given him the boot? "Jolynn, this is my job. I have connections. Trust me."

She grabbed hold of his shirt, right above the envelope, and tugged with surprising strength. "I'm getting really tired of watching men get themselves killed. Take the damned envelope if you want it and get out of here. Now. But you're crazy if you think I'm going to stay around for your suicide mission."

Her spine straight with fragile poise, she pushed away

from him, palm flat to the envelope. Turning on one heel, she left, the door closing with an almost imperceptible click. The following slam of the front door reverberated.

Chuck stroked along the envelope, nothing but a pack of papers. He knew what he would do, what he had to do. Just as he'd decided back at the cottage, he needed to show Jolynn once and for all that men could be trusted. *He* could be trusted to take care of her. "Okay, Taylor. I'll see what I can do with this . . . for her."

"Of course."

"If I find anything in here to incriminate you, you're going down with the rest of them."

"You won't find it." Taylor had the gall to smile, spinning the gilded globe beside his desk.

"And if I *do*?" Chuck pressed.

The smile faded. "All I ask is that you protect my daughter."

Taylor's green eyes locked on to his. He felt an odd kinship with the man, linked by their concern for the same woman.

"Yes, sir." For that second he gave Josiah Taylor the respect due him as Jolynn's father.

Chuck lifted the envelope, tucking it under his arm. Backing away from the desk, he stepped into the hall. He forced his stride to stay even as he looked around the colossal hall, up to the cathedral ceiling that sure enough had a mural of naked angels. Somehow he couldn't imagine his practical Jolynn growing up in a place like this.

Was she so different from his first impression of flashy, in-his-face confidence? Had their experiences changed her as they had him, or had he simply misjudged her from the start?

He charged past a maid on a ladder dusting the top of a statue and out the front door. The Fiat still waited where he'd left it and he started toward the car . . . only something caught his eye. Back in the days when he'd been a navigator, he could pick out the tiniest of dots on the horizon or the briefest blips on a radar screen. His flying days were over, but the instincts and the skills lived on. And right now, something definitely had snagged his attention.

He stared past the vehicle to a gazebo nestled in a far corner of the sculptured hedges. Vines twined through the latticework so densely the structure was almost impenetrable. A hint of red shone through, the unmistakable shade of Jolynn's hair.

The envelope burned his side where his arm held it secure. Jolynn confused him more than the most intricate of cases. She'd made it clear she wanted him to go. She may not trust in what they'd shared at the cottage but he couldn't turn away from her that easily.

By God, he would be sure she was safe, and the best way he could do that? Take Taylor's information back to the ship and see what he, Berg, and Nuñez could scare up through their intel networks.

Whether or not she wanted him, he would be watching her back, damn it.

Sinking behind the steering wheel, he tossed the envelope onto the seat beside him where Jolynn had been, where she belonged now. He cranked the Fiat and drove, the winding lane giving him too much time for regrets.

Throughout his career in the air force, he'd flown combat in Afghanistan. He'd flown test missions on aircraft the world didn't even know about yet. But he couldn't make one stubborn redhead walk away from her crooked father.

Beyond the front gate, he checked left, then right, not that there was much risk of oncoming traffic leading into the country estate. As he looked out the passenger window, something off-kilter snagged his radar eye, something on the opposite seat.

A thumb drive?

A thumb drive had slid from beneath the envelope, the edge just poking out. Chuck snatched the thumb drive from under the envelope, a slip of paper fluttering to the floor.

He opened a note written in Jolynn's scrawl. *Someone has access to the microprocessor timing code for the slot machines. The code is being used to launder money through the casino through rigged wins.*

Chuck twisted to look over his shoulder at the sprawling house. The armless statue poised in the middle of the fountain seemed to mock him across the distance, claiming Jolynn once and for all.

The gates clanged shut, locked, sealed. And what he held in his hand very likely didn't have a damn thing to do with money laundering.

But could well offer a clue about how data to build a dirty nuke was being shuffled through *Fortuna* slot machines.

★ ★ ★

Jolynn savored the caress of water streaming from her body as Chuck loved her. He held her close, safe. His hands now skimmed over her body, curving around the gentle swell of her stomach where she carried his child, their child.

The spray of the shower chilled to a biting sting.

He pulled away, his brown eyes filled with scorn.

"Chuck?" She tried to reach for him, but her arms wouldn't obey. She looked down and her arms were gone, just like on the amputated Venus statue.

"Good-bye, Jolynn." He backed up another step, their baby cradled in his hands now in that crazy senselessness of dreams.

"Chuck, come back. I don't understand."

"I want you, Lynnie, not some cold, stone statue."

His words rang like a gunshot through the maze of hedges, like the bullet that had taken down her uncle. Chuck's body blurred and became two men, just like that day, two faceless gunmen . . .

Jolynn startled awake, the wood planks of the gazebo uncomfortable beneath her. Exhausted from a night of no sleep and the wrenching emotions of the day, she realized she must have fallen asleep. She brushed a hand across her brow, smoothing her hair from her eyes.

She wanted to cry.

She needed to cry.

But the tears wouldn't come.

No great surprise since she felt dried up inside. Her head flopped back against the wall. He was gone. She could still feel the imprint of his lips on hers, smell him, feel him. Want him.

A month ago, she would have given anything to hear her father's explanation for why he had turned from her after Uncle Simon's death. Any joy was obliterated by the ache of having lost Chuck.

At least he was safe.

What if she and Chuck had met under normal circumstances, maybe at some vintage car show. She had often wondered if there could ever be a man for her, Jolynn

Taylor, a brainy, awkward girl who liked old cars and hated cooking.

From the middle of the garden, Venus de Milo showered water over the choir of fish at her feet. Jolynn studied the statue she'd thrown rocks at eighteen years ago, the day her uncle had died. The day she'd waited out here for her father, hoping he would finally notice her. Only now, she felt none of the inadequacies, none of the insecurities.

Again, she'd lost the most important man in her life, Chuck, instead of her father. However, this time, the man had left her something. A sense of her own self-worth.

"Hey, little girl."

Jolynn looked beside her and found Hebert waiting at the base of the gazebo steps. His beefy arms unfolded and spread wide. She flew into his embrace.

He patted her back with his clumsy paw of a hand. "You okay?"

"Not right now, but I'm going to be."

He held her tighter, the almost bruising force of his hug a welcome ache in exchange for the security of his love.

How many times had she run to Bear during her childhood? Even before her father had distanced himself after Uncle Simon's murder, Hebert Benoit—Bear—was the one she'd turned to with her problems.

She pulled back, staring up at his dear, craggy face. "Thank you, Bear."

He smiled.

She cried.

* * *

Wearing a ball cap and using one of the fake IDs Berg and Nuñez had cooked up, Chuck slipped back onto the *Fortuna* at this final stop before they reached Genoa. No doubt, Chuck Tanaka wouldn't be welcome. However, "Tim Kano" had been listed in the ship's computers as a guest for the whole cruise for just such a scenario if his Charles Tomas cover was blown. In fact, they all had a second name and room booked in case their identities were compromised.

Angry as hell at life, he charged down the corridor deep in the ship's belly, thumb drive burning a hole in his pocket. The engine room hummed louder and louder the closer he came to Berg's crappy cabin that most travel agents couldn't give away. Chuck keyed open the lock and shoved inside. Colonel Scanlon sat in front of the computers while Berg sprawled on the top bunk snoring lowly.

Chuck pushed the door closed tightly. "Where's Nuñez?"

"Mingling. Chasing down some leads the authorities got out of Grassi. Keeping an eye on our favorite row of slot machines, looking out for our three suspects. If anyone can spot a person in disguise, it's Nuñez. Today, he's pretending to be a French artist looking to win enough money to fund his own gallery showing."

"This may help you." Chuck slapped the thumb drive by the computers.

Scanlon's eyes narrowed. "Have a seat, Captain."

Chuck didn't budge.

"Sit. That's an order." His tone brooked no argument.

Too weary to argue, Chuck fell into the chair.

Scanlon reached across and raked the thumb drive to his side of the desk. "What do we have here?"

"Data straight from the *Fortuna*'s accounting office. Jolynn passed it along thinking it would help us with a money-laundering investigation. I suspect this may be why they were after her by the catacombs, regardless of what Grassi said."

He suppressed a yawn as he rubbed his neck. Glancing around the room, he wondered where they stashed the coffee machine. He could use a cup . . . or five. "There's data from the fund-raiser, which is funded by a percentage from the slot machines. The way those slot machines keep popping up in the investigation makes me wonder if they've been using the scholarship fund to move cash to fund the whole terrorist operation."

Colonel Scanlon plugged in the thumb drive, his brow furrowing while he waited for the data to upload. "Could well be. What's your take on Lucy Taylor? Do you think she worked with Adolpho Grassi in spite of what he says? He's her fiancé and she was in charge of the scholarship. She's got expensive habits. Big debts. Makes sense that Grassi would fall on his sword for the woman he loves. Quite frankly, I just can't see him pulling this off on his own the way he claims."

"My gut says it's not her, but you know my faith in my gut isn't at an all-time high right now." He had to believe Lucy hadn't known about the death threats, or he'd go crazy worrying about Jolynn alone with her.

The colonel turned away from the screens. "Are you all right?"

"Just make sure she doesn't get hurt." With a strange feeling of déjà vu, he heard himself utter almost the exact words Taylor had said to him the day before. Standing in the old man's shoes pinched.

"No."

"No?"

"That's your job. It's not me she wants, Captain."

"How about you tell her that." Bitterness crept into his voice.

The colonel looked heavenward. "Lord preserve me from ignorant company-grade officers." He jerked a thumb toward the computer screens behind him filling with encrypted data. "Think about who gave you this. I'm curious as to when she passed it over."

"When she pitched me out of her father's house."

"Why would she do that?" Scanlon's voice sounded suspiciously condescending. "What would you have done if she simply passed the information over to you?"

"Well, I sure as hell wouldn't have left her in that pit of vipers. She should be with me right now. This thing's bigger than Grassi, and they won't want Jolynn snooping around. If she stays with me while we find the proof, I could be there the next time they try to . . . shoot in her direction." He deflated into the chair. His arms hung limp, knuckles dragging the floor.

The colonel nudged. "She wanted to . . ."

"Keep me safe?"

"Bingo, Captain."

"Damn . . ." Chuck forked his fingers through his hair. "When did you go into the Match.com business?"

"Let's just say this cruise has been a real eye-opener for both of us." Scanlon clapped him on the shoulder, his assessing stare too insightful. "You have to know by now, Chuck, you're not only about the flying and techno details. You've got an instinct for this work. It carried you through that hellish time in Turkey and it's served you invaluably here as well."

Chuck looked away before the colonel could see just how much Jolynn had knocked him off balance. He studied the computer screen behind the colonel with the encryption decoder picking apart the puzzle like a car engine and . . .

"Holy shit, sir." Chuck shot to his feet and thumped

sleeping Berg awake on the top bunk. "Get up. Now. Grassi has been playing us with his confessions. I know exactly how they're moving the data, and if what I'm seeing is right, the final transmission will take place here on the *Fortuna* tomorrow night."

EIGHTEEN

★────────────────────────────────

"Who wants eight the hard way?"

"I'll take that. Give me twenty on eight."

"Come on, little Joe from Ko-ko-mo!"

Jolynn parted the pervasive smoke with her body, winding around slot machines and frenzied gamblers. Her eyes stung, and she tried to attribute the moisture to the cigarette haze.

Right now, she wanted to be done with the fund-raiser so she could ditch her high-heeled shoes and simple black evening gown—and figure out what to do with the rest of her life once she left Genoa. The nerve-tingling clamor of the casino contrasted in her mind with the quiet sterility of her empty future.

Amid the chaos of chiming bells and flashing lights, she elbowed through the crowd in search of her father. He was somewhere here sitting in a chair holding court. He'd done his best to persuade her not to come. But she had to, for her uncle's memory and for Lucy, who she hoped would find some peace in commemorating her father. Instead, her cousin was still hollow eyed from the betrayal, her olive green dress making her look all the more sallow and sad.

This wasn't the big event they'd all been hoping for. Five more hours of the required polite greetings and she could go back to her stateroom on the ship, peel off her basic black evening gown, and pack her bags with a clear conscience.

"Hey there, pretty lady!" A sailor extended one hand while he palmed her thigh with the other. "Come stand by me for luck."

She offered him a polite smile Venus de Milo would have disdained and kept her chin high, her emotions behind the staunch wall. "I think not."

How long before Chuck traced the information she'd given him and arrested—She didn't even want to guess who. Accusing anyone close to her seemed disloyal.

Like turning over the thumb drive wasn't disloyal?

But looking away, hiding would have made her just as guilty.

Her gaze scanned to the blackjack table. A wiry old man with a goatee encouraged the patrons encircling his area. Their faces, twisted with laughter she couldn't hear, seemed so surreal.

From behind the clutch of gamblers, a sleek dark head gleamed under the chandelier light. Lean and handsome in a white tuxedo jacket and black pants. She looked harder, studying the muscular figure, and oh my God, there was no mistaking it.

Chuck stood by a pack of heavily jeweled gamblers at the roulette wheel. Hope trembled low inside her. Had he come for her? Why else would he be here? He had the proof he needed, and yet still, here he was. As much as she wanted to shield him from her father's world, she should have known Chuck wouldn't give up on her.

And as much as she worried for him, she still couldn't hold back the joy at seeing him. Even a few hours away from him had been awful. How could she face a life without him?

The room was too noisy and packed for her to shout to him or push through quickly, so she called out to him with her eyes, her stare. He glanced over the heads of the well-dressed crowd, their gazes connecting with the familiar crackle of awareness. Memories of their time together at the cottage came rushing back. She couldn't have stopped her feet from moving toward Chuck if she'd tried.

The gleam of Hebert's bald head shone just beyond the clump of gamblers around the blackjack table as she walked. She stifled a smile. He looked profoundly uncomfortable stuffed into his tuxedo. Seeing Chuck and Bear so close, she was amazed that she'd ever missed the similarity in their strengths, a quiet steadfastness. Who needed flowery words?

Jolynn wove through the crush of people toward Chuck. What would she say to him? She wouldn't know if she couldn't get to him.

Jostled, she paused, looking over to apologize. "I'm sorry."

The aging Italian contessa who collected a different boy toy at every port gave an offhanded smile. *"Va bene."*

She seemed more interested in hitting the slots with the hard-bodied eye candy on her arm. Something niggled at Jolynn, but she couldn't think what. She stared back over her shoulder through the haze, but the woman was already out of sight. Farther across the room, Livia Cicero sang "Stardust" while her colonel boyfriend looked on.

The colonel? The man who worked with Chuck was still here?

Slowly, she realized Chuck wasn't here for her, but because of his investigation. Where was Bear? She searched for her rock in the middle of the rapidly disintegrating world, but he was nowhere in sight now. Neither was her father. So who did that leave for Chuck and the colonel to be watching? Not Bear. God no.

But oh Lord, please, it couldn't be Lucy either, although logic told her it had to be her cousin with her ties to Adolpho.

And as if her thoughts morphed into reality, the colonel pushed through the crowd in Lucy's direction. Chuck tipped his head to the side, then started walking away from her, toward Lucy.

Jolynn wanted to scream.

"No." The word slid free on the gust of a whisper. She gasped, confused and light-headed from lack of air. Grief constricted her breathing like a steel band around her ribs.

Like a male arm around her waist.

"Walk," a voice growled in her ear, a familiar voice.

A gun bit into the tender flesh of her side.

* * *

Chuck focused on Nuñez across the packed casino level, dressed as the replacement blackjack dealer. The colonel was pushing through the crowd, although his gaze never seemed to stray long from Livia onstage. Scanlon had wanted her off the ship tonight—but as predicted, she'd stubbornly declared otherwise.

Livia Cicero was the one who'd started this operation by approaching the colonel with her suspicions. She was the one who'd noticed the pattern of those three gamblers taking cruise after cruise, leading the team to see how those men always played the same rotation of slot machines as if making practice runs. But none of them could have foreseen how deep into the past this investigation would reach. Simon

Taylor's killer was here tonight, a player still jockeying for global power.

The thumb drive data had shown collected pieces of information to build a dirty nuke. Watching those cards slide in and out of the slot machines, it made sense now how the data had been uploaded bit by bit at different ports of call. No one having all the pieces of the puzzle, so if captured, that person couldn't tumble the whole operation.

But tonight, it wasn't a dry run, and the final handoff would prove disastrous. A simplified formula for building a dirty nuke placed in terrorist hands would create havoc around the world. No subway, so stadium, no mall would ever be safe again.

Failure was not an option. Chuck didn't have room for doubting his edge, especially not with Jolynn in the crosshairs.

And if—when—he got a second chance to talk to her, he wouldn't be screwing it up or taking no for an answer. Chuck mentally reviewed his speech for Jolynn, reminding himself to say "I love you" at least three times. Because damn it, there was no mistaking the feeling pumping through him.

While the husky crooning of the live music swelled across the room, the colonel crossed the last few steps, intercepting Lucy Taylor as she made her way toward the slots. Regret thudded into Chuck.

He would have sworn it wasn't Jolynn's cousin. This would be worse for her than if it had been her father. He didn't feel too good about it, either.

Livia's voice grew louder through the sound system. Chuck glanced back at her wondering what the hell was up with his old friend. Sure, her voice was huskier since her accident, but there was a strident sound . . . She was singing and pointing with her gloved hand as if addressing someone in the audience.

Someone by the slot machines.

The aging contessa was tugging her latest boy toy to the slots. A new face, but a familiar one all the same. Her young date was one of the three suspects identified by Livia from the international terrorist watch list. A student dissident from Albania.

Chuck launched through the crowd toward the machine. They were close, so damn close, and if that card was plugged in, the data would stream through the transmission cables and link up with the rest already floating out there. There would be no calling it back.

Livia screamed into the microphone, "Rex! Over there!"

On the other side of the contessa, the colonel froze, then charged into action. Just as they'd worked together in the airplane in the past, by instinct, through training, Chuck acted. Just as the colonel had told him before. It wasn't about the techno gear. It was about the person, the trained warrior. And right now, he was that person for the job.

He didn't even have to consciously tell his arm to lock around the burly student. Before he registered the thought, he snapped the man's wrist and whipped the card free a whisper away from the brightly lit slot machine.

A quick glance over and he found the colonel restraining the shrieking contessa, who wasn't even doing a decent job at hiding her culpability.

The room went still, the jeweled and polished partiers staring in shock, others silently scurrying away.

Nuñez leapt over the blackjack table and patted Chuck's arm, snapping him from his daze. "I've got it from here."

The fog of war clearing from his mind, he passed over the dissident to Nuñez just as security poured from all corners. Chuck backed a step, scanning the crowd for Jolynn, his arms hungry as hell to hold her now that the nightmare had finally ended.

He turned back to look where he'd seen her last and found nothing but faceless strangers.

Where the hell was Jolynn?

* * *

"Where the hell is that thumb drive?" a voice growled in Jolynn's ear.

Bear's voice. A voice that had soothed her hurts over the years now threatened her so unemotionally. Hebert Benoit, her father's trusted friend.

A gun bit into the tender flesh of her side right under her breaking heart. How could he do this? How could she have been so wrong about him?

The arm around her waist tightened. Melding them together, he shielded the weapon from view as he pushed her down the narrow service corridors of the cruise ship. No one to call for help. How had he cleared this area so completely?

The answer was all too painfully clear. Because he was in charge of security, of course. Grassi worked for him. Heat from his body seared her back. The stench of his breath mingled with her fear.

"Walk," he repeated, "and don't make a sound or I start shooting the second someone comes running to your rescue. And given the way your boyfriend feels about you, I suspect he would be first to round the corner. The first to die."

Chuck . . . She'd tried to do everything possible to keep him safe and had somehow only made things worse. But that didn't mean it had to end this way, damn it. She wasn't hiding from life anymore.

She wasn't going down without a fight. She jabbed an elbow into Hebert's thick gut and stomped his instep.

He grunted, his hold loosening for an instant.

She broke free, sprinting down the corridor toward the laundry rooms. Toward a door at the end of the hall. Ten more steps. *Chuck, I should have listened. I'm sorry.* Three steps.

Hebert grabbed the back of her dress. He twisted the fabric, yanking her to a stop. His arm sliced down and he backhanded her across the face. Bear had slapped her. Reeling, she slammed against the wall sideways. The scent of bleached sheets made her dizzy as heat wafted from the oversized machines.

Through a nauseating haze of pain, she stared at the face of the man who'd been like a father to her. Betrayal soured in her mouth. "I don't have your damned computer drive."

"Then you better hope you can tell me where it is. I don't need that out there floating around for anyone else to find and sell," he scowled down at her. "I don't like hurting you. But the people I work for will do a lot worse than this if you don't give them what they want. Now play this right and maybe we can work something out. I can convince them your daddy will pay big money to get you back."

She desperately wanted to believe him, but saw in his cold lifeless eyes that she was as good as dead already. In fact, this must have been the reason he called her to her father's bedside in the first place. *Bear* had been trying to kill her since she arrived. With her out of the picture, Bear would control everything.

Resisting the urge to throw up sapped her concentration. Her body hurt all over. Yelling wouldn't do a damn bit of good between the racket of the washers and the music playing in the casino.

"I'll do whatever you say. Let's please just stay calm." She pressed the heel of her hand to her forehead, steadying herself.

"Do whatever you need to do to keep moving and show me where you stashed the thumb drive. I know it's not on the ship. I've searched every square inch of the place."

She thought fast, needing to come up with a lie that would keep her alive and buy her time. "It's at my father's, but I'm not telling you where because right now I don't trust you to let me live if I do. Take me home and then you can tie me up, shove me in a closet to be found while you make your getaway."

"Good girl." He smiled, looking so much like the Bear she'd loved for years her heart damn near shattered. "That's a damn fine plan. Maybe you've got some of your father in you after all."

Unclipping his cell phone from his belt, he punched a number—speed dial?—and barked into the receiver. "I'm ready for pickup. Meet you on the top deck in five minutes."

Top deck? Pickup? The thought that he had a helicopter ready and waiting threatened to scare the starch right out of her spine. That kind of planning, those sorts of resources hinted at something on a much larger scale than low-level money laundering.

Rattled, Jolynn followed, praying some genius scheme would come to her. She feigned more dizziness and stumbled. She prayed Chuck would notice her missing and come for her. If only she could give him enough time. But she wasn't going to just sit around and wait to be rescued. She needed to do her part to help things along.

A trail to follow? It sounded almost too simple to work. She couldn't rig alarm systems as elaborate as his flares and electronic eye sensors, but then he'd told her that sometimes the simplest, low-tech plans worked best. With her free hand, she flicked her thumb in the clasp of her clutch bag and found her tube of lipstick, carefully, so damn slowly. But she was afraid Bear would notice as he hauled her through the maze of corridors. She got the lipstick open enough to . . .

Mark the wall.

And again.

Just a brush of red here . . . and there . . . like she'd seen spies in movies marking a post to leave a sign for another agent. It had worked for Hansel and Gretel, damn it. Such a long shot, but they were in a casino and Chuck was the best bet she'd ever been lucky enough to come across.

Now she just needed to keep Hebert distracted so he wouldn't notice what she was doing. "Why, Bear? Why are you betraying my family this way?"

"I'm a businessman, little girl. It's all about making the best deal and this one's the best I've ever come across. You're not going to mess that up for me. When you let it become personal, that's when things get screwed up. I'm in control of your father's dealings. Always have been. No one gets in the way and you're in the way now."

Realization iced the blood in her veins. "You. It was you all along. Your back may have been to me the whole time when Uncle Simon was murdered, but you were the one who shot him."

And all these years she must have blocked out the possibility, any sense of recognition. She thought of her dream the other night, of being in the garden, of gunshots. Had the full memory been working to the surface even then?

His beefy shoulders rolled with a careless shrug. "Simon was a threat to my power. He wanted me out so he had to go." He stroked the gun down her aching cheekbone. "Consider yourself lucky I let you live that day. You were a smart girl to keep your mouth shut when your daddy told you to, not that anyone would have believed you. But once your father got so sick before I finished gaining control, I couldn't risk you inheriting everything," he said, confirming her suspicions as to why he'd called her here, pretending her father wanted to see her. Hebert pushed through the final door onto the casino's upper deck. The humid night air felt sticky and heavy with danger. The muted outdoor lights reflected off the water. Wind roared overhead with a helicopter circling. The police? Could she be that lucky?

Hebert laughed lowly. "Sorry, little girl. That's my ride. Your ride, too, if you behave. So much faster and unreachable than making a getaway in a boat, don't you think?"

A rope ladder rolled down from the helicopter, still too high up to reach, but the chopper angled against the windy night gusts.

Jolynn considered flinging herself over the side. After gauging the distance between herself and the rail, she wasn't sure she could make it before being shot. And if she hit the deck below rather than the water . . . She shivered.

Not much time left and she was running out of options—

"Hey, Benoit. Over here." Chuck stepped from the shadows, his air casual, his hands stuffed in his pockets. The wind from the helicopter whipped his clothes around his muscled body, but his feet stayed planted as steadfastly as he'd stood by her this past week.

She'd known he would come, but grieved all the same. Her worst nightmare unfolded. Chuck's life was in danger because of her.

Bear pushed the gun deeper into Jolynn's already tender side. "Aw, look. The cavalry's come to save you. Except wait, cavalry's with the army, and your hero boy here's an air force man, right? Regardless, it's a shame he has to go, but at least he'll die a hero's death."

Chuck! She tried to reach him with her gaze.

He looked at her. His mocha brown eyes flamed with determination—and love.

Why hadn't she seen it before? Had she truly pushed him away for his safety, or because she'd been afraid to trust him? Too afraid to trust the love that coursed so forcefully through her body that it hummed with the power of it?

Chuck took a step forward, the rope ladder twisting in the wind just overhead. "We're both fight-to-the-death kind of guys here, so let's not make this any more painful than it has to be. I just want Jolynn. That's all."

"Then toss your gun away, real slow, and don't pretend you came without one."

Chuck withdrew his hands from his pockets. He held both palms up and reached under his tuxedo jacket. With two fingers, he placed his 9 mm on the ground and presented himself unarmed to a gunman. For her.

Repeatedly, Chuck had shown her his love. He had never said the words, but he'd protected her. He'd fought for her. He'd given her the answers her father had withheld for years. And when she'd asked, Chuck had let her go.

Chuck offered her what no man had before. He gave her choices.

"Not good enough, Tomas, or whatever you're calling yourself these days," Bear shouted over the roar of the chopper, sliding the gun from her side to under her chin. The cool metal bit into tender flesh. "Kick your weapon over the side where you can't get it back while I'm climbing up."

Chuck nudged the gun with his toe. Jolynn watched it slide across the deck, stopping at the rail then toppling over.

A dismal thud sounded on the deck below. She reminded herself to trust him, but she sure hoped he had another weapon tucked somewhere.

"Hmmm," Bear growled. "Now take off the jacket and turn around."

Chuck shrugged off the white tuxedo coat. The cummerbund hugged his lean waist without a gun in sight to mar the effect. They were out here alone and open. Where was everyone else? She didn't dare look left or right with the gun wedged under her chin.

"Well, Tomas or Tanaka or whoever you are tonight, it's been fun bringing down one of the big boys." Bear's smile faded. "Game's over and it looks like you lose." He swung the gun away from Jolynn. Extending his arm, he pointed the weapon at Chuck.

No! Rage, fear, and a strength she could have never imagined filled Jolynn. She shoved hard, knocking Bear's shot wide.

Chuck launched across the deck.

Two more shots reverberated, echoing in the night.

Chuck's weight slammed her against the running track along the deck. Their bodies tangled and rolled, jolting to a stop against the railing. Had he shoved her or fallen on her? Panic twisted within her.

He slid from her. Muggy night air blanketed her, replacing the warmth of his body. She struggled to breathe. Could they have both survived unscathed? Relief she almost feared acknowledging blossomed within her.

No one moved.

Scooting to sit up, she peered around Chuck at the bizarre scene before her. Bear clutched his gut, blood pouring between his fingers.

How? Chuck didn't have a gun.

But the colonel standing behind him did.

Horror and confusion and a sick relief swirled inside her. Gasping, Bear stumbled as the helicopter peeled away overhead. His knees hooked on the railing, and he flipped backward. The hollow thud of him hitting the deck shuddered through her. She buried her face in Chuck's chest.

Deadly silence echoed as loudly as his heart thumping against her ear for seven solid, blessedly alive beats. Then the drumming of approaching footsteps sounded up the stairs. Pandemonium exploded onto the upper deck. Agent Mike Nuñez led a group of men in dark suits, who pushed past the colonel.

Livia raced behind them, nearly tripping over her sequined evening gown as she threw herself into Rex Scanlon's arms. Two of Nuñez's guys blocked the stairs, keeping anyone else—especially any of Bear's so-called security force—from coming any farther. No doubt, her father would have his hands full sorting through his employee list, weeding out those corrupted by Hebert.

Chuck eased to his feet and extended one of his beautiful, strong hands to Jolynn. No more hiding. No more protecting her heart. Time to face life and take a chance on happiness.

She knew for certain Chuck was a sure bet.

Twining her fingers in his, she stood. She fell into his arms and held on, still hardly believing they were both alive.

"Are you okay?" He brushed a knuckle across her tender cheekbone where Bear had smacked her.

She would probably have a real shiner by morning. Who cared? They were alive. She would awaken in Chuck's arms.

"Yes, I'm fine." And she truly was. For the first time in eighteen years, she felt whole. "What about you?"

"Not a scratch. Nice job with the lipstick. God, you're

amazing." Pulling back, he cupped her face in his hands. "We're going to talk soon."

"Yes." Her hand gripped his as they turned to the crowd.

Her father cleared the top step, shaky and pale, leaning on his niece.

Lucy looked from Jolynn to Chuck and back again. "I guess only one of us has bad taste in men."

"I got lucky."

"You sure did." Lucy furrowed her brow. "For what it's worth, I really didn't have a clue what was going on."

Jolynn offered her a nod, not a hundred percent sure if she believed her right now when she'd been so wrong about Bear. No doubt, her father's business and everyone in his employ would be under some serious scrutiny.

The colonel tucked his gun inside his tuxedo jacket and turned to Chuck. "See you soon?"

Chuck's arm tightened around her shoulder. "We'll be down shortly. Okay?"

"Take your time. The Italian police have everything under control in the casino. The contessa and her accomplice should already be secured for questioning." The colonel slid his arm around Livia's shoulders and started down the stairs as police boats roared up from three sides.

Tucked against Chuck, Jolynn eased away from the remaining officers who were sealing the area and marking evidence, Agent Nuñez issuing orders as he peeled off a fake goatee. Once they reached a far corner, tension seeped from her body.

The silence echoed after the mayhem. Only a short time had passed. Such life-changing moments. She could feel the slight trembling of her body as aftereffects of the shooting rocked through her.

Leaning back against the rail, the familiar sea breeze lifting her hair, Jolynn faced Chuck. "This has been a surreal evening, to say the least. I guess I need to know if this is a dream. If you are a dream, or if you'll be gone when I wake up."

"I am real, what I feel for you is real, and God knows, if you'll have me, I'm not walking away from you again."

He spoke with such conviction she believed him, trusted the love in his eyes.

"I do want that so very much." Her voice hitched. "I want what we have to be more than some moment-in-time affair. I want it to be solid. Lasting."

"Then it is." Simple words, from a logical man.

And she believed him. She trusted in her judgment, in what she felt when she was with him. "Just so you know. You're stuck with me. Forever. No short-term commitment or maybes."

He pulled her close, a sigh of relief shuddering through him. She would make it up to him. Somehow. With a smile, she realized she had all the time in the world.

"Forever," he repeated. "We'll make it work. Nevada, or Dallas, we'll put the pieces together." Chuck palmed the back of her head and pinned her with his intense gaze. "I love you."

Before she could answer, he breathed the words over her cheek. "I love you."

Then he sighed them against her lips. "I love you."

Her heart caught somewhere in her throat. More than the words, she heard the depth of emotion behind them, a determined forever declaration from a man who didn't fail.

"There!" His chest heaved. "I said it three times. Did you hear me, Jolynn? Three times."

"I heard you." She brushed her fingers across his furrowed brow. "Why is it that love scares you more than bullets?"

"Good Lord, woman, bullets are commonplace. Being in love, well . . ." His voice grew hoarse. He cleared his throat. "This is a first for me."

"Me, too. I love you."

"I know."

"You do?"

"You told me already, back at your father's house when you trusted me with that thumb drive."

Peace settled over her. He'd understood. Yes, Chuck had given her an ability to trust in herself as well as him. But she had the feeling he'd learned something from her, too. He was learning to look with his heart. "I did, didn't I?"

"Loud and clear. You took a big risk handing that information over to me, not knowing who would be implicated."

"I trust you." She meant it. She'd trusted him with her body. She was ready to trust him with her heart. "For a guy who likes things nice and neat, you took a bit of a risk here yourself."

"And I'm ready to take one more." He stepped back, her hand clutched in his. Without breaking eye contact, he knelt before her just as he'd done the night she'd met him. Moonlight rather than chandeliers reflected off his gleaming black hair. The air, clean and pure, swirled around them. She stared into his unguarded eyes and saw straight into his heart.

His dark, infinitely intense eyes flickered over her with a passion she trusted would never wane. "Jolynn, Lynnie, Red, will you marry me?"

She gave him her answer in one of the simplest, most beautiful words of all. "Yes. Yes, and yes."

She loved his dimples.

Chuck lifted her hand clasped in his and pressed a kiss to her palm, sealing his commitment with a reverent kiss . . . a kiss that slowly changed. He took the tip of each finger between his lips, paying additional homage to her thumb. His teeth nipped the sensitive pad. He journeyed over her wrist, pausing at the tender crook of her elbow. Standing, he finally reached her mouth.

They kissed as if they had all the time in the world. He kissed her as if they were simply enjoying a lazy afternoon picnic. She kissed him with an ease that spoke of years' knowledge of each other. The beautiful connection of a couple blessed with forever to return for more.

Jolynn had considered herself down on her luck coming across the world to see her father. The whole trip had bad odds with the potential for massive losses.

But when she'd bet everything on Chuck, she hit the jackpot.

EPILOGUE

Newly promoted Major Chuck Tanaka loved living on the edge. And nothing dished up a bigger adrenaline rush than ending the day with Jolynn.

Hands on her waist, a scarf tied over her eyes, he guided her out to the front porch of their cabin in the woods. More of a cottage actually, the sunset streaking hazy warmth through the towering oak trees. They'd built their cottage on a larger scale than the one where they'd hidden in Italy. With an open concept living area, it sported three bedrooms—and a kick-ass workshop out back where he'd stashed his anniversary gift for Jolynn.

One year ago today, they'd met, a life-changing day for both of them that he looked forward to commemorating each year, along with their wedding date once they got married over the Christmas holidays. They would have planned the

ceremony for sooner, but they'd both wanted their big day
to be distanced from the mess uncovered on the *Fortuna*
last year.

Adolpho Grassi received multiple life sentences, without
parole, only dodging a death sentence by handing over
higher-ups in the terrorist food chain. He'd revealed the full
extent of a plan to set off a dirty nuke in a sports arena during the NFL kickoff game.

Lucy hadn't been dirty, but definitely "dusty" in the
casino's illegal dealings. She'd gotten off with parole and
placement in the witness relocation program, thanks to
ace legal help and complete cooperation. Josiah Taylor
had somehow managed to emerge from the whole ordeal
squeaky clean, only to pass away from a heart attack
six months ago. At least Jolynn had found some peace
in that relationship before her father died. She was still
wading through the Italian court system to sell off her
father's foreign assets and put the proceeds to more chari-
table use.

Peace was an interesting and elusive beast, but golden
when found. Chuck had realized something valuable in his
quest for vengeance against the people who'd kidnapped
him in Turkey three years ago. That greedy network of evil
was big and tenacious, sprouting tentacles faster than one
man could slice them off. He needed to come to terms with
the fact this was an ongoing battle, during which he needed
to live his life to the fullest.

With Jolynn.

He guided her around the back of their cabin, closer to
their workshop, which happened to be bigger than some
two-bedroom houses and they'd put the place to good use
together after hours. Chuck had transferred out of the dark

ops testing unit, too frustrated over pushing paperwork since he couldn't fly. Colonel Scanlon, a savvy leader, had shown him a new path for his uniformed service. Chuck worked undercover with the air force's OSI—Office of Special Investigations. His pal Nuñez had proven a great mentor when it came to investigative work.

A transfer to Randolph Air Force Base outside of San Antonio, Texas, offered the perfect locale for Chuck and Jolynn to build their life together. She'd taken a job at a local accounting firm. Life was good.

"How much farther?" she asked, a hand in front of her although she had to know he would never let anything harm her.

"Almost there." He guided her past the olive tree that Livia Cicero Scanlon had sent them as a housewarming gift. "I'm going to let go now. Stand still and don't look." Unable to resist, he swept aside her flowing red hair and pressed a kiss to the nape of her neck before stepping back. "Almost ready."

He squatted, lifting the garage door. The wooden door rumbled as it unveiled the contents. Parked alongside the 1965 Mustang they'd rebuilt three months ago, he'd added a vintage GTO today while she'd been at work. He pulled the scarf from over her eyes.

Her squeal of delight left no room for mistake. His gift was a big-time hit.

"Oh. My. God." Jolynn stared at the automobile, all but drooling over the original muscle car, a 1969 Pontiac GTO hardtop. She walked from front to back, all the way around, caressing her hand along the Starlight Black paint job.

Her hand hovered over the engine with reverence. "Four fifty-five, I assume?"

"Why, of course." He flicked on the overhead lights and closed the garage door.

"Dual quads?"

"Naturally. Even thrush mufflers."

Sighing, she pressed her hands to her chest. "A man after my own heart."

"That I am, Jolynn, that I am, because you most definitely have mine. Happy anniversary."

"It most definitely is." She looped her arms around his neck, angling her mouth over his.

Chuck's hands sketched lower until he cupped her bottom, lifting her off her feet and settling her on the hood of the car. Without removing his mouth from her skin, he hooked his hands under her knees. Her gorgeous long legs locked around his waist. He nestled between her thighs, the heat of her searing his hard-on clear through his jeans.

He whipped aside her tank top, tucked a hand under her bra, and thumbed the hooks free. Already eager for the feel of her skin, the taste of her, anticipation burned through him. Her breasts tightened in response just as his mouth closed over a peak.

She almost leapt off the car.

The way she wriggled and sighed sent liquid fire coursing through his veins. God, he loved the way she felt in his arms.

God, how he just loved *her*.

She brushed her fingers over his shorn hair, urging his head closer. She inched forward along the hood and rolled her hips against him. Sure, the physical side of their relationship rocked, but he knew he found so much more with Jolynn.

Easing his way back up, he traced the shell of her ear.

"Jolynn, Lynnie, Red, I want you. More than you can possibly imagine."

"I want you, too, Chuck." Her green eyes twinkling with promise, she pulled his face back to hers. "Now. And forever."

Turn the page for a sneak peek of
the next Dark Ops Novel by Catherine Mann

GUARDIAN

Coming September 2012
from Berkley Sensation!

★ ─────────────────────────────────────

Major Sophie Campbell had wanted to be a J.A.G. since she lost her father in elementary school. That didn't mean she always enjoyed her job.

Today, she downright hated it.

But come hell or high water, she would get some useful nuggets of information out of the witness for the defense—cocky aviator David "Ice" Berg.

"Major Berg, you are aware that the Fire Control Officer on your test team, a man under your command, made a serious error firing from an AC-130 gunship into a private citizen's home?"

"Ma'am, I was there," Berg drawled, his South Carolina roots coating each word. "It was tough to miss the flames. But Captain Tate didn't screw up."

Of all the test directors to be in charge of this particular mission, why did it have to be Berg? Sexy as hell with a sense of humor and unflappable calm, he managed to charm his way through life.

Not today.

"Let me rephrase the question." Sophie flipped through the pages of her legal pad.

Stalling.

She didn't actually need further information. She needed to decide the best tact for extracting crucial evidence from the rock-headed aviator occupying the witness stand for the past two hours. Based on prior encounters with stubborn Major David Berg, Sophie prepared herself for a protracted battle.

"Major Berg," she pressed, dropping her paper on the walnut table in the military courtroom, "in the month leading up to the incident, your team was under incredible pressure to complete testing on the gun mount system. You were being pushed to finish ahead of schedule so it could be used in combat."

"Objection!" Counsel for the Defense leapt to his feet. "Is there a question?"

"Su-stained," the judge, Colonel Christensen, monotoned. "Get to the point, please, Major Campbell."

"Yes, sir." She nodded.

Berg didn't so much as blink. He'd earned his call sign "Ice" honestly. The man truly was an iceberg under pressure, and today's stakes were high. Damn high. In order for a child to get justice, a young captain with a spotless record would have his life and career ruined with a court-martial conviction.

This case sucked on a lot of levels.

"I'll rephrase." A simple twist in wording would get the question before the witness, cast some doubt in the jurors' minds. "Are you certain Captain Tate didn't cut corners on crew rest before the mission in question?"

Berg quirked a dark, lazy brow. "Asked and answered in my initial deposition. I am certain."

Sure, she was pushing the envelope with badgering a witness, but her options had dwindled in the past couple of hours. She needed to win this case. Too many people counted on her, the child injured in the military testing accident. She also had a child of her own dependant solely on her.

She refused to consider that Berg might be right. Not that she doubted his honesty. His pristine reputation at Nellis Air Force Base carried whispered "awe" aura. As much reputation as anyone could garner working in the top secret field of dark ops testing. He was known as a by-the-book aviator with nerves of steel. No, she didn't question his ethics, but he must have missed something or been misled by those who worked for him. Maybe he had to cut a corner in the testing process that led to Captain Tate making this tragic—and too damn high-profile—military accident.

"Major Berg, do you acknowledge that there was immense pressure in the month leading up to the incident in question?"

"Stress is standard ops in the test world."

"And why might the pressure be higher during wartime?"

"Troops in the field need the technology we develop."

"And in times of stress, you agree that sleep can be difficult?"

Sophie neared the raised wooden stand. Berg radiated such raw strength she doubted any amount of months on the job would lay him low.

A long-banked heat within her fanned to life.

Her steps faltered.

Heat?

The slumbering numbness that had invaded her emotions

for the past year eased awake with a burning tingle. An almost painful warmth spread through her, begging to be fed by—

Major David Berg? David? "Ice"? No way!

What could have snagged her attention now, after she'd known him for at least a year and a half? Something about him today seemed different somehow.

His mustache. He'd shaved his mustache, unveiling a full, sensuous—

Sophie blinked once, twice. Had he noticed her lapse? A honking big unprofessional lapse.

She cleared her throat along with her thoughts. "Did Captain Tate receive the full eight hours of crew rest?"

"Twelve hours, ma'am," Berg answered smoothly. "Regulations state crew rest is twelve hours long, something I know, my crews know, and I'm sure you know."

"Of course, twelve hours." Well, it had been worth a try to trip him up, create a reasonable doubt. Moving on to plan B.

Sophie closed the last two feet between them, stopping just in front of Berg. Air-conditioning gusted from the vents above, working overtime to combat the Nevada summer heat. Her uniform clung to her back, the blue service jacket about as thick and stifling as a flak jacket right now.

Her nerves must be frazzled from the insane year of restructuring her life as a single mother. She needed to concentrate on her job, not . . . him. Since Lowell's death, she didn't have the time or energy for anything other than caring for her son and paying off the mountain of bills her husband had left behind.

She pressed ahead, placing an evidence bag with a scheduling log inside on the witness stand. "If it's twelve hours, then I'm confused how you fit in the missions and required rest without a single minute being off."

He picked up the schedule, scanned it, and placed it back on the stand. "The numbers are tight, but they work. Yes, we were on a deadline. A tight one with no wriggle room, not even a minute. That's what we do, year in and year out. When has the military not been overworked and under-manned?" Berg's drawl snapped with the first twinges of impatience. "So in essence, the crazy-ass schedule we work is actually standard."

Trained to watch for the least sign of weakening in her witness, Sophie rejoiced over the almost imperceptible clench of his jaw. Berg's pulse throbbed faster above his uniform collar, the reaction so subtle she felt certain only she noticed. She ignored her own quickening heart.

Time to press the advantage, if she dared.

A quick glance at the judge's bench reassured her. The jowly presider looked in need of some crew rest himself. She needed to move fast.

"Major, you can't be with your testers twenty-four/seven. So it's actually impossible for you to say with complete certainty that Captain Tate received the required amount of rest prior to his mission? I mean really, did you walk with him every step of the way?" Her words fell free with a soft intensity that curled through their pocket of space. "Eat with him? Follow him to the bathroom?"

If she could just piss off Berg enough, she sensed he would snap and slip, say one little thing wrong that would enable her to secure a conviction. It wasn't like he would go to jail—although somehow she knew he would rather go take the punishment on himself than see anyone in his command suffer that shame of a court-martial.

"Ma'am, I'm not required to watch my testers sleep. How-ever, I did see Captain Tate drive away, in the direction of his home after dinner—which I did watch him eat." His steely eyes glinted like the flecks of silver dusting his coal black hair. "However, I didn't follow him into the bathroom since we're not a couple of junior high girls."

Sophie snapped back a step.

Chuckles drifted from the jury. Damn it. Of course he played well to a crowd. In a military proceeding, the accused could choose either a judge or jury trial and just her luck, they'd gotten a jury.

"Order!" The judge's cheeks shook like a basset hound's. His gavel resounded through the military courtroom.

Part of being a successful attorney involved knowing when to retreat with grace, recouping for the next advance. Having foolishly depended on her husband for so many years, she now struggled with the concept of relinquishing control, of not delivering the last shot.

"Thank you, Major, for that . . . enlightening . . . information about the personal hygiene habits of your unit. I only wish you could be so forthcoming with the rest of your testimony." Sophie turned to the bench. "Withdrawn."

The judge darted a censorious glare her way. The jury laughed again, but this time she didn't mind.

Berg canted forward, his shoulders and chest seeming to enlarge, filling the witness stand with his muscular chest full of military ribbons—a Distinguished Flying Cross, a Bronze Star, and almost too many air medals to count. Each oak leaf cluster signified ten more combat missions. He didn't just put his ass on the line testing the newest equipment in the inventory. Berg served overseas, sometimes the first to use those new systems outside the test world.

Rumor had it, he'd received that Distinguished Flying Cross in Afghanistan. As the fire control officer in an AC-130 gunship he held off hundreds of Taliban fighters attempting to capture a pinned-down SEAL team. Berg had

stayed in the fight well past daylight, dangerous for the aircraft. He'd shot so precisely, so effectively his ammo had
lasted until a helicopter could arrive with pararescuemen to
scoop up and out the injured SEALs.

She accepted the inevitable. Any shot she could deliver
here today wasn't going to rattle a man who'd spent hours
flying over hundreds of Taliban fighters lobbing potshot and
aiming rocket launchers his way.

"Nothing further." Sophie effected her most efficient
walk, heels tapping back to the table. She pivoted on the
toes of her low pumps. "We reserve the option of recalling
this witness."

After two hours of cross-examination, she'd scored more
than a few points.

At what cost?

She and Berg had run into each other during early deposi-
tions. And even before that, they'd first met in a past investigation, but she'd still been married then. He'd been in the
middle of a messy divorce. She hadn't looked at him—
hadn't really seen him—the way she did today.

Regardless, stakes were too high for her to worry about
David Berg. If she won the court-martial proceeding, that
cleared the way for the young boy injured in the accident to
move forward with a civil suit.

The judge rested his cheek on his fist, the jowl shifting
to seal one eye. "You may step down, Major Berg."

Sophie averted her gaze from the witness, pretending to
jot notes. With an hour left until court recessed, she didn't
want to risk jack. No doubt when she saw Berg next the
unexpected attraction would have left as abruptly as it had
arrived.

Annnnnd, she looked at him anyway. Damn.

Her nerves tingled.

Tucking his wheel cap under his arm, the major circled to the front of the stand. His uniform fit his lanky body perfectly, accentuating each athletic stride.

She studied him from a more personal perspective. Sexy with jet-black hair, but not handsome, she decided. Not in the conventional sense. His angular features defied so mundane a label.

Deep creases fanned from the corners of his quicksilver eyes, attesting to a combination of years in the sun and ready laughter. His skin was a hint lighter where his mustache had been, drawing her attention back to his mouth. He wasn't smiling now.

Berg exuded the confidence of a man comfortable in his skin, his appeal making her distinctly uncomfortable in her own.

Sophie resisted the urge to tuck her thumb in the waistband of her skirt. Already snug, her uniform tightened as he narrowed the distance between them. She resolved, yet again, to eliminate midnight ice-cream sprees until she could afford to buy a larger size. He probably didn't even know how to count fat grams.

The hungry heat returned . . . and she didn't crave a pint of rocky road.

The last thing she wanted was some obstinate aviator cluttering her mind. She finally had her life on track, and she didn't intend to risk her hard-won independence simply because of a fleeting bout of hormonal insanity.

Level with her, Berg hesitated. His six-feet-four-inches dwarfed her five-feet-three. Five-four if she added the minimal lift of her shoes.

Even when not in uniform, she'd always disdained high heels, maintaining they gave her the look of a child playing dress-up. At that moment, she would have plea-bargained two *gallons* of rocky road for a pair of Tina Turner spikes.

Steel gray eyes pinned her for one slow blink before Berg shoved through the swinging wooden rail and out of the courtroom.

* * *

Major David "Ice" Berg cared about two things above all else: His daughter and his job.

Steamed by more than the Nevada sun, Dave leaned against the exterior wall by the front entrance of the court-house. At least Haley Rose was settled with his sister for the afternoon.

Five minutes alone with Major Sophie Campbell to straighten the facts and his world would be in order. With one of his tester's career in the balance, he couldn't just walk away.

He glanced at his watch, impatient from waiting in the heat, dryer than his South Carolina home state's humidity, but still a scorcher of a day. He still had to pick up Haley Rose from his sister's. Single parenthood left him with little time to waste.

What's taking the lady J.A.G. so long?

Jumbled voices swelled through the opening doors. Masses poured out and divided, easing down the courthouse stairs like the gush from an emptying aqueduct. Bluebirds feeding on the patchy lawn scattered, clearing a path. No sign of her.

Dave pushed away from the warm wall and jogged down the steps, exhaling his frustration. He would have to take a long lunch tomorrow and track her down, which would make him late picking up his daughter twice in a week. Crap.

He cut a path across the scraggly lawn. A fluttering blue-bird snagged his attention. He glanced back just as Sophie stepped through the door. She paused for a moment to put on her hat. He braced for the inevitable whammy—that wallop to his libido that came every time he looked at her.

Long ago, he'd learned to harness his reaction around her. From the first time he'd come across her eighteen months ago during a deposition on another case, he had wanted her. The glint of her wedding band had sparked regret. Not to mention he'd been in the middle of a hellacious divorce.

After discovering Sophie's ritzy address, he'd thanked heaven for the near miss. His single brush with a material-istic woman was one too many. His single brush with *marriage* was a mistake not to be repeated as well.

Her marital status may have changed, but her posh neighborhood remained the same. He didn't need any further incentive than that to resist her. Encounters focused solely on work offered security from temptation.

Sophie hurried down the steps, her pencil-straight uniform skirt hitching higher up her leg. Her legs had driven him close to crazy during his stint on the witness stand. And when his eyes travel upward to the best set of curved hips in the free world?

A man could lose himself in her softness.

Her sun-streaked blond hair was swept back into some kind of twist. Not for the first time, Dave imagined pulling out the pins and testing the silky texture sliding between his fingers. Her light hair contrasted with her golden glow, deep brown eyes, lightly tanned skin.

Tan lines.

Shit.

He knew the minute she saw him. Her gaze went from open to distant in a snap.

"Major Berg," she acknowledged before charging past.

Ego stinging, he watched her hips twitch in her brisk, twitchy walk as she left him in the dust. His whole body throbbed from viewing only two inches of skin above her knee, and she barely noticed him. He couldn't decide why her dismissal bothered him more than usual since he didn't plan to do anything about the attraction.

A good swift reality kick reminded him of his reason for seeking her out, and he resolved to take comfort from the chill of her greeting.

"Major," David called, catching her in three strides. "Wait a minute."

"I haven't got a minute." Sophie tossed the words over her shoulder without meeting his gaze.

"Make time."

She took two shorter, quick steps for his every long stride. "Call my secretary for an appointment."

"Hold on!" He gripped her arm and tugged her to a halt. "If I'd wanted an appointment, I wouldn't have spent the last hour waiting."

The combined force of her sudden stop and spin to face him brought them a whisper apart. The simple act of touching her for the first time sent blood surging well below the belt.

Down, boy.

Dave unclenched his hand, allowing himself a brief trail down Sophie's sleeve as he released her. A bubble of privacy wrapped around him as it had during the moment on the witness stand when she'd leaned a bit too close for a second past his comfort level.

A hint of uncertainty crossed her face before she stepped back. "This better be important."

"It is."

"You have exactly two minutes." She checked her watch, late-day sun glinting off the faceplate. "I'm late picking up my son."

He gestured toward the corner of the building, away from the crowd. "Let's step over here in the shade."

Following her, he almost cupped his hand to the middle of her back. Sophie stopped to face him just in time to prevent him from making *that* colossal mistake. Sophie Campbell was a J.A.G., an officer in the same air force he served. The Bronze Star on her uniform proved she was more than just someone sporting a bunch of "I Was There" ribbons. Right now, he wanted to know how she'd gotten that Bronze Star as much as he wanted to know the taste of her.

"One minute left, Major Berg."

Right. "We need to talk about your line of questioning upstairs."

"Do you have something to add to your testimony?"

"No."

"Then we have nothing to discuss." She moved to dart around him.

Dave braced a hand against a sprawling eucalyptus tree, blocking her escape. "I feel bad for that injured kid—Ricky—and for his family, too. Aside from how damn tragic the whole thing is, Professor Vasquez has got to be swamped with his son's medical bills. I'd like to help the kid win a hefty settlement, but I can't. You're on the wrong track."

"Major Berg—"

"Cut it out, Sophie. We're not in the courtroom." So much for keeping matters impersonal.

"This isn't accomplishing anything. If you have something

concrete to discuss, come to my office and we can meet in a more . . . professional setting." Her gaze skittered away from his. "David, I really can't do this today."

He concurred on that point at least. "Am I supposed to wait around until you can fit me into your schedule?"

"I'll be in touch."

"No good. I don't feel much like playing tag team with your voice mail."

Sophie watched undisguised frustration wrinkle David Berg's brow as he barricaded her exit. She needed to leave. Now. Rather than diminishing, the tingling she'd felt earlier had increased to something resembling a third-degree sunburn.

Much longer with him and she might launch herself at him like a sex-starved woman. Which, of course, she was, even if she hadn't realized it until an hour ago.

Sex. That's all it is, just a natural, physical reaction. After a nap and some ice cream, she would be fine. The reasonable explanation calmed her. As a normal, healthy woman, of course her body would inevitably react to enforced abstinence. She could push aside the unwanted attraction long enough to talk with him, for the good of her case.

"All right, I would like to go over a couple of points in the incident report. But I honestly don't have time this afternoon."

David's hand pressed to the tree trunk brushed mere inches beside her cheek. His heat reached to her like a furnace blasting on an already hundred-plus-degree day.

He shifted, his knee bent, his shoulders angling closer. "What if I meet you tomorrow for lunch?"

The offer tempted her. Hell, the man tempted her. She tried to focus on his tie instead of the flecks of steel in his blue eyes.

The rows and rows of tiny rectangular ribbons on his uniform jacket drew her eyes. An icy chill in her veins burned worse than the heat. How long before he too ended up cold and lifeless, like her husband, like her father?

She had no intention of waiting around to find out. "Your two minutes are up. Stop by my office after court tomorrow."

Sophie ducked under his arm in an attempt to escape his appeal.

Two cracks sounded.

David slammed into her, tackling her. Her briefcase flew from her grip.

Another pop. A gunshot? No time to question. Her head smacked the rocky earth, David Berg's body blanketing hers . . .

An enchanting new novel of richly drawn romance.

From *New York Times* Bestselling Author
Janet Chapman

Highlander
for the
Holidays

After a brutal attack, Jessie Pringle moved to the small
mountain town of Pine Creek, Maine, to start over. But
she never expected to meet Ian MacKeage, who had
seemingly stepped right out of the Scottish Highlands.
As drawn to Ian as he is to her, Jessie finds it more and
more difficult to deny her own desires—until a chance
encounter gives her a way to let go of the past . . .

M986T0911

DON'T MISS

Ladies Prefer Rogues

Janet Chapman, Sandra Hill, Veronica Wolff, and Trish Jensen

Out of time, out of place, but still searching for true love.

New York Times bestselling author **Janet Chapman** writes about a band of twenty-third-century warriors on a mission to save mankind . . .

USA Today bestselling author **Sandra Hill** plunges a woman back in time to post–Civil War Louisiana, where the poor Southern belle must make a living as a matchmaker . . .

National bestselling author Veronica Wolff tells of a seventeenth-century Scotsman who avenges the death of his greatest love . . .

USA Today bestselling author **Trish Jensen** spins a fetching fable about a woman from the Wild West who lands in modern-day Nevada . . .

penguin.com

Penguin Group (USA) Online

What will you be reading tomorrow?

Patricia Cornwell, Nora Roberts, Catherine Coulter,
Ken Follett, John Sandford, Clive Cussler,
Tom Clancy, Laurell K. Hamilton, Charlaine Harris,
J. R. Ward, W.E.B. Griffin, William Gibson,
Robin Cook, Brian Jacques, Stephen King,
Dean Koontz, Eric Jerome Dickey, Terry McMillan,
Sue Monk Kidd, Amy Tan, Jayne Ann Krentz,
Daniel Silva, Kate Jacobs...

You'll find them all at
penguin.com

Read excerpts and newsletters,
find tour schedules and reading group guides,
and enter contests.

Subscribe to Penguin Group (USA) newsletters
and get an exclusive inside look
at exciting new titles and the authors you love
long before everyone else does.

PENGUIN GROUP (USA)
penguin.com